T0104570

Crowe's Bait

Chernobyl: The Explosion that Brought Down the Iron Curtain

Ed W. Nickerson

Order this book online at www.trafford.com
or email orders@trafford.com

Most Trafford titles are also available at major online book retailers.

Print information available on the last page.

ISBN: 978-1-4907-8166-2 (sc)
ISBN: 978-1-4907-8168-6 (hc)
ISBN: 978-1-4907-8167-9 (e)

Library of Congress Control Number: 2017904325

Trafford rev. 08/04/2017

www.trafford.com

North America & international
toll-free: 1 888 232 4444 (USA & Canada)
fax: 812 355 4082

I would like to thank my wife Judy for editing and general advice and my friend Bob Helbrecht (whose name I use in the story) for his technical support on nuclear power; in this my sixth novel.

Previous novels in the Ed Crowe series

First Flight of the Crowe (Trafford 2009)
Crowe's Feat (Trafford 2012)
Crowe's Nest (Trafford 2012)
Something to Crowe About (Trafford 2013)
A Murder of Crowes (Trafford 2015)

CHAPTER ONE

Friday, April 25th, 1986
5:45pm
Oakville, Canada

They sat in her car outside The Queen's Head. It was a clear evening, with the evening sun still in the sky. Vicky looked lovely with her blond hair held back with a clip, and her make-up just at the right level to show off her beautiful blue eyes. Ed was always impressed with Vicky's ability to make the most of an awkward situation, and he needed her to lead the way now. It was his personal circumstances that had led them to where they were today, and he didn't want to seem rushed. Both were nervous and unsure how to get their required roles in motion. Finally Vicky closed her eyes, took a deep breath, and opening her eyes wide turned to Ed.

"A few comments before we proceed, if I may?"

Ed nodded and took her hands in his to help her begin the plan they had agreed upon eight weeks earlier.

"So, Edwin William, my favorite bloke, here are a few comments about our relationship that we are about to end; blow into the air; toss into the wind or any other flippant expression you might suggest."

"Reluctantly accept as inevitable," Ed quickly added.

"That's nice," Vicky smiled. "Thank you. I appreciate that. But we must! So here I go." She leaned across and kissed him gently on his cheek. "In the two months we've been boyfriend/girlfriend, we have cruised the Caribbean; visited both New York and San Francisco; been bird-watching several times; eaten at some lovely restaurants; spent some time getting to know each others' strengths and weaknesses, and made love twelve times. A wonderful time, bloke, and one I will never forget. Now please start the process and let's get this over and done with."

Ed raised his index finger.

Vicky nodded. "Okay, just the one comment please."

"Every time I said I loved you, Vicky, I meant it."

Vicky gulped to hold back a tear. "You can be so nice, bloke. Now go!"

Ed leaned across, gave her a quick kiss on her lips, got out of the car and walked into the pub. Vicky looked at her watch. Five minutes was their agreed-upon time.

Ed entered the pub and walked to his regular spot at the bar. Seana was working the bar and waved hello to him. Seana had worked at The Queen's Head for several years, and was a friend of Vicky's. Like Vicky she was five-eight and slim, but with long dark hair, tied up in a pony-tail tonight. It was always a pleasure to be served by her. Ed nodded for his regular pint of Double Diamond, and said his hellos to his fellow regulars.

Seana delivered his pint. "Is Vicky joining us today?"

"I'm not sure," Ed replied with a shrug. "She said she might."

Several minutes later Vicky walked into the pub and headed for Ed. Her tall slim figure always attracted attention, but this was a different Vicky from just a few minutes earlier. Her hair was hanging loose around her shoulders, her lipstick was gone and her eye make-up was smeared. There was no smile on her now serious looking face. Seana couldn't believe her eyes.

"Ed, outside!" was all Vicky said, and turned back toward the exit. No wave to Seana, no recognition of friends she knew. Ed followed quickly.

Outside Vicky turned to Ed and immediately started waving her finger at him. "This makes me feel pretty stupid," she said, but her actions were not related to her words. She continued pointing, waving and gesturing to Ed and motioned as if she was shouting. "Okay, I'm going to jab you now, and then I'm gone." She jabbed Ed in the chest, threw up her hands in frustration, turned and left.

Ed motioned as if he was calling to Vicky to return. "Speak to you later," he said. Looking down at the ground, he turned and walked back to the pub entrance.

Those watching through a window from inside the pub quickly returned to their places and went back to their own conversations. They would discuss what had just happened later.

He walked back to the bar, ran his hands through his dark too-long hair as if searching for answers, picked up his drink and took a long swig of beer. Putting his nearly empty glass back on the bar, he looked at Seana and motioned for a second pint. Seana pulled his pint but didn't rush to deliver it. She could see he was upset.

"What was that all about?" she asked, sliding his beer across the bar.

Ed shrugged and frowned. "I think it could be said that Vicky just dumped me. In no uncertain terms, I might add."

Seana leaned closer and spoke softly. "Vicky? Dump you? She's crazy about you. She told me so last week."

"Things change, I guess. Whatever happened to that shy, unassuming Vicky you were always telling me about?"

Seana nodded her understanding. "When her ex-fiancé dumped her and she met you, that changed everything – and mostly for the good. I can't believe she would do it right here and right now. Yikes!"

Ed finished his first beer, took a mouthful of his second beer and shook his head. "I think I'll finish my beer and go home," he said. "I don't want her to come back and finish me off."

Seana nodded. "I understand. The beers are on me. Go home and relax."

Ed did as he was told and was home by six-thirty.

Seven-thousand-four-hundred-and-eighty-seven kilometers to the east, just outside the town of Pripyat in the northern area of Ukraine SSR, at 01:23 local time, Saturday, April 26th, the Chernobyl Nuclear Power Plant, Reactor Unit 4, reached 33,000 MW thermal and exploded. The 2000 ton upper plate of the reactor was blown up and through the roof of the building. Several seconds later a second explosion, the equivalent of ten tons of TNT occurred. This explosion released super heated lumps of graphite, reactor fuel and fission products that resulted in unprotected workers receiving fatal levels of radiation in less than a minute.

At exactly eight-forty-five Ed's phone rang and he picked it up immediately. "How are you doing?" he asked.

"Not bad for a broken-hearted ex-girlfriend. The tears have stopped flowing." Vicky paused. "Just kidding, I'm doing fine. Seana phoned to say you left early and heart-broken." She laughed. "We agreed it was because you had only two pints instead of your regular three."

"Thanks, I'm sure," Ed replied. "So when did you take acting lessons? Everyone seemed impressed, and most likely felt quite sorry for me."

"I'm not *just* a pretty face," Vicky said proudly.

"No you're not for sure. But you are most certainly pretty."

"Okay quit that nice-bloke stuff. It's going to be sad enough not spending my Friday nights with you watching 'Heartbeat', and then having you seduce me into your bed."

"Me seduce you? That'll be the day."

She thought for a second before she replied. "Not now it won't, not now."

He cringed at his poor wording. "Sorry. I wasn't thinking. Bad choice of words."

Vicky responded quickly and firmly. "Hey, I knew the rules of the game when we started all of this. In fact I made most of them up. Next weekend after Pat and Roy's wedding in England, you're going to ask your lady-friend to marry you. We'll always be friends, as they say, and that's fine with me."

Ed closed his eyes, not quite sure how things had happened as they had. He was sad but happy at the same time. His main goal had been to ensure Vicky's feelings were not hurt, which had not been the case when her ex-fiancé had ended their relationship with a note on her birthday card several months earlier. She was obviously fully accepting of their new relationship as of tonight. "Thanks, friend," he smiled.

"Good night, Ed."

"Good night, Vicky. I meant what I said in the car."

They hung up.

Ed turned on the TV and sat back to watch 'Heartbeat'. Alone.

Fifteen minutes later his phone rang again, and Vicky spoke before he had a chance to speak. "You're on the nine-thirty Air Canada flight on Monday, right? Well I'll pick you up at six downstairs and drive you to the airport. And don't tell me I don't have to, because I want to. Bye."

Ed hung up without speaking.

Vicky hung up the phone and then pointed to it with a devilish grin. "Just you wait, 'Enry 'Iggins, just you wait."

At 4am, Sunday, April 27th, Oakville time, 11am local time in Pripyat, Ukraine hundreds of buses were arriving to start the evacuation of the town. Residents were told that the evacuation would last only three days. Most would never return. By 3pm, 53,000 people were evacuated to various villages of the Kiev region. There was a 10km exclusion zone set around Pripyat. Eventually the exclusion zone was expanded to 30km and has been in effect ever since.

CHAPTER TWO

Monday, April 28th, 1986
6pm
Oakville

A stretch limousine pulled up in front of Ed's apartment block, where he stood with his luggage. He didn't realize it was for him until Vicky exited as the driver held the door open for her.

"Jump in, bloke," she said enthusiastically, "Charles will get your luggage."

Ed entered the passenger area that was built to hold ten comfortably. Vicky sat at the back of the area and patted the seat next to her. Ed joined her and they buckled up as the driver stored Ed's luggage.

"Gees, Vicky, you didn't have to…"

She slapped his leg. "Hey, it's my father's limo. My pleasure; actually our pleasure. My father asked me to use it since he knows we're not going out together any longer, or not 'a team' as he likes to say, and he wanted you to know that he has a high regard for you. Besides, I don't get to use it very often."

Ed picked up her hand and kissed it gently. "You're a very sweet person, young lady. Thank you."

"Hey, I'm sweet to all my ex-boyfriends."

Ed raised an eyebrow. "You only have one ex-boyfriend, Miss Kilgour."

She shrugged. "Whatever! I suppose *he* is *technically* an ex-fiancé and now enjoying his new life in San Francisco with his boyfriend."

"Partner is the correct terminology, Vicky."

"Partner, smartner! Sounds more like a cowboy thing to me."

Ed jabbed her with his elbow. "Moving on then?"

"Yes," Vicky agreed, "moving on then. Do you have your best-man speech ready for the wedding? You know the wedding between your best mate Roy and your, shall I say, 'good friend' Pat, and where the maid of honor is your lady friend whom you intend to ask to marry you...that speech!"

"If you put it that way, yes I do. Thank you for clarifying the situation so clearly."

Vicky took his hand in hand in hers. "Seriously I do hope the wedding goes well. I like Pat, and not just because she's my client." She paused and then smiled sweetly. "Don't forget you'll need to review your life insurance needs if Carolyn accepts your hand in marriage."

Ed tried to remove his hand, but Vicky held on. "Okay that was unnecessary," she added. "Let's just relax. We'll be at the airport in twenty minutes."

Little was said during the last few minutes, with Ed feeling quite uneasy about the fact that Vicky was with him on the way to the airport. The personal inter-relationships Vicky had touched on were messy enough, and he was looking forward to getting on the plane to somehow allow the distance make it all easier to accept.

The limo pulled up at the departure gates and Ed and Vicky waited while the driver walked around to open the trunk. He seemed to be taking a long time. The trunk lid finally opened and Ed looked down with a feeling of unease. Beside his well-travelled basic black and battered suitcase was a new looking pink-colored hard covered case that looked like it belonged in Hollywood.

Ed looked sideways at Vicky. "Going somewhere?"

"Oh, yeah. You're not the only world traveler, Mr. Crowe."

The driver removed both bags, tipped his hat, got in the limo and drove away.

Without speaking they entered the airport. Ed moved the bags to one side and turned to Vicky for direction or support, he wasn't sure which.

Vicky stood her full five-feet eight inches. "But I'm flying first class."

Ed nodded. "Very nice for you. May I ask…?"

"You're flying first class also. You're sitting next to me, my treat."

"Can we sit down for a minute?" Ed asked.

Vicky held her confidence. "Sure, why not. Let's have a coffee at Tim Hortons, just over there."

Five minutes later they sat at one of the few empty tables drinking their coffee, their bags dragged up beside them.

"So what's new?" Ed asked politely.

"You're mad at me aren't you?" She was losing her bravado.

Ed shook his head. "Vicky, I promise you I am not mad at you. Confused as all- get-out maybe, but not mad. You have to look after yourself first, pretty lady. Obviously I have been doing that lately, so you must do the same. Can I, may I, simply ask you to explain what the story is? I'll shut up and listen."

Vicky closed her eyes, took a deep breath, and told the story that she knew she had to tell – hoping that Ed would understand.

"About three weeks ago, I received the invitation to the wedding. I couldn't believe it! Pat and I are good friends, but an invitation to her wedding? Like wow! I immediately phoned her. Now she knows you and I are good friends and all, but I wasn't sure how much she knew. I tried to touch on the issue, but she quickly reminded me, as only Pat can, that the invitation was for me *and* a guest. Obviously that wasn't intended to be you. I thought about it, Ed. I was worried sick for a while. And then Pat phoned me to help make arrangements for me while I'm in England, and then it just happened: I accepted! She was excited, I was excited, but I asked her not to tell you. I told her I would tell you – which I just did. I know I'm a coward, but I so much wanted to be there, to visit England, to meet your friends, to meet Roy and…" she licked her lips nervously, "and to meet Carolyn. God this sounds awful, doesn't it? You must think I'm so selfish."

Ed nodded his understanding. "One question then."

Vicky closed her eyes and waited.

"Will you have the third dance with me?"

She threw he arms around him, almost spilling both cups of coffee. "Oh God, yes! The third dance, the tenth dance, whichever dance numbers you want!"

Ed stood. "Then let's get going. We've got a plane to catch."

CHAPTER THREE

The plane was forty minutes into the flight, they had reached the flying altitude and the 'Fasten Seat Belt' sign had been turned off. Ed and Vicky were sitting in row one, with Ed on the aisle and Vicky by the window. The seats were wide and comfortable, something Ed was not accustomed to. Vicky had not upgraded their seats when they had flown to San Francisco and Miami. She had explained to Ed as they had taken their seats that she wanted *this* trip to be special. Ed was sure it would be *special*, but that had nothing to do with the seat selection. He couldn't decide how to explain the full circumstances of the personal relationships between himself, Pat, Carolyn, Roy, and eventually the circumstances of the wedding being held at Stonebridge Manor, the home of Lord and Lady Stonebridge. It wasn't just the actual location, but the fact that Lord Stonebridge was the head of the British Secret Intelligence Service – better known as MI6 – and complicating matters more was that that Carolyn Andrews was the daughter of Lord and Lady Stonebridge. Andrews was her mother's maiden name; the name Carolyn used as a mid-level MI6 representative, with her business card simply identifying her as a representative of the Foreign Office. He shook his head and decided to let things take their natural course. Vicky was suspicious that Ed was more than 'just a simple travel agent'. He knew that and she knew that he knew that.

The stewardess offered a variety of drinks, but they decided on a pot of hot tea.

"This is so much fun, Ed," Vicky giggled. "I feel like a teenager on her first date with an older man."

"Hey I'm only a couple of years older that you, young lady."

"I know," she whispered, "but you're so much more experienced in worldly affairs, aren't you now?"

Here we go, Ed thought.

The stewardess delivered the tea and biscuits, and Ed decided to take the lead.

"So tell me, where does Pat have you staying in London to befit your expensive First Class approach to this once-in-a-lifetime trip?"

"I was wondering when you would ask that. Actually I'm staying in a nice part of London, not far from downtown so I can do some shopping before the wedding."

"Oh, do pray tell." He sipped on his tea.

"I'm staying with your mother."

Ed spilt his tea and gasped. "You're what?"

"Yes, your mother has agreed to let me sleep in your room."

"Never! My mum would never..."

"Of course not," she grinned. "You're staying at the Polish lady's house down the street."

"I don't believe it," Ed groaned. "Actually, I do. Pat does have a way of organizing matters to her own taste." He laughed a little. "Good for Pat. You and my mum will get along very well, of that I'm sure."

Vicky nudged him gently. "Just keep in mind I'm Pat's friend. Nothing to do with you, except I'm your life insurance agent. Pat doubts that you mentioned me to your mother, so she didn't talk about us either. But on the other hand, when your mother and I are doing some Oxford Street shopping, perhaps I'll let it slip that I'm your; ex-girlfriend, ex-lover, ex-Friday-night date. What do you think?"

"I think she would think you're a lucky girl to be my triple-ex, and I'd be a fool not to try and get you back."

Vicky smiled and nudged him not so gently. "Smart ass! So can I ask you a few questions about where we're going, who's who and stuff? Pat said it would be better for me to ask you, and not her. She actually chuckled when she said that. Now keep in mind that I know some of what you do in your travels is not for my ears. I think your getting a phone call from the president of the U.S. after your most recent trip makes that rather obvious, but help me put things into perspective. I don't want to be asking embarrassing questions at the wedding, do I?"

Ed nodded. "That makes sense. Fire away."

"The wedding is at a Stonebridge Manor. Is that some kind of rental wedding location?"

Ed closed his eyes to think. This was not going to be easy. "Stonebridge Manor is the ancestral home of Lord and Lady Stonebridge. It's about fifty miles north of London."

"Wow. So they're friends of Roy?"

"No."

"So?"

"They are the parents of Carolyn."

"But her name is …"

"She uses her mother's maiden name for certain occasions."

Vicky sat up straight. "Are you telling me that the lady friend you're going ask to marry you is the daughter of a Lord and Lady?"

Ed nodded with a shrug.

"Holy poop! Is he like a Lord as in the House of Lords?"

Ed nodded again.

"Good lord," she laughed. "Get it? Good lord!"

"I got it, smarty."

Vicky sat back in her chair. "Okay, give me time to think."

"One more thing," Ed said quietly. "He is the head of MI6; the British Secret Intelligence Service. So you may see security types around."

"You're not kidding me are you? I wouldn't appreciate…"

"No kidding. Honest."

"Whoa! Give me more time to think."

Vicky sat and looked straight at the wall ahead of them. She had a lot to think about trying to piece together, as best she could, all the information that was available to her without asking Ed questions that she knew he could not answer honestly. Eventually she arrived at her final question. She turned to Ed. "So here's my final question, and then I'll shut up."

"I'll be sure to answer it as fully as I can."

Vicky nodded her thanks. "So the last time you returned from one of your special trips, I picked you up at Hamilton airport – at four am I might add – and drove you home. You were somewhat beaten up and it was later the next day that you spoke to President Reagan. Now it was Carolyn who phoned me to ask me to pick you up etc. because Pat was flying to England to finalize her wedding plans."

"Correct," Ed replied quickly.

"That wasn't the question. The question is; is Carolyn a travel agent, and is that why she was involved?"

"No."

Vicky punched his arm. "C'mon, Ed, give me some credit here."

Ed leaned over and spoke quietly. "Carolyn is a representative of the British Foreign Service Office. She helps Brits that need assistance from time to time, and don't forget I am still British." He was more than satisfied with his answer. It was the truth. Not the full truth, perhaps, but the truth.

"Hmmm," Vicky mused. "So Pat works for Export Development Canada, Carolyn works for the British Foreign Office, Lord Stonebridge is the head of MI6, and you're just a lowly Canadian travel agent flitting around the world from time to time…and that's not a question thank you very much!"

Ed nodded anyway.

Vicky reached for her blanket, curled up her feet on her seat, and leaned toward Ed. "May I lean on you, oh world traveler?"

"It would be my pleasure, young lady."

She covered herself with the blanket and snuggled up to Ed. "Put your arm over me please."

Ed reached over as she snuggled in closer. "I do believe your wearing my favorite perfume," he commented.

"Really? What a coincidence." She reached over under the blanket and squeezed his leg. "Goodnight, bloke. When I wake up four hours from now, I'll stop asking questions and will act like a young lady for the rest of the trip."

He gently squeezed her arm. "Goodnight, Vicky."

She looked up at him with a sad frown. "Hey, I'm snuggled up to you. There are rules, you know."

He bent down slightly and kissed the top of her head. "Goodnight, pretty blue eyes."

She shivered nicely. "Good night, bloke." She closed her eyes and within a minute was asleep.

CHAPTER FOUR

Tuesday, April, 29th 1986 Flying over the Atlantic

Almost four hours to the minute later Vicky awoke, threw off the blanket and was wide awake. Ed was still trying to nod off without disturbing his 'pretty blue eyes'. She stood, grabbed her small carry-on bag and left. "I'm off to powder my nose," she offered as she left.

Fifteen minutes later she returned looking refreshed and quite beautiful. "Your turn," she said taking her seat. Ed took advantage of the mostly sleeping passengers and went to 'powder his nose'.

As soon as he was in the washroom area, Vicky picked up Ed's small carry-on bag and found his passport. For several minutes she flipped through the pages of his passport making mental notes of the countries he had visited since arriving in Canada less than two years ago, while noting again that his passport was issued four year before he arrived in Canada, and was issued for ten years and not the normal five. It was only when she flipped back to the inside cover that she noticed a second interesting variance in his passport to the norm. She smiled at the find, put his passport carefully back in his bag, slid the bag back under his seat grabbed an Air Canada in-flight magazine and started reading. She gave the appearance of an angel when Ed returned, and he was no wiser to her new-found information.

Tea and coffee were poured, and breakfast was served as the plane flew over Ireland and across central England. Ed was happy to point out the cities and landmarks. Luckily there were few clouds which was a good sign of the weather in store for them. Vicky was excited asking all types of questions about England, its history and what were the correct ways to address people, especially Lord and lady Stonebridge, at the wedding.

Ed interrupted her questions as he pointed below them. "That's Windsor Castle," he announced, and Vicky was unusually speechless as she took it all in.

"Will you take me to Windsor Castle?" she asked enthusiastically. "Please, please?"

"Let's see how much time you have after you've finished your Oxford Street shopping with my mum."

"I'll find time, I'll find time," she replied quickly. Then she took a breath and asked carefully. "Will you find time, Ed?"

"I'll find time, Vicky. What are good friends for, eh?"

She reached over and gave him a big hug. "You're a great ex-boyfriend, Ed. I wish I had more like you." She shrugged. "Maybe I will soon." She shook her head. "Nah, you're sorta special. To me anyway." She went back to looking out of the window and back to asking questions.

"So what is Roy like," Vicky asked.

"Well, let's see. He's sort of short like Pat. Perhaps a tad heavy, and somewhat balding early. Great guy, of course. Pat wouldn't marry just anyone, would she?"

"Well she wouldn't marry you, if that's what you mean."

Ed laughed. "Thanks"

"Hey, just kidding. I know she likes and respects you a lot…a BIG lot that is."

The plane started its descent. Vicky kept her eyes looking out of the window taking everything in, while Ed grinned slightly to himself.

As they touched down, Vicky sat up and turned to Ed with a smile. "He'll be here you know: Roy that is. He and Pat are picking us up."

"Even better," Ed smiled. "Any other surprises for me?"

"I'll let you know," Vicky responded with a shrug. "Us girls have sorted out all the details. Just come along for the ride."

"Yes, miss. As you say, miss."

They passed through passport control without a hitch, picked up their bags and, to Vicky's surprise, walked through the 'Nothing to Declare' Customs line. As usual Heathrow was busy with thousands of passengers moving as quickly as they could to get out of the airport and into the real world.

Pat saw Ed and Vicky and came running to give them both a hug, especially her new friend Vicky. They were both so excited about seeing each other, especially with the wedding as the main attraction.

"Vicky, this is Roy," Pat said as an introduction.

Roy was two inches taller than Ed, slim to thin, and with a full head of hair. He shook Vicky's hand that was offered and then gave her a gentle hug. "Welcome to England, Vicky. It's a pleasure to meet you."

Vicky bowed her head slightly. "It's even a greater pleasure for me, Roy. I wouldn't have recognized you given that Ed said you were short, fat and bald!"

Roy laughed heartily. "No matter. Pat described you perfectly; pretty, charming, and way too nice for the likes of Ed."

Vicky turned to Ed. "So there, bloke!"

Ed shrugged. "What are friends for?"

A lengthy walk through the airport got them to Roy's car. Pat and Vicky jumped into the back seats and immediately started talking about the wedding plans. Ed and Roy caught up on a variety of matters with Ed speaking softly for a few moments. Roy nodded and smiled.

Forty-five minutes later Roy pulled over and stopped the car. "There you go, Vicky," he said leaning into the back, "Windsor Castle."

Vicky couldn't believe her eyes. Up on a hill was the castle; beautiful and dramatically located, surrounded by acres of neatly kept grass with a pathway with trees in full spring color on either side that led up to the castle. She jumped out and stood transfixed at the beauty.

In the car Roy turned to Pat. "Ed and I will go for a cup of tea and pick you right here in an hour and a half?"

"Thanks, guys," she beamed. "You've just made her day, maybe her trip." She got out of the car; put an arm through Vicky's and led her up the Long Walk to the castle.

The tea lady delivered their pot of tea. Roy looked at the cups and then at the lady.

"You'd like larger cups, wouldn't you, sir?" she asked.

"Would you mind," Roy replied with a smile of thanks, "my friend here is rather clumsy. He's from Canada and they use big cups so the tea doesn't freeze too quickly."

"I have a friend in Canada," she said enthusiastically. "She lives in Vancouver. Lovely city, but so far away. I'll get you some other cups."

She returned two minutes later with two large cups and saucers celebrating the Coronation in 1953. "There you go, gents," now speaking with a strong London accent. "Don't drop 'em; they're worth a bob or two."

Ed poured the tea carefully, being sure to add the milk after the pour. This was an English Tea Shop in Windsor. Things had to be done proper like!

"So are you all ready for your role as best man?" Roy asked, but knowing the answer.

"Ready to go."

"Good speech?"

"Seventeen minutes long."

Roy gagged. "Nothing about other girls now."

"Then it's only seven minutes long."

"Fine. She's very pretty you know."

"Yes, you're a very lucky man."

Roy topped up their tea. "I was talking about Vicky, and you know it. She also did a super job on our life insurance needs. Very knowledgeable."

"Yes, she is. Very pretty and very knowledgeable."

"Have you spoken to Carolyn lately? You know, the English lady you're crazy about…Or are you; still crazy about her that is?"

Ed rubbed his chin, wanting to be careful with his answer. "We spoke last week. Just to make sure we didn't cover off the same issues in our speeches."

"And?"

"We didn't."

"And?"

"And I don't know. As I'm sure you're aware Carolyn spent some time in France with her mother. Had a slight touch of depression, I'm guessing. She sounded just fine last week. I'm meeting her on Thursday."

"Just fine? People recovering from heart surgery are 'just fine'."

"Let's leave it at that. I will find out on Thursday how she is, how we are…or not!"

Roy stood to leave. "That's a deal. Let's go meet the ladies and get you and Vicky to your mum's place."

Pat and Vicky were a few minutes late, and both visibly excited about their visit to the castle. Vicky jumped in the back seat next to Ed, bouncing with eagerness and excitement. "Oh, Roy, thank you so much. That was wonderful."

Roy smiled. "Don't thank me, I'm just the driver. It was Eddie's idea to show you the castle."

Vicky turned to Ed with a grin. "Eddie? Who's Eddie? I know an Ed Crowe and I know an Edwin Crowe…but an Eddie? That sounds so young and…and…"

"Sexy?" Ed offered.

Vicky shook her head. "Nope. Definitely not sexy."

Roy pulled into the traffic. "He was always Eddie at school, so the name stuck. In fact he hadn't been called Ed until his first trip to Canada. Much more of a lumberjack's name, I suppose."

Vicky nodded her head slowly. "Ed the lumberjack! That works."

"Are we done?" Ed wondered.

Vicky nudged him with her shoulder. "We're done Eddie; Eddie the travel agent."

Pat turned with a wink. "I like him whatever we call him." She knew that it was Carolyn that had first called him Ed, and only after he had asked her not to call him Edwin. That had been his trip to Ankara; the trip that had resulted in his becoming a consultant with MI6, and had also resulted in his first meeting Pat in Canada. Pat from CSIS, not Export Development Canada as was indicated on her government business card.

As they entered London traffic they slowed down as the number of cars and vehicles of all size increased. Ed pointed out interesting features spending some time explaining to Vicky how roundabouts worked.

"So tell me, Vicky," Roy enquired, "you decided not to bring a guest to the wedding. Any special reason, other than cost, that is?"

Pat jumped in. "That's his way of asking you if you have a boyfriend. Don't feel obliged."

Vicky thought for a few moments. "Well in answer to your question, Roy, no I don't have a boyfriend. Not at this time anyway."

"Lot's of eligible men at the wedding," Roy offered.

Vicky looked at Ed sideways and continued. "I was engaged at one time. My fiancé had a wooden leg, so I broke it off"

Ed rolled his eyes, Pat giggled to herself, and Roy almost lost control of the car as he laughed and banged his hand on the steering wheel. "So you broke it off! Now that is funny. That is very funny. What do you think, Eddie?"

Ed smiled, remembering the day he suggested she use that expression whenever her broken engagement was discussed. It worked every time. The fact that her fiancé had broken off the engagement with a brief note on her birthday card had never arisen. "I'm sure it was a step in the right direction," Ed replied. "At least for Vicky."

Vicky gave him a wink, they all laughed, and the discussion was over. Un-noticed by Pat or Roy, Vicky slipped her hand over to Ed's and gave it a 'thank you' squeeze.

As they drove slowly through the west end of London, Pat's mobile phone rang. She quickly grabbed it from her handbag and answered it with a single word. "Go."

She listened and spoke little except an occasional "Okay." When she turned off the phone, she waited before she spoke. Eerily no-one asked. They somehow knew not to enquire.

She turned to Ed and Vicky. "Not sure if you've heard, but there was a nuclear reactor accident in Russia a couple of days ago – in Ukraine actually. The soviet authorities announced it, two days after the event, and only after radiation levels set off alarms at a nuclear power plant in Sweden. The initial announcement was, to say the least, lacking in details. The latest report has announced that the local town of Pripyat has been evacuated." She shook her head. "There's a bit of a kafuffle about what happened and the Canadian nuclear power authorities have made some serious insinuations. So there's a bit of an international crisis in Ottawa. If it's okay with you guys Roy will drop you off at Mrs. C's and we'll head somewhere where I can make a few phone calls confidentially. Ed, I know your mum will be expecting us to stop in for a cup of tea, so perhaps you could convey our regrets?"

"Of course," Ed replied, nodding his head. "Business must."

Vicky looked sideways at Ed, but said nothing. The mood in the car had changed and nothing needed saying.

Ed and Vicky retrieved their bags from the boot of Roy's car and the four hugged and shook hands.

"The manor?" Ed asked as he hugged Pat.

She extended the hug, "Yep. Bit of an issue. I'll be in touch." She reached in her handbag and slipped him a mobile phone. "My number is listed."

Pat and Roy quickly jumped into the car and drove away.

Vicky turned to Ed with a sneaky look. “What was that all about?”

Ed shrugged his ignorance. “Search me.” He took her arm and opened the gate to his mother’s house. “Come and meet my mum.”

“Stonebridge Manor?” Roy asked as he turned north.

“Yes please, sweetie,” Pat replied with a nudge.

“I understand,” he added, “I’ll ask you no questions…”

“And I’ll tell you no lies,” Pat replied.

Mrs. Crowe opened the door and waved Ed and Vicky in. “Come in, come in, the kettle’s on the boil.” No more than five-foot-four, and with her hair recently cut and colored, she both looked and acted younger than she was. She turned to Vicky. “Well, Victoria aren’t you a pretty one.” She hurried them past the stairs and into the family room. The table was set for five and Ed explained that Pat and Roy had to rush off to a meeting.

“The meeting is about the wedding, Mrs. Crowe,” Vicky offered. “And it’s Vicky please.”

“Thank you, Vicky. And it’s Mrs. C., please. Edwin, make the tea please. I want to get to know Vicky a little more before we head off to do some shopping in the next few days.”

Ed cleared the table of two settings and headed into the small kitchen to do as he was asked. It gave him a few moments to wonder why a nuclear accident in Ukraine could have any bearing on MI6; but something was afoot, of that he was sure.

He poured the tea as Vicky outlined to his mother how she had met Pat and how close their friendship had become over the past few months. He thought she did well in describing the process while keeping Ed’s active involvement limited, when in fact he had been the friend that had introduced them to each other. Vicky didn’t lie; she just didn’t add all the related details. Ed added only a few nods to the outline, and delivered the cups of tea when there was a break in the conversation. The three enjoyed their tea and biscuits.

Ed's mother broke the ritual of silence. "Perhaps, Edwin, you could show Vicky to her room."

Ed nodded, collected Vicky's bag and headed up the stairs to 'his' bedroom. Vicky entered the small room, enjoying the surroundings. There was a single bed to the right, at the end of which was the window that looked over Queen's Park. The remainder of the room was limited to a small desk and a chest of drawers. Throughout the room were photos of Ed at various ages, mostly as a member of a football or cricket team. A few trophies added to the sports background.

Ed smiled and turned to Vicky. "Not like your bedroom, eh?"

She laughed. No it wasn't like her bedroom at all. Her bedroom, in her parent's large Oakville house, with a view of Lake Ontario to the south and beautiful Lakeshore Road to the north, was larger than the entire main floor of Mrs. Crowe's home.

"I think your room has more flavor," she nodded. "And likely has had more romantic activity than mine by a country mile."

Before Ed could respond, the mobile phone in his trouser pocket rang and vibrated. He lifted a finger to excuse himself. "Hi, Pat," he answered, and then listened.

Vicky was determined not to listen or show interest, and went about the room moving items that would help in her unpacking when she was ready to do so. It didn't matter: Ed only grunted and said 'yes' a couple of times before he turned off the phone.

"I have to go," he said quickly. "A car's picking me up in half an hour."

"I'm going with you," Vicky announced clearly.

Ed shook his head. "Vicky, you can't…It's kind of business."

"Oh yes I can. I know what 'kind of business' it is. I'm going with you, or more to the point, you're taking me with you." She raised a hand. "If you don't take me, I'm going downstairs right now to tell your mother that I'm pregnant with your child."

"Whoa...I er, you're not er…"

"Of course I'm not! Do you think I'm an idiot?" She pointed at him. "Yes, it's a lie and yes it's bribery. Big deal! I'm going with you."

"Your mother accepted your comments without question." Vicky said as they sat in the limo. "Maybe she's used to your lying to her?"

Ed chuckled and he turned to face her. "Let's just say she doesn't ask any awkward questions. I don't lie to Mum."

"Glad to hear it, Edwin."

The town car was speeding north on lesser used back roads, staying clear of the busy motorways and main roads. Ed and Vicky sat in the back seat of the very large vehicle, and there was room for two more just on that one seat.

"I didn't know there were this many roundabouts in the world," Vicky said as the driver barely slowed down to move through the many roundabouts, both large and small.

Ed nodded. "Increases gas mileage, or petrol mileage if you will, by five percent, I've heard tell."

"There's another weird one," Vicky said, jotting a note on a note pad. "Who in heaven's name wants to live in a place called Stoke Poges, or Cryer's Hill, or even Walter's Ash? Do you have an addiction for strange sounding names in England? Look at that sign, 5km to Loosley Row for God's sake."

"Moose Jaw," Ed countered with a grin. "Swift Current, Come By Chance," he added.

"Okay. Let's call it a tie." She reached over and they shook hands. "You're not mad at me are you, Ed? For insisting you drag me along."

"Glad to have you with me, Vicky. Just remember…"

"Yeah, yeah, I know. It's 'kind of business.' Probably funny business I'd bet."

"Just a young travel agent's business in today's day and age, Miss Kilgour."

CHAPTER FIVE

"Holy cow!" Vicky gasped as the town car sat at the gate of Stonebridge Manor. The driver spoke quietly on his mobile phone and the gates opened.

Even at the quick speed that they drove, it took several minutes to drive to the entrance of the manor. The grounds were a beautiful mixture of finely trimmed grass, outstandingly designed flower beds, and stands of trees of every size and shape. The beauty of it all took Vicky's breath away and she couldn't stop looking in awe until the car pulled up sharply in front of the manor house. Ed exited as Vicky quickly touched up her make-up, not exiting until she was satisfied everything was in place. She thanked the driver who was holding the door open for her, wondering if she should tip him. He was back inside and on his way before she had time to decide.

Vicky brushed down her dress, adjusted her hair, and as casually as she could she walked the few steps to Ed. "Look okay?" she asked.

"Beautiful," Ed replied honestly, and turned to head up the steps to the front door.

"Whoa, hold on," Vicky said. She looked up at the manor, gently shaking her head. The manor was similar to structures out of a BBC television program on historical structures of the distant past. "Not exactly like 'Coronation Street' is it? How many rooms are there?"

"Fifty plus."

She looked around at the gardens and landscaping. The flowers were in full spring blossom and the trees were filled with young and vibrant colors.

"What do I do when we get inside, Ed? I'm beginning to regret your letting me come along."

Ed chuckled. "Vicky, my dear friend, just act yourself. I can assure you as grand as the manor is, and as stately the interior is, you will feel as comfortable and relaxed as when you met my mother."

As he spoke, the double doors to the manor opened and Lady Stonebridge walked forward.

"Why, Mr. Crowe, what a pleasant surprise. Please introduce me to your friend and our special guest." Lady Stonebridge was dressed, as was her style, as if the Queen might be dropping in for an afternoon cup of tea. She spoke with a correct, but not posh, accent.

Ed introduced Victoria Kilgour as Pat's friend, his friend, and also their life insurance agent. She curtsied slightly as she shook Lady Stonebridge's hand.

"None of that required," Lady Stonebridge said quietly, as she ushered them into the manor's large and beautiful hall. "I was not 'to the manor born'," she continued. "In fact I was born and raised in Neasden, in north London."

"That would be just north of Kilburn," Ed added mischievously.

"We prefer to think of it as just south of St. Albans," Lady Stonebridge retorted quickly.

Vicky didn't understand the difference, but was in awe at the manor and its surrounding.

Pat ran down the stairs and gave Vicky a hug. "Oh, I'm so glad Ed convinced you to join him for the drive. Come on into the library where Roy is waiting."

Vicky gave Ed a sideways look. "Ed insisted. Wouldn't have it any other way."

The four walked to the library, and explaining that she and Ed had a short meeting to attend, Pat led Ed upstairs to Lord Stonebridge's office.

"I'll have tea sent up in twenty minutes," Lady Stonebridge offered, then led Vicky to one side of the room to find out as much as she could about Ed and Pat's friend.

The library was large and held hundreds of books on each wall. Roy sat at the far end reading a huge copy of an old and beautifully bound copy of the Encyclopedia Britannica. He waved hello, and when Lady Stonebridge turned her back to him as she sat down, he zipped his fingers across his lips and pointed to her. Vicky got the message and replied with a small smile.

"So," Lady Stonebridge began "tell me all about yourself, Victoria. Pat speaks very highly of you."

Twenty minutes later Vicky summed up her background, spending a considerable amount of time relating the story of her ex-fiancé now living with his boyfriend in San Francisco. Ed's name was never mentioned. Vicky spoke quietly, Lady Stonebridge was almost in tears, and Roy was proud of his new friend Vicky.

Lord Stonebridge stood looking out the window overlooking the beautifully landscaped grounds of Stonebridge Manor, but he had other thoughts on his mind at the moment. As head of MI6 the recent, and urgent, request of Prime Minister Thatcher to assist the USSR, was not a comforting thought. There were lots of changes happening within the USSR since President Gorbachev had been elected General Secretary of the Communist Party, but no one person could change history, and the Soviet history was not to be taken as un-important or irrelevant. He turned his tall slim body and sat at his desk that was large and appropriate for the immense size of his office. He spread his hands on the top of the desk and faced his fellow attendees with a smile.

"Perhaps I should sum-up where we are at?" suggested Mr. Cooper, better known in the department as the General. He sat to the right of Lord Stonebridge, while Ed and Pat sat to the left.

Lord Stonebridge nodded. "Please do, General. And if there are any questions in the room, they must be asked and answered if possible."

Ed and Pat nodded their understanding, and sat a little higher in their chairs to give the General their full attention.

The General combed his hand through his grey and thinning hair. Ed thought he looked younger and healthier since his retirement. He had run his own travel agency, the travel agency where Ed had worked before getting involved with MI6 as a consultant. The consulting job that had ultimately led to Ed's moving to Canada.

"So to the big picture," the General started, "and that must, by the nature of the beast, involve politics. Only this time at the very highest levels."

Lord Stonebridge waved him on with a knowledgeable smile.

"President Gorbachev and his close advisors are now sure the 'accident' was in fact not an accident. For that matter, no-one in the Soviet nuclear power regime believes it was an accident. The problem they face now is they cannot trust anyone in their own operation to search out the obvious culprit – more on him later. Gorbachev initially considered asking the US to do the investigation, but the huge mistrust of the US by the KGB makes that impossible. Further, Gorbachev fears an internal up-rising if he went the US route and that would be an international disaster. Australia, always the good guy, said 'no thanks'. They don't want to annoy their new friend China. So Canada was suggested by President Reagan, and Gorbachev agreed. Interestingly the Canada/Ukraine connection made it a fully acceptable solution. There are more Canadians of Ukrainian descent than in any other western country, a fact I was not aware of."

"So why are we not meeting in Ottawa?" Ed asked.

Pat answered quickly. "That meeting was held this morning by phone. Prime Minister Mulroney spoke with Mrs. Thatcher and Lord Stonebridge. The Canadian nuclear power authorities are sending one of their nuclear experts to see the Chernobyl disaster as we speak. He will visit briefly and obviously under full nuclear fall-out protection. But he cannot be involved in finding and confronting the man that pressed the button so to speak. That is my job." She turned to Ed with a smile. "And yours."

"Whoa," Ed groaned loudly, "you're getting married in four days for heaven's sake. That makes no sense. And I'm the best man!"

Lord Stonebridge raised his hands to slow things down. "Let the General finish his up-date before we raise some very serious matters surrounding this challenge, except let me stress that we must have this resolved in less than four days. If it isn't," he emphasized, "there is a concern there will be a second 'accident'."

The room went silent. Pat shrugged, with a nod of thanks to Ed.

The General continued. "So once again, Eddie, your Canadian passport is part of the solution. Let us hope we can use it, along with Pat's of course, to address this major concern." He turned to Ed. "To address the question you raised earlier Miss Andrews is currently on her way to Istanbul. She is headed to Istanbul because Mr. Alexi Umarov is also on his way to Istanbul. He, of course, is the man we think – are almost positive – created the explosion and the resulting melt-down at Chernobyl. He is Chechen, I'll get into that later, and his activity since the explosion convinces one and all that he is our man. He is not trying hard to hide. He flew to Istanbul only hours before the explosion. He left a note which translated from Russian into English means 'More to come'. He has not hidden the fact that he has booked a seven day cruise from Istanbul to Rome, in fact he has made it obvious what he is doing. It's the message that worries us all. We could catch him in a matter of hours, but we know that even the KGB, especially the KGB, could not make him talk. Like many Chechens he despises Russia and everything they stand for. Like almost all Chechens he is a Muslim – not what you would call devout, but Muslim nevertheless. And Islam is a, no 'the', major difference between Chechnya and most other republics of the USSR."

"What is the plan?" Ed asked enthusiastically, now intrigued by the background.

"In simple terms," the General continued, "it is to meet and get to know Mr. Alexi Umarov and convince him to explain his 'More to come' comment. By 'convince' I mean persuade, influence, and win-over even. It is not our plan to beat him into submission." He looked at Pat and Ed. "Obviously you wouldn't be here if the goal included beatings. The fact is he's a very intelligent man, and not what we would normally think of as a terrorist. In addition to being educated as a nuclear physicist, he speaks fluent English, Chechen, Ukrainian, and Russian. He is single, was born in Grozny, the capital of Chechnya, thirty-four years ago. He, like many Muslims, drinks alcohol occasionally and is a dedicated cigar smoker. He imports many high-quality cigars - if that is not a contradiction in terms – mostly from Cuba, where he has visited several times."

Lord Stonebridge's phone rang, and he held up his hand indicating he had to take the call. He listened intently, nodding his head from time to time. His only words were 'thank you,' and he hung up.

"Good news," he smiled, "Miss Andrews is now an employee of Princess Cruise Lines, and her first role is Senior Activities Officer on the Sun Princess cruise ship that leaves tomorrow from Istanbul to Rome. The stage is set, but we must act fast. The ship pulls up anchor tomorrow at 6pm."

"Pulls up anchor?" Ed enquired.

"Okay, leaves the dock," Lord Stonebridge shrugged. "Not quite as romantic for a love boat as outlined in the television series."

As they shared the humor, the door opened and Vicky walked into the office pushing a trolley filled with tea and biscuits. She stood upright with a formal look on her face. "Tea time with biscuits," she said in as posh an English accent she could manage without laughing.

Lord Stonebridge quickly stood and bowed his head in thanks. "Ah, tea. The answer to all of the world's problems." He walked toward Vicky with his hand extended. "Miss Victoria Kilgour, I presume?"

Ed and Pat jumped to introduce Vicky to Lord Stonebridge and the General: whom they introduced as Mr. Cooper. After the official introductions, Lord Stonebridge invited Vicky to join them for a relaxing cup of tea. She sat close to Pat, while Ed sat nervously hoping that the visit would be short. It wasn't to be.

Lord Stonebridge led the discussion. "So I hear tell, Miss Kilgour, that you are a life insurance agent, and a very successful one at that, and you use our Mr. Crowe as your travel agent. I trust he does a good job for you?"

Vicky stood, Ed assumed to leave, but instead she moved her chair closer to Lord Stonebridge's desk. "Yes and quite a travel agent he is. A regular world traveler no less." She was enjoying her opportunity. "Why he visited Turkey in April 1984 then spent some time in Canada, before returning to Turkey for another visit. Later that year he visited Libya of all places, stopping off at Malta on the way. Then a quick trip to Sofia, Bulgaria, and then to Paris for goodness sake."

Ed raised his hand. Vicky was touching on the stops he had visited in his role as a consultant for MI6, and he needed her to stop. "Gee, thanks, Vicky…."

"No, no," Lord Stonebridge interrupted, "please continue, Miss Kilgour. You seem to have a good handle on our Mr. Crowe's travels."

Vicky nodded with a wide smile. "Now his next trip was less interesting." Ed groaned. "He was back to London, and then off to Amsterdam, Holland in early 1985. Just a quick visit this time and then back home to Canada." She looked at Ed and then, almost apologetically, to Pat. She took a long sip of her tea.

"Moving on the next trip is really interesting," Vicky continued. "Ed visits Paris in August 1985, and guess what? Why he's there on a honeymoon with my friend Pat, who is, as we all know, getting married to Ed's best friend on Saturday. Like wow!"

"That is interesting," the General acknowledged with a slight chuckle.

Pat shrugged and blushed.

Ed had given up hope and sat with his eyes closed.

Vicky spoke quickly. "Now I know it was not their honeymoon, and in fact my father had to convince the CBC not to extend their news coverage on the facts involved during their time in Paris – including the street fights that erupted during their 'honeymoon'. Something to do with the French government during the Second World War, but what do I know, I'm too young to know about these things."

Lord Stonebridge replied knowingly. "You obviously know a great deal more than you're letting on, Miss Kilgour, and I appreciate your delicate and guarded telling. Please do proceed."

Vicky now spoke carefully, not wanting to appear to be bragging, while accepting Lord Stonebridge's carefully worded invitation to continue. "Well shortly after I first met Ed at our local pub, he headed out to Damascus, Syria in early January 1986 for his usual travel agent trip, no doubt to learn more about a very interesting part of the world. What made this trip so personal to me was that when he returned home on February 26th – at 4am I might add – I was asked by Pat and your daughter…er, I mean Miss Andrews, to pick him up and get him home safe and sound. It was, of course, my pleasure to help him, and made sure not to ask questions about his freshly bruised face." She paused. "No doubt he accidently walked into a door."

Ed nodded.

Vicky summed up. "So yes a very interesting travel agent, and indeed a very interesting new Canadian. His passport is interesting in that it was issued for ten years instead of the usual five, and dated four years before he ever came to Canada. And while my passport, indeed most Canadian passports, offer the usual basic information regarding the carrier, Ed's is very special in that it has Pat's office telephone number on page three." She smiled. "That, of course, would be Pat's number at Export Development Canada in Ottawa. Makes sense to me."

Lord Stonebridge stood and moved around his desk to shake Vicky's hand. "Thank you, Miss Kilgour. I appreciate your candor and, no doubt, confidence in your, shall we say, discretion."

"Cross my heart and swear to God – so to speak," she responded, crossing her heart as she spoke. With a gentle bow of her head, she wheeled the tea trolley out of the office and quietly closed the door behind her.

Lord Stonebridge returned to his desk and as was his nature he spread his hands across the large desktop, obviously thinking about what had just occurred. "Well now, that went well as unexpected as it was. Let's move on."

Ed raised his hand. "One more thing, sir. The day after Vicky picked me up and baby-sat me, she answered the phone from the White House when President Reagan phoned to thank me, us that is, for our work in Damascus. She stood and listened as I spoke to the president. She has never mentioned it since. My point is, sir, that I think we can absolutely rely on Miss Kilgour to keep things to herself."

"Absolutely," Pat added enthusiastically, "she is absolutely reliable."

"Excellent," Lord Stonebridge added, "I feel ever better knowing that."

Pat waited a few seconds before she continued. "Actually, sir, there is more to it than that. I had our department do a complete background check of Vicky Kilgour several months ago, and she passed with flying colours."

Ed peeked sideways toward Pat with a look of intrigue and concern.

"Pray tell us more," Lord Stonebridge insisted.

Pat knew she had to tell all. "Well without going into too much personal data, sir, Vicky introduced herself to Ed..er..Mr. Crowe late last year at his local pub. She was a friend of a friend, but it would be fair to say that she had recently had some personal issues in her life that could have, and I stress could have, had her wittingly, or unwittingly, shine some light on Mr. Crowe's activities that would have been very embarrassing for both your organization and my own."

Ed gulped with a smile, knowing that Pat would choose her words carefully.

Pat continued. "So I felt obliged to follow departmental orders to a 'T' and do a background check on her." She sat up straight and continued. "Vicky Kilgour comes from a very good family in the town of Oakville, which is a very nice area west of Toronto. Her parents had a nice mid-size home in Oakville, until several years ago when her father's investments portfolio increased substantially. He sold fifty-percent and that took him into the very rich class. That was all above board and he has spoken many times about his investment strategy in public. She still lives with her parents in a large and beautiful home that backs onto Lake Ontario, has two swimming pools, one in the basement of their home. She lives in her own third of the house with her own access."

"Sound lovely." The General offered,

"It is," Pat continued. "Now she has her own interesting background. She has an MBA from the University of Toronto and is an accomplished life insurance agent. She has done very well for herself, and is a constant winner of all sales contests. What I'm trying to say is that money is not an issue for her, and she recently took her parents on a Caribbean cruise as a thank-you; in lieu of rent. She is Mr. Crowe's life insurance agent, and after meeting her, she is now also my agent. She knows her stuff."

Ed jumped in. "And she made twice my earnings last year... including my consulting fees from here, sir."

Lord Stonebridge nodded his understanding and turned to Pat. "Could I just ask...?"

"Allow me," Ed interrupted. "Until late last year Vicky was engaged to be married. Her fiancé broke of the engagement in a rather crude manner – a comment on her birthday card – and then left town. It was with Pat's assistance that we tracked him down." Ed shrugged awkwardly. "He now lives with his boyfriend/partner in San Francisco. It was a complete shock to Vicky, but somehow she felt sorry for him when she heard the news. She was sad that he had, prior to his move, lived a life that fit into the norm, while privately loving a person in a way that is sociably unacceptable. She is a fine person, sir."

Lord Stonebridge closed his eyes to think, while holding up a hand to cease the discussion. Ed, Pat, and the General each knew what he was thinking. He lowered his hand, opened his eyes and smiled. "I have an idea," he said.

"I like it," the General said.

"A bit risky," Ed added.

"Too risky," Pat said with authority.

Lord Stonebridge turned in his chair to face Pat. "Miss Walker, I do understand your concern. However it would be totally unreasonable of me to ask you to take on a role so close to your wedding, especially since there appears to be a reasonably acceptable alternative, and given that this assignment has little, if any, risk. I think I must insist."

Pat nodded her acceptance glumly, yet inside was happy knowing that she now had the time to arrange every small detail of her wedding...even if the best man was soon heading off to Istanbul for a Mediterranean cruise.

Lord Stonebridge turned to Ed. "Perhaps you could ask Miss Kilgour to join us."

Ed left the room and headed down to the library where Vicky and Roy were looking through the oldest encyclopedia from the expansive choice.

"Hello, Eddie, what can we do for you then?" Roy asked.

Ed spoke with just a touch of upper-class. "Lord Stonebridge would request the pleasure of Miss Kilgour's company by re-joining him upstairs in his office for a quiet la-di-dah conversation." He bowed slightly and motioned to the door.

"Oh, God," Vicky gasped, "did I get myself into trouble? Please help me, Ed."

Ed motioned to the door again. "Perhaps. Let me lead the way, miss."

"You're a rotten friend," Vicky mumbled as she followed Ed up the stairs to the office.

Ed opened the door with a slight bow and followed Vicky into the office. He led her to a chair in front of Lord Stonebridge's desk, and sat behind her along with the General and Pat. Vicky sat up straight with her arms on the leather arms of the chair. She could feel the lack of tension in the room, and almost instantly relaxed.

"How may I assist you, Lord Stonebridge?" she enquired.

"You may indeed assist both my department and your wonderful country Canada," Lord Stonebridge replied, "if I might ask you..."

"Yes," Vicky interrupted.

"What I want to ask..."

Vicky spoke-up. "You misunderstood my answer, sir. I agree in advance to your asking, as long as I don't have to sleep with, or shoot, anyone. We ladies have our limitations. Isn't that right, Pat?"

"Right on!" Pat laughed from behind.

Lord Stonebridge accepted the comments and nodded his understanding.

Vicky continued with a shrug and a cheeky grin. "Actually, sir, I was just kidding. If I have to shoot someone, I will."

Everyone in the room accepted her sense of humor with a chuckle, and Lord Stonebridge continued, and turned to Ed. "Miss Walker tells me your luggage and Miss Kilgour's luggage is at your mother's house. If so would you please arrange to have it transferred as soon as possible to Chief of Security's office at London Heathrow, Terminal One."

Ed quickly left the room to make the necessary call.

Lord Stonebridge turned to Vicky. "Do you know where Chechnya is, Miss Kilgour?"

"Well I couldn't show you exactly where it is on a map," Vicky answered, "but I know it is part of the USSR, and *generally* where it is."

Lord Stonebridge motioned to the General who spent ten minutes reviewing with Vicky the basic history of Chechnya and its relationship within the USSR. As he finished summing up, Ed walked into the room and nodded that all was in order.

The General sat straighter in his chair to make a point. "Now what I need to tell you all about is what we believe is the main reason for the Chernobyl explosion. During World War Two there was Operation Lentil. Stalin approved Operation Lentil and it was ordered to begin on February 23rd 1944. What it resulted in was the expulsion of the entire Chechen and Ingush populations of the North Caucasus to remote areas of the Soviet Union. We're talking about more than 500,000 people here. Tens, or possibly hundreds, of thousands died or were killed during the round-ups and transportation. The Soviet government had accused them of co-operating with the Nazi invaders, in spite of the fact that more than 40,000 Chechens and Ingush were fighting for the Red Army."

Ed shook his head. "That's unreal. Why have we never heard of this?"

"You must understand," Lord Stonebridge answered with a reluctant shrug, "that the war was still raging, the Allies were still in the planning stages of D Day, and what couldn't be seen, couldn't be addressed. At the same time, thousands were dying in concentration camps, whose existence was still unknown to the outside world. It was a terrible, terrible time in human history."

The General took a deep breath and continued. "There was some retribution in the 1950s after Stalin's death, but nothing that would ever convince Chechen's to have any respect for Russia. There was none then and there is none now."

Vicky shook her head, holding back a tear. "I'm sorry; I don't know how I can help…what we're here for…why…"

Lord Stonebridge raised his hand, picked up the phone and ordered tea and biscuits. "Let's take a break and over tea the General will explain how that terrible time in history may be part of the facts for what brings us here today. Please rest assured that our plans are to see if we can eliminate a second Chernobyl in spite of this terrible event that happened so many years ago."

Both Pat and Ed wanted to walk over to Vicky and offer her a touch of comfort, but both knew better so the five sat quietly waiting for the answer to all problems – a hot pot of tea and some biscuits.

The tea trolley arrived and they all helped themselves.

Vicky took a sip of the very hot tea. "Maybe I should have limited my assistance to delivering tea?" she offered.

"You weren't raised to be a tea lady," Ed said with a grin. "An important part of their job is to keep opinions to themselves, something you couldn't do about my international travels, it seems."

"Well it was all the truth wasn't it?" she replied quickly." I am not in the habit of lying."

"That will have to change, I'm afraid, Miss Kilgour," Lord Stonebridge cautioned. "Do you have your passport with you?"

"Yes," Vicky replied reaching into her purse and handing it to Lord Stonebridge.

He turned to Pat and handed her the passport. "If you would be so kind as to bring us a UK passport for Miss Kilgour under the name of

Vicky Crowe, and it would be wise to include at least some of the trips the Mr. Crowe has recently taken."

Ed handed his passport to Pat, who left the room to head down to the special MI6 offices in the basement of the manor.

"So is this my honeymoon with our Mr. Crowe, sir?" Vicky chuckled.

"Not a honeymoon this time, just a happily married couple on a pleasant cruise in the Mediterranean. But General, please proceed to the details of the plan, keeping in mind the ship leaves from Istanbul tomorrow at 6pm., and our new Mr. and Mrs. Crowe must be aboard at least two hours before that."

CHAPTER SIX

Vicky waved her new passport as the limo sped south to Heathrow Airport. "A brand new passport, some Turkish cash, a brand new husband, a borrowed wedding ring, and now I'm heading for a Mediterranean cruise. Could life be any better than that? I don't think so." She leaned over to Ed with a cheeky grin. "But this cruise will be sex-free, mister, and don't you forget it!"

"You're enjoying this way too much, Mrs. Victoria Crowe," Ed smiled back. "And don't forget I'm the lead operative on this trip. I'm the boss, and you do as I say."

"Oh, yes, oh master. I'll do exactly as you tell me…except no sex!"

Ed smiled. "We'll get along fine then, Vicky." He reached over and touched her hand. "Seriously, let's see what we can do about finding out about the possibility of a second 'accident' from a gentleman who sounds like he's slightly lost his mind."

Vicky gave a serious nod. "Of course, Ed. I'll work with you as you direct and hopefully we can make the world a much safer place." She paused and turned to look out the window as the English countryside flashed by. The driver was keeping to the B roads which were surrounded on both sides with hedgerows, hiding the pastures and green fields beyond. The driver could turn on the roof-top swirling blue police lights if he needed to clear traffic ahead; which he often had to do.

Vicky turned to Ed, took a deep breath and continued. "So our luggage is on its way from your mother's home to meet us at the airport. We have air tickets. We have Turkish Visas which somehow were 'available' at Stonebridge Manor. We have a large cabin with balcony, and Carolyn will be ready to meet us and bring us up-to-date once we're on the ship. Am I missing anything?"

Ed closed his eyes to think. "Remember the borrowed wedding ring is Lord Stonebridge's mother's wedding ring, and I'm told it's worth a pretty penny."

Vicky looked the band that was gold and set with five medium sized diamonds. Suddenly the penny dropped. "Hold it! Hold it! Are you telling me that this is the ring Pat wore during your so-called honeymoon in Paris?"

Ed shrugged with a sneaky smile. "Seems so. But hey, it was just a prop. All part of working with MI6."

"How much?"

"Ten thousand...pounds, that is."

Vicky's eyes widened. "Wow! That's...that's..."

"That's a lot of money," Ed said, nodding his head. "A lot of money indeed."

After a long, crowded, and noisy walk through one of the busiest airports in the world, they found their luggage waiting for them at the Turkish Airlines gate at Terminal One, Heathrow. They boarded the Boeing 707 with only minutes to spare. Much to Vicky's surprise the Turkish flight crew and cabin staff could have been on any international airline, especially when they all spoke English. They took their First Class seats, sat back and relaxed.

"So who is this guy again?" Vicky asked quietly.

Ed opened up his wallet and showed the photograph. He was somewhat thin faced with a very trim moustache. His hair was black and combed back, with not a hair out of place. He was olive complexioned, almost southern European in coloring. But it was his eyes that one noticed first. They were set back slightly and glaring straight ahead, which gave him an almost threatening look.

"Good looking guy," Vicky whispered.

"And super intelligent," Ed added. "A doctorate in nuclear physics by age twenty-six."

She nudged him in the arm. "Hey, you're twenty-six aren't you? What do you have to say about yourself?"

"Well, I'm flying to Istanbul with a good-looking young lady, and we hope to save some lives…from that nuclear physicist no less."

"Okay, you win."

"Let's hope that 'we' win."

"We will. He's already made the mistake of letting us know there is more to come. He has a weakness. We just need to find out what it is. You'll see."

"You're the MBA."

Vicky nodded. "Exactly. And we're trained to determine and understand people's strengths and weaknesses…and use our knowledge to our advantage. Basic psychology."

"Oh my," Ed groaned. "What are my strengths and weaknesses, or dare I ask?"

"Honesty and honesty...in that order. Looks like they're about to start serving dinner."

The plane landed at Ataturk International Airport fifteen minutes past midnight, Wednesday, April 30th. Ed wondered what they could accomplish in just a couple of days.

Vicky was too excited about the next few days with all the unknown risks, while understanding this was a once-in-a-lifetime experience. She knew she had to remain professional and serious, but the thrill of it all was difficult not to enjoy.

The security and passport control was no different than at other international airports. After showing their confirmation certificate for the cruise, little else mattered. Their visas were in order, their passports were stamped, and they moved on to pick up their luggage in what was a very busy airport. When they stepped into the public area a Princess

Cruises representative met them, holding a sign with CROWE neatly printed.

"This way," the young lady indicated, taking Vicky's luggage from her and rolling it toward the exit. Ed lugged his suitcase, telling himself he would have to get one with wheels. Both Ed and Vicky were most impressed with the representative's positive attitude and followed her onto a bus that had twelve other customers aboard.

The representative spoke into microphone. "This bus will take you to your hotel, and at twelve noon tomorrow, it will pick you up outside the hotel for the short drive to your ship." She spoke briefly to the driver in what Vicky assumed was Turkish and she left the bus with a smile.

The drive to their hotel was less than an hour, as there were few people on the roads and streets. As they got closer to the Beyoglu district of Istanbul where their hotel was located, things got busier. There were more cars and carts filling the streets and the sidewalks were busy with the late-night crowd. It was even busier as the bus pulled up in front of the Pera Palace Hotel. The hotel was large with seven floors and was beautifully set in a luxurious location at the top of one of the many hills of Istanbul. Vicky, Ed and all of their follow passengers were impressed at the outside, and even more impressed as they entered the hotel's huge and elegant lobby. There were many wonderfully designed chairs and sofas for the hotel guests to enjoy in their comfort, with flowers, paintings, and walls of books to add a modern touch to 19th century designed building.

"Yikes," Vicky whispered, leaning toward Ed, "I thought we were heading to a Holiday Inn. This place is spectacular."

"Never been to a place like it," Ed nodded. "Now this would be a place for a honeymoon," he added with a straight face. He got an elbow in the ribs anyway.

They signed in as Mr. and Mrs. Crowe and followed the bell boy to their third floor room. It was only when they entered the room with its unique design and furniture – with a named plaque on the wall – did they understand they had been booked into 'The Agatha Christie

Room'. The bell boy gave them the keys and left before Ed could find some coin to hand him with his thanks.

"Oh my God," Vicky gasped. "Just look at the photos, memorabilia and books about Agatha. They are just outstanding. Who will we have to thank for this?"

"Probably Carolyn," Ed guessed.

"Good thinking on her part. Keeps your mind off other things, eh?"

"I'm sure I don't know what you're talking about," Ed replied quickly.

Vicky waved off his response. "Here are the rules for tonight. I'm going to shower and get ready for bed, while you go down to the lobby for twenty minutes. When you return I'll be on my side of the bed ready for a good night's sleep. You shower or whatever and, keeping your underwear on, take the other side of the bed. In the morning, you get up and out first, and I'll join you for breakfast half an hour later. If we can eat on the Orient Terrace, so much the better."

"Yes, dear."

"And please don't call me 'dear'; unless you mean expensive." She laughed. "Now go."

"Good night, then," Ed said picking up the keys and walking to the door.

Ed waited for half an hour to return to the room. He showered quickly and keeping his shorts on turned off all the lights and got into the empty side of the bed. Vicky didn't make a sound, although he doubted she was asleep. He lay on his side with his back to Vicky, and she lay with her back to him. He tried unsuccessfully to sleep moving as little as he could.

Vicky sat up straight, holding the sheet to her body. "Oh, for God's sake give me a kiss good night will you!"

Ed sat up, they kissed quickly without passion.

"Thank you," Vicky said. "Now good night."

"Good night, Vicky."

They both went back to their neutral positions and were both asleep within minutes.

CHAPTER SEVEN

Wednesday, April, 30th 1986

Vicky kicked backwards and hit Ed in his leg. "Get moving, bloke. It's seven-thirty already. I'll see you downstairs for brekky in half an hour."

Ed rolled out of bed, decided he'd shower later, dressed casually and headed down to the main floor. The large cafeteria was busy and as Ed looked around, he could tell there were guests from around the world. The majority were men. Some wore flowing robes that seemed to reflect their wealth and status in life, while the majority wore business suits of many varieties that were reflective of the many languages of the guest's native lands. A terrific place to people watch, Ed thought, and was happy to be escorted to a table for two by a window with a lovely view of the hotel's garden. There were flowers and trees he had never seen before. More interestingly, he could see birds he didn't recognize. Knowing he wouldn't have time to do any bird watching, he ordered English Breakfast tea and sat back to enjoy the sights and sounds of a new world.

To no surprise Vicky entered the room nearly an hour later. She was wearing a blue dress with a high neckline and a sweater that covered her arms. Many heads were turned her way as she walked confidently to join Ed.

"Good night's sleep?" she asked as she sat and picked up the menu.

"Like a baby; but without the crying."

"Me too."

Ed leaned forward. "If you don't mind my saying so, that is a perfect outfit to wear. Not too showy – so to speak, but very fashionable. The color suits you."

Vicky nodded. "Thank you, or tesekkup ederim, as they say in Turkish."

Ed's eyes widened. "Wow, as they say in English."

Vicky gave a quick wink. "I asked the lady at the front desk. When in Istanbul..."

Ed poured her a cup of tea from the second pot he'd ordered. "A pleasure to know you, young lady, or perhaps I should say thank you, sweetie? After all we are married now."

She took a sip of her tea. "Vicky will do, thank you, or I'll start calling you honeybunch."

He toasted her with his cup. "As you say, Vicky. Shall we order?"

They ordered a light breakfast, knowing that in a few hours they would be on the cruise ship where excellent food would be available anytime of the day.

"So while I was waiting the half-hour for you to join me here, I did a little research about our hotel," said Ed with enthusiasm. "It turns out that the hotel was built in 1892, and was used by the passengers from the Orient Express. At the time, of course, Istanbul was known as Constantinople. In addition to Agatha Christie some well-known clients included Ernest Hemingway and Alfred Hitchcock. Lots of history in such a lovely city, don't you agree?"

Vicky nodded. "Lovely indeed. Perhaps one day when I get married – if I get married – I'll suggest this hotel as our honeymoon location. What do you think of that?"

"Well what I also found out, during the second half-hour I waited for you to join me here, is that Room 101 was recently converted into an Ataturk Museum, as an honor to the founder of modern Turkey."

Vicky leaned across the table with a smile and a twinkle in her eyes. "Was it worth the wait?"

"Every minute, Vicky, every minute."

Their breakfast was served with Turkish apple tea, instead of English Breakfast, and Ed manage to drink it without comment. Vicky thought it was wonderful and ordered a second cup.

"So tell me, Vicky, would you like to go on a quick walking tour of Istanbul? From here we can visit the Bosphorus, Galata Tower and the famous shopping street of Istiklal Avenue, and still be back in plenty of time for our bus ride at twelve."

"I'm for shopping any time. Let's go!"

"Okay, we'll head to the tower first since there'll probably be a line-up to go to the top, then we'll walk over to the Bosphorus to look across at Asia, the come back via the Istiklal and maybe buy a Turkish carpet."

Vicky gave him a not-a-chance look. "Maybe I could buy a bikini for the cruise. I wasn't expecting to go swimming in England for the wedding."

"Let's ask at the desk where to buy what. We don't need to look anymore than a couple of tourists than we are. And we'll use my credit card."

"Excuse me, mister! I have my own card thank you very much."

Ed leaned forward. "Don't forget my card is registered as international, and I'm pretty sure you didn't phone your card company to let them know you were going to Turkey. And don't forget you're here as Vicky Crowe."

"I don't know..."

Ed spoke quietly. "Besides if I use my card, it will be a requirement of the cruise, and paid for by...you know who."

The thought of having a bikini paid for by MI6 was too much to argue against. It would forever be her little secret. "Done!"

The lady at the front desk recommended that Vicky buy her bikini on the ship. That being settled they headed down the beautiful streets of the Beyoglu district. The streets were busy with shoppers and business people. There was such a huge variety of clothing worn by the citizens and visitors that they did not feel at all out of place in their regular comfortable outfits. Vicky particularly enjoyed the feel and smell of the street life. They reached the Bosphorus and sat and watched the many large and small commercial ships heading to and from the Black Sea. It was only when they walked along the river front that they realized they could see their cruise ship, Royal Princess, just a few hundred yards to their left at the docks. They walked back to the Galata Tower, and looked up at the stunning circular structure with several viewing areas toward the top, beyond which the steeple added a serene elegance of character. They waited only a few minutes before the elevator took them to the top, taking a brochure of the sights at the top with them. As they walked onto the observation deck which circled the tower, Vicky grabbed for Ed's arm.

"Whoa," she said. "This is high."

Ed looked at the brochure. "Hey, it's only 67 meters, or 219 feet, depending on how you look at it. And we're not even at the top!"

"We'll I'm going to look at it holding onto you. And don't get any ideas."

Sideling around the tower on the rather narrow observation deck the views of the entire city were outstanding. Ed pointed out the Haghia Sophia, the Topkapi Palace, and the beautiful Blue Mosque. After enjoying the historical city's sites and sounds from such a relaxing location, they decided to take the stairs down and were happy to head quickly back to their hotel. Both were excited and nervous about the days and challenges ahead.

They were ready in the hotel lobby 15 minutes early, as were the other passengers and all were eager to begin their cruise on The Love Boat. It was the discussion everyone was sharing when the driver entered the hotel lobby. He quickly ticked off names on his sheet and then handed everyone a slip of paper with their seat number on the bus. He counted the number of pieces of luggage, explained they would see them again outside their cabins and invited all to enter the bus for a short ride to the ship.

Ed's and Vicky's seats were the last row of seats while the remaining passengers were all toward the front end of the bus. Ed was wondering what the reason was, but realized quickly when the bus driver opened the front door and a Princess Cruise ship's officer joined them. She was dressed in a white uniform with golden buttons and officer's epaulets on her shoulders. The uniform enhanced her height and full figure extremely well.

Vicky nudged Ed. "I bet you wish I had a bosom like that when we were boyfriend-girlfriend, eh?"

"No comment." Ed whispered.

"Good answer. Just remember we're officially married, so no sweet-talking her."

"I promise," Ed nodded.

The ship's officer picked up a microphone as the bus slowly moved on. "Good morning, ladies and gentlemen, and thank you for being early. My name is Nancy Watson; I'm your Cruise Director and a big welcome to Princess Cruises. I will be handing each of you your cabin keys, and answering any questions you may have at this time." After accepting a nice round of applause she started the key distribution.

Vicky looked around. "Why are we sitting back here? I don't feel we've been invited to the party."

"Maybe because we're special," Ed hinted.

"Yeah, maybe."

Finally Nancy Watson walked up to them. "Mr. and Mrs. Crowe, welcome aboard. How are you today?"

"We are fine thank you, Nancy. It's a pleasure to meet you." He turned to Vicky and spoke in a whisper. "Vicky, meet Carolyn. Carolyn, meet Vicky."

Vicky put her hand to her mouth to suppress her surprise. She spoke in a hush. "Oh, my God, Carolyn. I…I don't know what to say…I…"

Ed interrupted. "Vicky was just saying how nice you look in your uniform, isn't that right, Vicky?"

Vicky swallowed and took a deep breath. "It really is a pleasure to meet you," she said extending her hand which Carolyn shook.

Carolyn smiled with a nod. "Thanks for the compliment, Vicky. I can't stop for now. Here are your cabin keys. It's a very nice cabin in the middle of the ship. I'll stop by in an hour or two." She gave them a quick thumbs-up and walked to the front of the bus.

Vicky turned to Ed, still in a bit of shock. "Thanks, Ed. But she really is so nice, so pretty. No wonder you…you know."

He put his finger to her lips. "Loose lips…."

Vicky grinned. "Okay, boss. Business it is."

Ed winked. "Besides you're pretty too."

"Don't get cute with me, bloke. We're on a business trip, and don't you forget it!"

"Well said," Ed laughed. "We're going to get along great as a business team."

The bus pulled up on the dock, directly in front of the gangway. Nancy Watson directed them on board, presenting each passenger with a small booklet that showed the blueprint of each deck, so everyone could see where their cabin was in relation to other decks, and outlined the locations of the ship's restaurants, pools, libraries and all other passenger amenities. Ed and Vicky made their way to their cabin 228 on the starboard side of the ship.

The cabin was not large, but well designed. The bathroom was on the right as one walked in, and to the left was just enough room to hang their clothes. The queen bed took up most of the room, with a desk and chairs at the far end. There was, to their great delight, a small balcony that had two chairs and a tiny coffee table. Having cruised before, they knew that a balcony offered them fabulous views of the world outside. They agreed who would have which drawers and waited for their luggage to arrive. They didn't wait long and thirty minutes later they were unpacked and their luggage bags were slipped under the bed and out of the way.

"What a team," Ed said looking around at the well organized cabin.

Vicky gave him a quick, strictly professional, hug. "Way to go, boss."

Ed nodded his thanks. "Well we can't just sit here. Let's order a nice pot of tea." He picked up the phone.

"Surprise, surprise," Vicky said. "What's a better way to get the action moving to help save the world, than a good cup of tea?"

The tea arrived and they sat out on the balcony, with the view of the Bosphorus and the Asian side of Istanbul straight ahead and the massive Topkapi Palace to their far right. It was sunny and warm. It was beautiful. Neither spoke. There was nothing to be said.

Carolyn knocked on their door an hour later. Ed quickly ran to the door, opened it, and welcomed Carolyn in with a short bow and a wave of his hand.

Carolyn curtsied and entered. "Hi, Ed. Hi, Vicky. How are you both doing?"

Vicky responded with a smile. "We're doing great, Carolyn: or Nancy perhaps. It really is nice to meet with you, having chatted with you a few times about Mr. Travel Agent here." She motioned to Ed.

Carolyn nodded. "He needs help from time to time, but then he's a male isn't he? But you were good enough, Vicky, to do those things no-questions-asked, and that was very noble and trustworthy of you. However now that you've crossed the secrecy line, perhaps we should chat – the three of us, that is?"

Vicky closed the door to the balcony. She and Carolyn sat on the two chairs and Ed sat on the bed.

"Where are we at, Miss?" Ed asked. He used her operational name to make the discussion totally official.

"Well first things first, Mister," Carolyn replied, now using his operational name, "I think we need to agree on an operational name for Vicky." She turned to Vicky. "Pat's name, by the way, is Boss. Who would you like to be?"

Vicky thought for a moment. "How about Slim?"

"Slim it is," Carolyn agreed. "Welcome aboard – in more ways than one." She shook Slim's hand firmly.

Vicky took a deep breath and turned her mind to the challenge at hand.

"Here's where we're at," Carolyn began. "Our man was one of the first to board and he is in a large and expensive cabin. He has spent most of the time since he got on board smoking some rather large, and horrible smelling, cigars. Apparently they are from Cuba and top-notch. He sits on the starboard side of the Promenade Deck. It's a smoker's paradise, while watching the world go by with the walkers and joggers, and there are a few of those already. He seems nice enough and gave me a smile as I walked past him. I didn't speak, just gave him a nod of welcome. I spoke to his steward and told a lie. I told him that Mr. Umarov is a wealthy regular customer of Princess and he should let me know of anything that he requests or orders. So far nothing, so he hasn't eaten since he came on board."

"Speaking of which?" Ed said, raising his hand.

"Of course," Carolyn said. "If you sit on the starboard side of the Promenade Deck in the Wheelhouse Bar, you might catch a glimpse of our man." She winked to Ed. "And you'll be happy to hear that they're serving English style fish and chips."

Vicky rolled her eyes. "Salads available?"

Carolyn nodded. "Of course, this is Princess. Almost everything is available. Just one more thing," she stood to leave. "We – you – do not have a lot of time to meet and get to know him. If you don't succeed quickly, then we have move to Plan B."

"Which is?" Ed asked.

Carolyn shook her head. "I don't really know. We don't have one. We can't arrest him, and we certainly can't force him to speak. If we try that, we'll all be in the brig."

Vicky stood. "Not to worry, Miss. With Mister's charm and gourmet choices, we'll be sure to make friends with him quickly."

Carolyn offered a smile, shook their hands, wished them luck and left their cabin.

Ed rubbed his hands together. "Let's go 'ave a gander at the nosh then, yeah?"

"God help us," Vicky groaned, slapping her forehead in resignation.

They walked down to the Promenade Deck and entered the Wheelhouse Bar, and as directed by Carolyn, sat on the Starboard side. While Vicky ordered Ed's fish and chips and a salad for herself, Ed strolled casually along the inside walkway, keeping his eyes on the people sitting out on the deck. Their man was easy to find. He sat smoking a large cigar, nodding 'hellos' to those walking or jogging by. Through the window Ed could only see the back of Umarov's head and his outstretched legs. He had a full head of dark hair that was cut short and brushed back in an old-man's style. He was one of the few on the deck wearing full length pants, and his sandals were heavy and out of style. Ed wandered back to their table just as the meal arrived. He dug into his meal which was nice and hot, while Vicky picked at her salad.

"You ever eat salads?" Vicky asked.

"All the time," Ed replied, offering her a small piece of fish with his fork.

She was about to decline his offer, but leaned forward and took it carefully in her mouth. She nodded. "Hey, that's good. Let's share!"

Happily they shared the rest of their meals in silence.

"He's out there," Ed said as he put his knife and fork in the finished position. They waited while the server took away their plates and delivered the 'required' pot of tea.

Ed rubbed his hands together. "A healthy salad, fish and chips, a pot of tea and thee. Whatever could be better?"

"What a nice thing to say," Vicky smiled. "I'll never have fish and chips again without thinking of this occasion." She paused. "Of course I may never have fish and chips again, anyway."

Ed poured their tea…milk first. They toasted each other.

Vicky nodded toward their man. "What's he like?"

He leaned forward and spoke quietly. "From what I could see, which wasn't much, he appears much older than his age and rather over-dressed for the weather and occasion."

"Sounds like a gentleman to me. So now what?"

"Let's take a walk around the Promenade Deck, and give him a nod as he is nodding to everyone else. Might as well let him see us casually for the first time."

They started walking on the far side. Ed strolled 'Prince Philip' style with his hands clasped behind his back. Vicky was by his side, but not too close. They walked around the aft of the ship and passed their man several minutes later. He nodded and they returned his nod with Ed adding a quiet, "Afternoon."

Twenty steps on Vicky spoke quietly. "Well aren't you the gentleman?"

"Even gentlemen eat fish and chips," Ed added, his nose just slightly in the air.

"Touché, dear sir."

They wandered back to their cabin and sat on the balcony.

"I have two ideas." Vicky said.

"Fire away."

"One. I think we should get the queen bed changed to two singles."

Ed looked surprised. "Won't that just raise issues?"

"It's not 'issues' I'm worried about rising when we're in the same bed, young man."

Ed chuckled. He was tempted to tell her he'd been in similar circumstances before and managed to control himself, but decided against it. "Okay, but you speak to the steward. Not sure what you could tell him that makes sense."

Vicky thought about it. "No problem, I'll tell him that you suffer from major nightmares from your experiences in the navy during the Falkland's War, just a few years ago."

"That likely would be the case if I had been there, and no doubt it is the case for many who were. I don't like to use it as the reason, but at least the timing works."

"Thanks. And if I need to snuggle, I'll join you in your bed...but only to snuggle!"

"Done. And your second idea?"

"I think we should be on the Sun Deck at sail-away, just in case our man is there. Gives us another chance to be seen by him."

"Good idea, Slim. Great thinking."

She jokingly saluted. "Thanks, Mister. I want to help out as best I can." She thought for a moment, chewing on her lip. "Okay I've changed my mind. I won't even think of joining you to snuggle. Not with Carolyn on board. That wouldn't be right."

Ed nodded his understanding. "Let's get ready to join the rest of the passengers on the Sun Deck for sail-away...and the start to an important operation."

They changed into more comfortable clothing and headed to the Sun Deck. Many passengers were waiting for the big moment and enjoying a complimentary glass of champagne. To Vicky's surprise Ed did not partake of the champagne, but instead looked around the crowded deck, searching for their man. When he saw him on the other side of the ship, he motioned to Vicky and they casually walked around the deck and took a position on the railing, ten feet from him, looking out across the Bosphorus. It was a wonderful sight watching small boats and large ferries crossing such a busy waterway, in such a well organized fashion. Things changed when their ship's horn blew several times and the passengers raised a toast as the ship's ropes were disconnected from the pier and it gradually slipped away from its mooring. Vicky was excited and gave Ed a big, but quick, hug and pecked him on his cheek. "Anchor's away, matey...or ex-matey as the case may be. Let's do the job and enjoy the process, eh?"

"That's the spirit, partner. And speaking of spirits..." He helped himself to a glass of champagne as the waiter walked by.

"I knew that was too good to be true," Vicky murmured.

They walked past their man, and Ed toasted him with his glass of champagne. The man toasted Ed back with a smile and a raise of his hand with his cigar. Vicky nodded, and she and Ed continued their slow walking. When they were back to the other side of the ship they stood comfortably by the railing looking out to sea. From the small boats and ships below, the people waved farewell and as is required in such circumstances, they waved back. Reluctantly they headed back to their cabin and started to get ready for the early sitting for dinner. It was a formal dress-code night, and they each changed seperately in the confines of the not very large bathroom.

CHAPTER EIGHT

"You look lovely, young lady," Ed said as they were ready to leave for dinner.

Vicky was wearing a full length blue silk dress with a low cut, but appropriate, front that showed off her slim figure beautifully. Her diamond necklace and bracelets added a touch of glamour and finesse.

"Thank you," she said bowing gently. "But keep in mind I ordered this for the wedding, so I'm afraid it will look rather older on Saturday."

"You'll look wonderful in that, Vicky, no matter how many times you wear it.'

"Hmm," she smiled, "maybe I'll wear it to your wedding? If I'm invited that is."

"Shall we go?" Ed offered his arm as he opened the door.

She took his arm. "You look pretty fine also, I might add. You look good in a tux."

"And this is the only shirt that goes with it. I'll have to be careful not to spill anything on it."

She laughed. "No worries, matey. We'd have it laundered tomorrow. Charge it to MI6, eh?"

He gave her a quick kiss on her cheek, and they left for dinner.

They indicated their room number and were escorted to a table for eight in a nice quiet corner of the lavishly decorated dining room. They were the last couple to arrive and Ed introduced himself and his wife, using their Christian names only. There were two American couples, and one Australian.

Ed ordered himself a glass of red wine and a glass of spring water for Vicky.

"So where are you guys from?" asked one of the two American men, with an east-coast accent.

"We're from Canada," Vicky responded, as Ed gave her a gentle kick under the table.

"Really from Britain," Ed added quickly. "Moved to Canada recently to work with the Canadian government to promote exports to the old country."

"So you have socialized medicine up there?" the American asked.

"All twenty-five million of us," Ed replied with a nod. "About the same number of Americans that don't have any medical coverage I understand."

The American clapped his hands. "Well said, Ed. Well said. Why don't you tell us how it all works?"

The four couples spent the next hour and a half enjoying a wonderful meal while discussing the different health care systems. Australia had introduced federal health coverage in 1984, which was a combination of federal and private coverage. The discussion was both interesting and informative, and all eight of them learned something new about such an important issue. They all left as friends looking forward to tomorrow's discussion on politics in each country.

Vicky held on to Ed's arm as they walked back to their cabin to change and then to attend some of the entertainment, casino, and socializing events throughout the ship. When they entered their cabin there were now two single beds. Ed opened the curtains to the balcony. There was a beautiful full moon high in the sky with stars shining through the immense clear, clean heavens.

"Come see this," Ed said as he stepped back.

Vicky stood in front of him and crossed her arms and shivered slightly at the amazing view. "So wonderful," she whispered.

Ed stood closer to her. "May I put my arms around you?" he asked quietly.

"No," she replied.

Ed nodded his understanding. He waited several seconds and was about to turn.

"Okay, but nothing sexy. That's final."

He put his arms around her and joined his hands below her crossed arms. "I was going to say that we should hold each other like this once more before we mentally converted full time to Mister and Slim. Honest."

She opened her arms and held her hands over his. "Good idea, Ed." She counted to thirty. "Okay, Mister, let's get going to the business at hand."

Just as they separated there was a knock on the door. Ed walked to the door, checked outside through the peep-hole, and opened the door to let Carolyn in. She wore her white officer's uniform and her Nancy Watson badge. She noticed the two single beds, but said nothing.

"We're just about to head out and check out our man," Vicky said, grabbing a change of clothes and stepping into the bathroom. "Carry on," she laughed from inside, "I can hear everything in here."

"Part of the joys of cruising," Carolyn chuckled. "But don't sweat it, my cabin is about one quarter the size of this, and I sleep in a bunk."

"Not quite the manor," Ed quipped.

"Not indeed," Carolyn agreed. "But to business if I may?"

Vicky exited the bathroom dressed in a knee-length dress with mid-arm length sleeves. "Okay?" she asked.

"Perfect, Slim," Carolyn replied.

"Then to business, Miss," Vicky said taking a seat on her bed and offering Carolyn the chair by the desk.

Carolyn spoke slowly. "Here's the latest up-date. As of now, twenty people are dead from the accident, mostly workers at the plant of course. But there will be more. The emergency workers went in not properly covered. Some of them know they will die. One described it as being kamikaze-like. Rather sad to say the least. We also know that the Russian authorities are aware that our man is on the ship, and while the plan is to let us do what we can, we are positive members of the KGB are waiting in our ship's first stop, Izmir, and they're not going to wait for us do our part. They want him dead, and they want him dead now. So we have tomorrow and Friday to find out where the 'More to come' location is. And one more thing; apparently our man is not a healthy young man. We know he has some type of illness, but we're not sure what exactly, or how bad it is. His doctor in Chechnya refused to open his medical files to the KGB...and then burned them. He won't speak for love nor money, and I can assure you the KGB aren't offering either of those two incentives!"

"Then we'd better get going," Ed said, taking a change of clothes into the bathroom.

Carolyn looked around the room smiled at Vicky and asked quietly. "How's it going, Vicky?"

Vicky nodded. "Pretty good, I suppose. I am rather nervous. I don't want to do anything stupid."

"You won't, Vicky. Just use your natural common sense. That's the only thing we can all do. Some day I'll tell you a few stories about my learning process in this business. We'll both have a bit of a laugh."

Vicky reached over and touched Carolyn's hand in thanks.

Ed came out of the bathroom in casual pants and a short sleeve shirt. "Okay, ladies, let's go get a man!"

The 'ladies' gave him a look, but didn't speak.

He raised a hand. "Okay, bad choice of words. Let's go get *our* man."

The three left the cabin. Carolyn went down the hall to the right. Ed and Vicky turned left, heading toward the ship's many activities.

Ed and Vicky stopped at one of the bars by the Grand Foyer to keep a lookout for their man. Ed ordered himself a beer, while Vicky ordered a glass of water. Many of the passengers were still dressed in their suits, tuxedos and long dresses and danced to the gentle music of a quartet. They relaxed and enjoyed their drinks, nodding to other passengers as they walked by enjoying their own drinks. Ed then noticed Vicky's eyes raised as she looked over his shoulder. Ed turned slowly and through the windows to the outside deck saw their man holding a drink and cigar, take a seat by himself at a small table. He leaned back, took a sip of his drink and a deep relaxing drag on his cigar.

"Let's take our drinks outside for some nice fresh sea air," Ed said, motioning to the exit closest to their man.

"What a wonderful Idea," Vicky agreed, "I was just thinking the same thing myself."

They slowly walked past the dancers to their left, and Ed opened the door with a slight bow. They took a separate small table, three away from their goal.

"Now what?" Vicky whispered, watching over Ed's shoulder.

Ed shrugged as he took a drink of his beer. Their man just sat and enjoyed his cigar and drink.

"Oh heck, let me try something," Vicky said, remembering Carolyn's comment. She picked up her drink and walked toward to their man. Ed didn't want to make a fuss, so watched as Vicky left him sitting alone.

"You know, sir," Vicky began, "that a person who smokes will, on average, live seven years less than a non-smoker? That is a fact, not just point of view."

The man stood having put down his drink and cigar. He gave a friendly smile. He spoke with a slight accent, less pronounced than Vicky had expected. "That is very nice of you to say so, ma'am. I appreciate your interest. May I ask…?"

"I sell life insurance, sir. There are many actuarial studies that prove this unfortunate fact. I am considering becoming an actuary, so have seen the statistics myself."

"Ah, I see," he replied. "Your concern is that those that die earlier than you expected causes your company to lose money, perhaps?"

Vicky shook her head. "No. The life-expectancy tables we use include deaths of all nature. Besides people are constantly living longer than what our some-what out of date tables predict, and additionally more and more people are quitting smoking, except perhaps in France and China. Now I apologize for bothering you. I realize it is none of my business. Excuse me."

He raised his hand. "No, please stay a minute." He leaned over and poured his drink onto the lit end of his cigar in the ashtray. It sizzled and died. "That, madam, is the last cigar I shall ever enjoy, and while you are helping in that fashion, I will now drink one less glass of white wine." He smiled. "But it will not be my last glass of wine; with your approval, madame?"

Vicky laughed. "Well I do not drink myself, but I do understand that a glass of wine can be relaxing." She was about to turn and walk away, but had a sudden brainwave and without thinking she spoke. "And I am not married, sir. It's Miss. I doubt I would walk over to you if I were with my husband."

He looked at her left hand, and then to Ed. "But…?"

Vicky stood a little taller to ensure she made her point. "He, sir, is my brother. He recently lost his wife and we are taking the cruise to help him recover from his loss."

He looked at her left hand and offered a questioning shrug.

"I wear that, sir, to ensure that I do not have men hitting on me."

His head went back. "Hitting you?"

She waved her right hand. "No, no, no. Hitting on me. Trying to flirt with me. It happens from time to time."

"Ah, flirting; yes, now I understand. And, if you don't my saying so it is normal for a young man to want to flirt with such a pretty young lady, yes?"

Vicky chuckled. "Yes, of course it is. But not under the circumstances." She motioned gently to Ed.

"Yes, of course. But please invite your brother over for an introduction. No mention of his loss." He offered her his hand. "My name is Alexi Umarov. I am from Chechnya, an engineer, and I assure you, a gentleman. Invite him. Please?"

She waited, feigning indecision, and then nodded. "My name is Victoria Crowe. We're from Canada, but originally from England. Please give me a minute."

She turned and walked over to Ed, who had his back to the encounter. He looked to Vicky, eyes wide open in amazement.

She sat with Ed between her and her new friend. She spoke quietly. "You're my brother. Your wife died recently and we're cruising for a bit of relaxation from your loss. He knows I sell life insurance and he just had the last cigar he will ever smoke. I'll explain over there. He wants to meet you. No mention of your loss. He knows we're from Canada, originally from England. I didn't say where, but let's go with Queen's Park."

Ed closed his eyes momentarily to take it all in. When he opened them he smiled. "Christ! You are a great liar. You should do this for a living. Okay, but let's also go with; our father died when we were kids and you went to university in Canada – hence your accent. Try and speak some British-English once in a while. My mother is 'our' mother. No other brothers or sisters. Make sense?"

"One hundred percent. I'll do most of the speaking, so play along. I won't mess up, I promise."

Ed stood, brushed himself off and followed Vicky to their future of telling lies.

Vicky led the way with Ed following just a step behind. He didn't want to look enthusiastic, when in fact he was. This was the meeting they needed in order to create the appropriate connection with their man.

Vicky led the introductions. "Ed this is Alexi Umarov. He is from Chechnya and an engineer. Mr. Umarov this is my brother Ed. Ed is a travel agent in Canada, but was a travel agent in England before he joined me in Canada."

They shook hands and Umarov invited them to sit at the small but comfortable table. "Please call me Alex," he said quickly. "It is a pleasure to meet you both. There are very few Chechnian immigrants in Canada. It would be interesting to learn more about your wonderful country."

The three chatted for an hour about travel in their respective countries, during which time Ed saw Carolyn, some fifty feet away, taking note of the three of them being together. She nodded slightly to Ed with a smile. When he thought it was appropriate Ed excused himself for an early night's sleep.

"Your brother is a very nice gentleman, Victoria," Umarov said.

"Please call me Vicky, Alex. Only my mother calls me Victoria, and then only when she is annoyed with me."

He bowed his head slightly. "Thank you. Then perhaps I might call you Miss Vicky. That sounds very nice. Did you know that your Queen Victoria was the first child in England to be named Victoria?"

"No I didn't know that," Vicky replied, suddenly realizing she was thinking of her real mother, not Ed's mother; her 'now' mother. She clenched her hand to keep her head straight, realizing that this slip-up didn't matter.

"Would you like to take a walk around the ship, Miss Vicky?" he asked, standing.

"I would like that very much," she replied, accepting his hand to help her from her chair. He held her hand for just a few moments as they strolled along the outside deck. When they arrived at a quiet spot, they turned and stood at the railing overlooking a calm sea with a full moon high in the clear sky. Vicky didn't want to be the first to speak and set the discussion in the wrong direction.

He turned to her. "My English is not perfect, Miss Vicky, and I do not know the difference in the words pretty and beautiful. But I do want to say that I think you are one or both of these words." He raised his hand, as Vicky's eyes opened wide. "My intention is not to make you feel in any way awkward; however I would not be honest if I could not say this to you. Please know I have never said that to any lady before. I am not married and never have been." He shrugged with a smile. "Am I allowed to stay your friend now, Miss Vicky? Please."

Vicky didn't have to act surprised; she was stunned. Men had said nice things to her before, but none had sounded as sincere, yet she worried about what her reaction might be. She closed her eyes. She had to think. Lying about her marital status was easy. Lying to such an honest and gentle person was difficult. She decided to go half-way.

"Alex, to say I am taken aback is what we English would call the understatement of the year. Can I simply respond by stating that yes we are still friends, new friends, but friends anyway. And let me add by saying that I am honored by your very generous comments. Perhaps I should head to my cabin and see how my brother is doing."

"Yes, of course. May I walk you to your cabin, Miss Vicky, and I will talk only about the weather?"

"That would be lovely, Alex. Thank you." She immediately wondered if she had made a mistake, but was sure Ed had fixed what needed to be fixed.

They didn't speak until they were on her deck and walking to her room.

"Does it always rain in London, Miss Vicky?" He asked.

She chuckled at the question. "Not all the time, Alex. But let me say that I saw much more sun when I moved to Canada to go to university than one sees in foggy London. It's colder, of course, and I miss visiting my favorite castle in Windsor, but one cannot have everything in life, can one?"

"No we cannot," he agreed as they approached her cabin.

She peeked at the names by the door:

'Mr. Edwin Crowe. Miss Victoria Crowe.'

She had almost prayed it would be okay, and was now totally relieved.

He offered his hand and they shook hands. "May I join you and your brother for breakfast in the morning?" he asked, still holding her hand gently.

"My brother will not be eating breakfast tomorrow, Alex. He will be jogging around the ship. But if you like..."

He responded immediately. "I shall save us a table. Shall we say seven-thirty? Eight o'clock? Your choice, Miss Vicky, and I look forward to joining you."

"Seven-thirty would be fine, Alex. I shall see you in the morning." She leaned forward and gave him an air kiss. "Good night, Alex."

He bowed as he stepped back. "Good night, Miss Vicky, and thank you. Knowing I will be seeing you in just a few hours, I will indeed have a good and restful night." He turned and left.

Vicky entered the cabin to face Ed and Carolyn standing in the middle of the room.

"Wow!" Carolyn whispered, "bloody wow!"

"Crikey," Ed added, "bloody crikey."

Vicky shook her head, sat on her bed, and sniffed back her tears. "That was awful," she managed. "He is such a gentleman, and I like him. Now I have to go through it all again tomorrow. I feel like a real…"

Ed backed off and motioned to Carolyn.

Carolyn sat with Vicky and put her arm around her. "Vicky, you're a wonderful loving person. Too nice perhaps." She gave her a hug. "Slim, that was a wonderful job. Because of you we are one step closer to potentially saving some people's lives. People we don't know and people Alex likely doesn't know. Well done."

Vicky stood and wiped away her tears. "Thank you, Miss. Where do we go from here?" They all sat ready for the work ahead.

Carolyn led the discussion. "Here's my plan. I think it will make life easier, especially for Slim. What I want you to do, Slim, is wear a microphone tomorrow for breakfast. I will record your conversation, and that way you don't have to worry about trying to capture any details that you may be able to find out. Keep in mind that tomorrow will be our last full day alone with him."

"Really?" Vicky asked with a chuckle. "How do I, where do I?"

"Close you eyes, and turn around please, Mister," Carolyn asked.

Ed did as he was told.

Carolyn undid the top buttons of her ship uniform and held it open. A small microphone was attached to the centre of her bra. She removed it, gave it to Vicky, did up her buttons and told Ed he could turn around.

"Yikes," Vicky said. "That's neat. I'll put it on first thing tomorrow." She thought for a moment. "How do I know…?"

Carolyn interrupted her. "I will turn it on at my end and start recording at twenty past seven, and I will turn it off five minutes after your conversation with Alex is ended. That will give you the five minutes to say anything into the microphone you want me or the records to show. I will be doing the recording in my cabin, so Mister will not be listening in. I don't mind breaking a few rules, but a guest in crews' cabins is a big no-no."

Vicky turned to Ed with a smile. "You'll be jogging anyway won't you, Mister?"

"I will now," he answered.

Carolyn continued. "Somewhere along the way, Slim, Alex will have to know what you are looking for. Somehow you will have to do that and not totally put him off at the same time. I confess I have no suggestions that might help you out. You understand him better than we do so unless Mister has an idea?"

Ed rubbed his chin, thinking. He tried to put himself in Alex's position and wondered what would help soften the blow. "Okay, here's what I think. Slim, you think he's a very nice person. You should remind him of that as you lead into the true details, and try to rely on his niceness and his role as a gentleman to understand why you are doing what you are, and the way you are doing it."

Vicky and Carolyn looked at each other, somewhat stunned at his response.

Vicky spoke first. "Like wow! Have you ever been dumped like that?"

"Not yet," Ed replied. "But if I ever am…"

"Excellent thinking, Mister," Carolyn added. "I didn't know men could think like that."

Ed shrugged it off. "Well I'm way too smart to respond to that."

"Indeed you are," Carolyn offered. "Now any other questions before I leave you both to a good night's sleep?"

Vicky replied quickly. "Just my thanks as a friend, Carolyn. And my appreciation for your comments, Miss."

Carolyn nodded and left the cabin.

"I do want to say that I agree with Miss that you did a terrific job," Ed said.

"Thanks. I appreciate that."

He handed her a sheet of paper. "This is what makes sense about your being born in England and then moving to Canada for university. I've listed schools you would have gone to, and mine that were different. That will explain your university attendance. I've also listed things about London that you would know having been born and educated there."

Vicky scanned the information. "Hey, that's great. Well done. You know, it seems a little like we are being used as…bait almost"

Ed nodded. "I think you're right. Crowe's bait, eh?"

"Good one, Ed."

"So where does the microphone go?"

Vicky shook her head. "Go get changed for bed, Ed. And don't forget to keep your underwear on."

Ed did as he was told.

CHAPTER NINE

Thursday, May 1st 1986
7 am

There was a gentle knock on the door and Vicky opened it quickly. She took the tray from the waiter and placed it on the table between her bed and Ed's bed. She tapped him on his shoulder.

"Wakey, wakey," she said.

He rolled over with a groan. "What the heck time is it?"

"Seven o'clock, sleepyhead. Don't forget you're to be out jogging in a few minutes. We all have a role to play you know."

He sat up, holding the sheet up to keep himself covered. "Okay, give me a minute."

She poured their tea and handed him his cup. "Milk in first of course. Just like a true Brit."

"Thanks, pretty blue eyes…oops, sorry I forgot. Thanks, Slim." He took a gulp. "English breakfast; perfect."

"How do I look for a breakfast date?" she asked, standing up. She wore a white blouse buttoned at the back that offered her more protection from anyone seeing the microphone, and a knee-length light blue skirt.

He smiled. "You look very nice, and I think I now know where the microphone is located."

"Maybe," she replied, "but that is for me to know and you, and every one else, not to find out."

"Of course. I do hope it goes well and look forward to hearing the recording later. Can I only encourage you to say what you want to say, and not worry about me or anyone else that may hear it; and that will not be many people in any event. This is business, as strange a business as it is."

Vicky nodded, looking at her watch. "Thanks, Mister. I'll keep that in mind. Look the mic is on and I have to leave. I want to be no more than five minutes late. Men appreciate that, believe me. And thanks again for the information on my schooling in London etc. I think that will help big time."

For the first time in a long time, they shook hands and she left the cabin. Ed looked at the phone, and ten seconds later it rang. It was Carolyn.

"Well said, Mister. I'll keep in touch. I suggest you pass on the jogging and sit by the phone, just in case."

"Will do, Miss." He hung up the phone and headed to the bathroom to clean up, knowing he should not take the time for a shower.

Vicky held her head high and put on a smile as she walked into the breakfast room. It wasn't very busy, with most of the passengers preferring the buffet. Alex sat at a table for four with a window view at the far end of the room. He stood as she approached and held a seat out for her, and then sat himself. She nodded her thanks.

"Good morning, Alex," she said, keeping her hands on her lap. "How are you this fine morning?"

"Life is wonderful," he replied. "A lovely day, a calm sea, and if I may, a most charming guest to enjoy breakfast with."

The waiter offered them menus and asked if they would like tea or coffee.

"I would love some English Breakfast tea," Vicky replied.

"Coffee for me," Alex added.

They looked at their menus. When the waiter returned with their drinks, Vicky ordered dry toast and strawberry jam. Alex ordered two poached eggs and toast. The waiter left them to themselves.

Alex spoke first, as Vicky had hoped he would. "I do want you to know, Miss Vicky, that I appreciate your joining me this morning. I do hope we can sit and find out more about each other, without being too personal of course."

"That would be nice, Alex," she replied, taking a sip of her tea. "Should I begin perhaps? Not that I have a very exciting tale to tell."

He waved her on. "Please begin, Miss Vicky."

"As I mentioned yesterday," Vicky started slowly, "I went to school in England. Ed and I went to different schools, hence my ending up in university in Canada."

"You passed the 11 Plus then?"

"Why, yes I did. I didn't realize you would know that sort of detail."

"You might be surprised what I learned in my very unusual education back home. But I interrupted, please continue"

The waiter delivered their meals and it gave Vicky time to settle down. She decided to go all the way. She took a nibble of her toast.

"I went to Kilburn Grammar School and Ed went to Aylestone Secondary Modern School. Actually his school was only a few years old while mine had been built a hundred years before. Of course we both wore uniforms, very English that way."

Alex nodded. "School uniforms are very good for the education system. It limits the what-do-I-wear-today situation. They should be worn more often in the US school system."

"Agree entirely," Vicky added wiping her lips. "I didn't mention that our father died rather young. Ed was four and I was only two. A sad time for our mother."

Alex pushed his plate away. "Very sad indeed. May I ask?"

"He died of a heart attack. That's why Ed likes to jog and keep in shape."

Sitting in her cabin Carolyn nodded her head in respect for Vicky's style. 'This lady's a winner all the way,' she said to herself.

Vicky didn't want to push her luck too much further. "So I ended up in Canada at the University of Toronto, graduated with an MBA, and finally chose to go into life insurance sales, which I totally enjoy. Ed joined me in Canada to add to his travel agent background and ended up staying. All not very exciting, but I have a good life." She finished her tea and motioned to Alex to take proceed.

"Perhaps more exciting than my background," Alex said, waving his hand to order more tea and coffee. "We may need a second cup," he offered.

Vicky nodded, while Carolyn began to worry.

"I was born in Grozny, the capital of Chechnya. My parents are both of Chechen background and I say that because they are both medical doctors; a profession usually saved for Russians in my country. Under the current Soviet government Chechens are looked down upon, almost second class citizens in their own country." He shrugged. "Perhaps you are not aware of that, but it is important to my background. I went to very special and expensive schools as a child and eventually went to Grozny University. The university specialized in Agriculture and Aviation Design. One specialty to feed the nation and the other to get us to the moon and beyond."

The waiter delivered their tea and coffee. They each poured their own.

"That sounds rather interesting," Vicky said, sipping her hot tea.

"Indeed it is," Alex agreed, "but alas the country also needed specialists in nuclear energy, and that is the course I selected, and indeed the course selected for me. It was a wonderful opportunity for me to use my English, since English is the main language of the nuclear energy business. It also allowed me to learn a profession that I could use on a global basis, and not be limited to just the Soviet sphere. That was important to me."

"No doubt there are lots of jobs around the world that would require your skills," Vicky said.

"Indeed. However I spent time in several of the Russian built nuclear stations throughout the Soviet Union, and seven years ago I moved to the nuclear station in Chernobyl." He leaned forward with a smile. "But then you already know that, don't you, Miss Vicky?" He leaned back in his chair and waited.

Vicky rested her hands on her lap and took a breath.

In her cabin, Carolyn crossed her fingers, closed her eyes and hoped for the best.

Vicky sat up straight in her seat, and held her hand across the table. "Hi, Alex. My name is Vicky, but Vicky Kilgour." He stood, shook her hand, and then sat back down with a nod of acceptance of her apology. Vicky continued. "I'm sorry I've had to lie to you, but duty must. I've never lived in England; in fact I've only been there for a few days before we flew to join this cruise. I regret having to lie to you for two reasons. First I'm not used to lying and secondly I didn't think I would have to tell lies to such a nice person, such a gentleman in fact."

"You flatter me," he said.

"Not really, Alex, I think you have a certain je ne sais quoi." She laughed. "That's French, it means…"

"I know what it means," he laughed back. "I speak a little French, Ukrainian, and Russian in addition to my English and Chechen. But I thank you for the compliment."

"So there," she said, "I don't know everything about you, but yes I do know that you worked at the Chernobyl plant, and in case you haven't heard over twenty people have died thus far from the accident."

Alex took a long drink of coffee. "So Ed is not your brother?"

"No, he is not my brother. He's a very good friend who works from time to time with a special agency. We were going to a wedding when he was asked to work on a special assignment – I think that's the word. His regular associate is the lady getting married, so I was asked to fill in for her." She shrugged. "So here I am. And by the way it is 'Miss'. I am not married. At least I didn't have to lie about that part of the story. And with your permission, Alex, I do hope we can stay friends, no matter how the rest of our discussion, or discussions, go?"

"Of course we're still friends, Miss Vicky. I do appreciate your honesty and I can understand why neither you nor Ed could just walk up to me and say you want to talk about the Chernobyl accident. Indeed I gathered that by the fact that you, and not Ed, made the first move. Good planning on his part perhaps?"

Vicky laughed. "No. I just did it on the spur of the moment when I saw you smoking that cigar. The information I gave you is accurate by the way. I didn't make that up."

"May I suggest the following," Alex asked with a smile. "Why don't we go for a nice stroll around the deck, and then I will walk you back to your cabin. But let us have lunch together today, after which you and Ed can approach me about the accident? This way I get some time with you as a young lady, and not as an inquisitor."

"Perfect, Alex. That would be very nice. Let's do that."

They stood and went for their walk.

Carolyn phoned Ed to make sure he was still in his cabin and to stay there for a while. Carolyn would join them as soon as Vicky returned.

"How's she doing?" Ed asked.

"She's magic, Mister. Bloody magic."

Just over an hour later Vicky and Alex stood outside her cabin.

"May I meet you here at noon for lunch? I will arrange a special lunch in a special location in order that we can speak in private after a relaxing meal."

She shook his hand. "I look forward to lunching with you Alex. Now that we know each other just a little better, perhaps we will be able to enjoy the meal in a more comfortable setting."

He bowed, kissed her hand, turned and left. She watched him for just a few moments and then entered her cabin.

Ed sat reading the ship's newspaper, as if nothing special was happening.

"How'd it go?" he asked casually.

"Okay I think. Let's see what Miss thinks. I need to freshen up."

She entered the bathroom and held onto the sink with both hands. Her body was shaking nervously and only now could she let her emotions show. She reached into her make-up bag, pulled out an aspirin bottle and quickly popped one into her mouth and swallowed it with a sip of water. After willing herself to relax she went back into the cabin just as there was a knock on the door. She opened it and Carolyn entered the room quickly. She was wearing her ship's uniform, and entered holding a small tape in her hand and a broad smile on her face.

She pointed to Vicky. "You are one of the smoothest young women I have ever known, Miss Vicky. Well done, in fact very well done." She turned to Ed. "Some time I'll play you the tape, but in the meantime let's think through our next move. Slim's next move that is."

Vicky relaxed in a second and had to stop herself from crying in happiness and relief.

"Okay, here's where we are," Carolyn began, leading the discussion. "Alex now knows exactly who Slim is, and he knows that Slim is aware of his having worked at Chernobyl. No hidden secrets thus far, but worth noting that he also knows that Slim is working with Mister who is himself representing an agency; as yet un-named, but I'd be amazed if he didn't realize it is MI6. My pure speculation is that in his mind dealing with MI6 is more comfortable than dealing with the CIA. He and Slim are going to talk about the accident after a nice lunch. He now knows over twenty people died, and while I couldn't see his reaction, I doubt that was in any way a surprise. Most importantly he has accepted Slim in her role, and continues to regard her as a friend. That relationship is what will allow us to carry on. Slim, anything I've missed?"

"I don't think so," Vicky replied, "except I've never been so happy to tell the truth. I sure couldn't do this as a full time job."

"Well done, Slim," Ed added, shaking her hand. "Does he know about the KGB in Izmir?"

Vicky shook her head. "No. I wonder if I should tell him"

"Absolutely," Ed replied quickly. "Not only will it enhance your friendship, it will also put him on his guard. Whatever happens we don't want him to be used as an internal political-pawn in Russia. Gorbachev has enough problems as it is."

Carolyn nodded. "Good thinking, Mister." She smiled. "You are thinking more like a spy every day."

"I wonder if that's a good thing," he pondered.

"I don't know," Vicky said. "But I'll have to remember your new skill-set when we're back to our 'boring' lives in Canada."

"The sooner the better," Ed replied.

Carolyn raised her hand. "I've gotta go. I have to get a message to London about how things are going. And, Slim, as it has been said in many other similar important messages, your name will be mentioned in the dispatch." She left the cabin.

"Wow," Vicky beamed, grinning from ear to ear. "Do you hear that, Ed. Maybe I should do this full time, eh?" Before Ed could respond, Vicky shook her head. "Nah, I'm way too nice a person to lie all the time aren't I?"

"Way too nice, Vicky. Way too nice. Shall we chat about what to say after lunch with Alex?"

"Sure, Mister. Back to reality."

They sat down, Vicky on her bed and Ed on the desk chair.

"Here's my bottom line," Ed began. "I don't think Alex is going to tell you where the next, and hopefully only, accident will be. Agree?"

Vicky nodded. "Using your expression; not a snowball's chance in Hell. But I do think he will tell us, whether or not there is to be another accident, and if so is it just one more. What do you think?"

Ed closed his eyes to think, and then nodded. "Yes, I think he'll tell his new friend that much. But what would be a huge additional help is if you could get him to give us a clue. Something to think about, as it were."

"That will be our goal then," Vicky agreed, "but I'm not going to, you know..."

"I know you're not going to, Slim," Ed interrupted, "and I know you're not going to, Vicky."

"Thanks. Now if you'll give me some privacy, I'll get ready for my luncheon date, as it were."

Ed gave her a thumb's up, and sat out on the balcony with his back to the cabin.

When Vicky called Ed back into the cabin, she had changed her clothes, make-up, and hairstyle.

"Well don't you look nice," Ed said, noticing the blouse she wore was buttoned up in the front, with several buttons at the top open. She was wearing a gold chain with a Maple Leaf pendant.

"Nice necklace," Ed said.

Vicky touched it with her left hand. "And look," she said, "no wedding ring."

Ed nodded. "Right. Pretty short marriage, eh?"

Vicky's face turned glum. "Yeah, a failed engagement and now a marriage finished, and I never even got to kiss my husband. What a loser I turned out to be."

"Hey, come on," Ed smiled, wishing he hadn't said what he had said.

Vicky shook her head, and then looked up. "Okay, ex-hubby and ex-boyfriend get over here and give me a hug. And that, Ed, is an order."

Ed stepped over and took her in his arms, giving her a solid hug and a kiss on her forehead. "Any man would be happy to marry you, Vicky. And I suspect Alex would be first - or second - in line."

She decided not to go there, but gave him a quick kiss on his cheek. "Thanks, Mister. Now let me get my head in gear for an all-important lunch date."

As they separated the phone rang. Ed picked it up. It was Carolyn. "Two points, Mister. Alex is arranging for a very nice lunch in his very nice suite, and so far thirty-one people have died. Tell Slim I'll start recording at twelve sharp unless you phone me to tell me other-wise. Speak to you later." She hung up.

Ed passed along the message to Vicky as she adjusted her hair. "Got it!" she said with confidence. As a last minute thought she put her business card in her small purse.

CHAPTER TEN

At exactly twelve noon, there was a knock on the cabin door. Ed was, conveniently in the bathroom. The shower was running, but he wasn't in it.

Vicky opened the door. Her head was held up; she was feeling confident. Alex stood with a beautiful bouquet of red and white roses and bowed slightly as he presented them to Vicky.

"Oh my goodness," Vicky exclaimed, "how perfectly lovely of you. Please come in." Alex entered and stayed by the door. The roses were in a glass vase and Vicky placed them in the centre of the desk and stood back to admire them. She turned to Alex. "I should say that you shouldn't have, but I'm so happy that you did. They are lovely, truly lovely."

Alex waved his hand gently. "Lovely flowers for a lovely lady."

Vicky grabbed her purse and joined him at the door. She stood on her toes and quickly gave him a kiss on his cheek. "And a generous message from a generous man."

"Shall we?" he asked as he opened the door and motioned for Vicky to lead the way. Outside he turned to Vicky. "I hope you do not mind, I have ordered lunch in my suite. It is a large suite and the food will be served. I hope you will not worry..."

"I will not." Vicky took his arm. "Lead the way please."

To say the suite was large was an understatement. It was one of the two Royal Suites on the ship. The bedroom was off to one side and there was a separate sitting area with two comfortable armchairs and a love seat. Lunch was to be served on the extensive veranda, and the waiter was ready for them when they arrived. Vicky's wide eyes expressed her amazement, especially about the size of the cabin.

"One has to enjoy life to the fullest at this time in one's life," Alex explained. "Shall we take a seat at the table?"

Vicky didn't ask for an explanation, but led the way to the veranda. The waiter held their chairs as they sat and with a nod from Alex he served the soup and walked into the main cabin area for discretion's sake.

"The soup is wonderful," Vicky said after her first sip.

"And hot," Alex added. "Soup should always be hot."

Vicky reached into her purse and handed her business card to him. "I want to give this to you to prove I really am who I say am."

"Why, thank you. Perhaps I'll write to you sometime."

"That would be nice," she replied, "very nice."

Vicky took the opportunity to look around. The suite was on an upper deck, at the aft of the ship and the veranda was almost the size a standard cabin. The view was beautiful and they could have been the only passengers on the ship. There was only sea visible from their view, and the ship could have been hundreds of miles from land. She knew it wasn't but she enjoyed the possibility.

"I am happy to see your enjoying the view," Alex said.

Vicky finished her soup and gently wiped her lips. "Thank you, Alex. I do feel rather spoiled at the moment."

"I am happy to hear that, Miss Vicky, very happy. So tell me, are you wired?"

Vicky patted her lips again with her serviette, giving her a second to think. "Why, Alex, do I look at all agitated?" She held a gentle smile.

He laughed and pointed a friendly finger at her. "You are not only a very lovely young lady, but a very smart and quick-witted young lady also. I am so happy to have met you."

In her cabin Carolyn punched the air in approval.

"You say such nice things, Alex. Thank you."

They enjoyed the rest of the meal without discussing any related subjects and when they were finished the waiter collected everything together on a trolley and rolled it quietly out of the suite.

"Shall we move inside where it is more private?" Alex asked.

"Of course, and thank you again for such a lovely lunch."

They sat across from each other in the comfortable chairs. Vicky crossed her legs ensuring not too much of her legs were showing. She needed the discussion to be strictly professional, while understanding that Alex was likely happy to keep it as friendly as the rest of their conversation had been thus far.

Alex sat up straight and interlocked his hands in front of himself. "So what would you like to ask me, Vicky?"

"I'm reluctant to ask you anything actually, but really feel I must. Our friendship..."

"Our friendship is solid, but business 'must' at times, and this is the time. You will be the only person I will speak to on this subject and there are, of course, limitations to what I may say."

"Yes of course there are. So I will ask only what I think you will feel comfortable telling me."

"Then the rules are set, Vicky. Please proceed."

"Was it an accident?"

Alex thought about the question. "Yes."

"Was it preventable?"

"Yes."

"You could have prevented it from happening?"

"If I had been there, yes."

"Did you know it was going to happen?"

"I had expectations that it would happen, but it was not a certainty; no."

"Would you explain that a little later, please?"

"Of course."

Vicky was now getting nervous, and Carolyn was sitting in her cabin with her eyes closed.

"You said there would be 'More to come'?"

"Yes."

"Is it one more, or more than one?"

"To my knowledge, just one."

Vicky relaxed somewhat. "Will it be an accident?"

"No."

"So it will not be of the same or similar cause?"

"No."

"Will you be responsible for the one more?"

"No, but I know of it."

"Could you stop it from happening?"

Alex shook his head. "Not by myself, no."

"But if you told other people…"

"Yes."

Vicky held her breath for a second in an effort to relax, knowing she was getting to the most important question. "Now I will not ask you where or when, but may I ask you one more question that would, might I say, make life somewhat easier for everyone; including perhaps yourself?"

He shrugged, unsure of what was coming. "Of course," he finally said, "what are friends for?"

Vicky gulped. "Could you give me a clue? A hint perhaps?"

He adjusted himself in the chair and thought for thirty seconds, which seemed like a lifetime to both Vicky and Carolyn.

He shook his head. "I'm not sure I can do that, as much as I would like to."

Vicky looked at him straight into his eyes. "I'll give you a reason you might want to, Alex. There will be KGB agents looking for you when we arrive at Izmir. That is the truth. I did not make it up."

His eyes opened wide and he took a deep breath. He was fully aware that if the KGB got hold of him they would stop at nothing in order to get him to betray his fellow Chechen collaborators. "That is good to be aware of. Then yes, I will give you a clue. But you must give me some time to think about that. It will not be a simple solution."

"I understand, Alex. Thank you for that."

Carolyn excitedly phoned Ed in his cabin to pass on the excellent news.

"What a lady!" was all Ed could think of in response. They hung up.

Alex walked to his small fridge. "May I have a glass of wine, Miss Vicky?"

"Oh, please do," Vicky replied, her heart beating fast as she tried to calm down, reminding herself to congratulate Ed on his 'clue' suggestion…or was it an subtle order? She didn't care, there was more information coming.

Alex sat down with a glass of white wine and a relaxed look. "Perhaps I should give you some background to everything?"

"That would be most interesting, Alex. Please do."

"The Russian and Chechen people have never got along well, and likely never will. The history goes all the way back before the 15th century at which time Chechnya converted to Islam in an effort to receive protection from the Ottoman Empire in its struggles against Russia. Thus the large majority of our people are Muslim, as I am of course."

Vicky looked at his glass of wine and then back to him, with a smile.

"Ah," he nodded with a shrug, "you noticed that of course. I think of myself as a democratic Muslim. I'm not sure exactly what that means, but it works for me. I notice you do not drink alcohol. Is there a particular reason?"

She grimaced. "It's a long story, Alex. Another time and place perhaps?"

"Of course. My apologies. I do not mean to pry. But let me return to my story."

"Before you do, perhaps you could explain what made you realize we were not just a couple of married passengers on a cruise ship?"

"Ah," he replied, "I always have to be careful. After I saw you and Ed several times on the deck, it struck me as unusual that we would see each other as often as we did on the first day of the cruise. So one time I followed both of you to your cabin, and sure enough your names on the door were Mr. and Mrs. Crowe. And then shortly thereafter you gave me some good advice on my cigar smoking, and introduced yourself as Ed's sister. And sure enough when I walked with you to your cabin, it was Mr. and Miss Crowe. Now one doesn't have to be a Sherlock Holmes to know something was up. You were obviously not KGB, so I was interested in finding out who you both were...especially you."

"I'll keep that in mind if I am ever involved in a similar circumstance," she laughed. "But of course I never will be. Sorry to interrupt."

Alex continued. "There are two really important events that have happened between Russia and my people in the last fifty years. We never got along for centuries, but these two sum up the current lack of respect and distrust we have for the Russian people. The first occurred during the Second World War. Because of the lack of respect for Russia by some of our people, many sided with Germany. The belief was that we would do better if Germany beat Russia. As the Russian army was pushing back the German army in 1943, in October of that year some 120,000 Chechens were moved to Checheno-Ingushetia Republic, with the promise that they were to work at mending bridges and that they would return. But on February 23, 1944, which happened to be Red Army Day, the entire population was deported as punishment for their collaboration with the Germans. Up to 50% were children. They were driven to Kazakhstan and Kyrgyzstan, and thousands died on the way. In one instance some 700 people were crowded into a barn, and the barn was then burnt to the ground. The general who ordered that received a medal. Villages were eliminated and everyone killed. While the exact numbers cannot be determined, it is thought about some 480,000 Chechens died, plus thousands of Ingush, Kalmyks, and Balkars. These murders were ordered and approved by the NKVD, which is now the KGB. That is to say they were responsible for internal security; a government agency. And, of course, with the approval of Stalin, probably the worst human to ever walk the face of the earth. It was officially referred to as Operation Lentil." He paused in order to settle down somewhat. "Would you like me to continue?" he asked.

"Not really," Vicky replied. "But perhaps you should. If nothing else there will one more person in the world who will know what happened."

"Or more perhaps?"

Vicky shrugged. "Perhaps."

"In 1957, four years after Stalin's death the Soviet Government approved an act that allowed repressed nations to officially travel freely within the Soviet Union, and while this does not sound like much, it was of huge importance and an acceptance by Khrushchev that what Stalin had done was wrong. By 1959 nearly all Chechens had returned home. They could not recover their previous homes, which were now owned by Russians. Chechens and the Ingush returnees were considered second or even third-class people, and to many Russians they are still so today. However in August 1958 there were riots in the city of Grozny. It all started, alas, as a result of a Russian soldier asking an Ingush lady to dance. Her fiancé started a fight with the soldier and killed him. There were then major riots by the Russian population throughout the city and many Chechens died, including one old man who was beaten to death while the authorities watched. The riots lasted four days, and while this may not sound as bad as what happened in 1944, I should remind you that my family lived in Grozny, and I was just six years old myself. I saw the riots from my window, although I did not leave our house for over a week. So it is very personal for me. There is still no respect shown between the two populations and to be honest, I doubt there ever will be. And the fact remains that Chechens are still treated like peasants in their own land. When a Russian calls someone a 'Chechen', what they mean is 'bandit' or 'thief'. They have no respect for us, and we have no respect for them."

Vicky shook her head. "That is scary to say the least. But, Alex, isn't the Soviet Union going to change under Gorbachev? How does this accident and any further similar occurrence help?"

He nodded his head wisely. "Excellent point and a significant question. Yes things are shifting somewhat under Gorbachev, and they will continue to do so. But keep in mind he is just one man, and many members of the KGB do not want change. Any change will eliminate some of their power. The changes proposed are what you might call a political hot potato; in the Soviet Union I would call it a potential political disaster. And while this may not sound very reasonable, I believe the accident will help change the Soviet Union in a positive fashion. Now as you no doubt are aware Gorbachev has two main thrusts, from which all changes will be driven. They are Perestroika and Glasnost. Without going into detail, Glasnost translates easily into English as 'Openness'. Perestroika translates as 'Restructuring'. Easy words to understand, but to the peoples of the Soviet Union they represents a massive change. Many see these words as their future. A future they do not know and cannot see or fully understand, but it will be immense. This accident will show the people, just within the nuclear power business, how poorly managed the Soviet Union is. Now a poorly managed agriculture business is easy to see and feel. Our people go hungry and line-up for hours to get the basics of bread and milk. Serious indeed, but a poorly managed nuclear power business, and I can assure you it is extremely poorly managed, leads to what happened last week."

"But, Alex, you said it wouldn't have happened if you were there."

"But I wasn't, was I? I planned this trip knowing that something could go wrong, not that it would go wrong. Let me try and summarize, please. When the accident happened the plant was going through what is known as a steam turbine test. The test is to ensure the plant can still run when there is an electrical power failure. There are three emergency back-up diesel generators at Chernobyl that would replace the lack of electrical power due to a power failure. It takes some

60 to 75 seconds for these generators to replace the megawatt output. Now during this very important delay the goal is to use the power generated directly from the steam turbine of the plant as it wound down. In other words, the plant's closing down created sufficient power for the minute or so that would to be used to maintain the ongoing operation of the plant. Simple in theory, but not in practice. The steam turbine test has been tried three times before in the years preceding, and it did not work. Several issues were at play last week. The test was planned over three shifts, which should never have happened. Several of the operators were not qualified to run the test, and the plant manager was not sufficiently knowledgeable of what to do if something went wrong; which it did.

"So what went wrong?"

"In speaking to my friend and associate from the plant an unusual, but certainly not rare, instance occurred. The Kiev power plant went offline and Chernobyl was requested to postpone the reduction of its own power in order that the peak evening demand for Kiev be met. This simply added to the complicated process of testing and in the confusion there was not enough power being produced by its own steam engine to, in plain English, stop the plant from boiling over. And just like a kettle boiling over, the lid flew off. It tore a hole in the roof, and…"

"All hell broke loose," Vicky added sadly.

"Indeed, all hell broke loose." Alex nodded. "But the worst is yet to come. Those that died, and I suspect I knew most of them, are at rest. The real hell to come is for those people that received an overdose of the highly radioactive fallout, who will suffer for many years to come, and that will include many from the local town of Pripyat. In typical Russian fashion the town wasn't evacuated until the following day, some 36 hours after the event. Totally unacceptable, but who is to be held responsible?" He shrugged. "No-one of course. But, and maybe just a 'but', things will change as a result. That is a sad expectation to hope for."

Vicky nodded, understanding. "I really should be getting back now, Alex. I do want to thank you for a wonderful lunch, and without seeming too pushy, I do look forward to your agreeing to give me a clue; no matter how complicated."

"Must you rush?"

Vicky nodded. "Ed and I have to leave the cruise tomorrow when we dock in Izmir tomorrow morning. We have a wedding to attend in England on Saturday. I wish it were the following Saturday and we could stay on the cruise...but?"

"Of course, Miss Vicky. I fully understand, and thank you for the KGB warning."

"My pleasure, Alex." She turned to leave.

Alex touched her arm. "May I speak to you privately - for just a few seconds?"

Vicky bit her lip. "I can't let you kiss me, Alex."

"No of course. That wasn't my goal. A dream perhaps, but not a goal for today."

Vicky decided to take the risk. She undid the top three buttons of her blouse, opened it wide enough to remove the small microphone from her bra between her breasts. She placed it in her left hand, closed it fully and held it behind her back. "What are friends for," she smiled.

"Thank you, Miss Vicky. Thank you sincerely. I want you to know that I am dying; cancer alas."

Vicky gasped and tried to speak, but couldn't.

He held up his hand and put a finger to his mouth. "I understand, Miss Vicky. I have been diagnosed with a very rare and deadly case of cancer. And before you feel in any way awkward, it has nothing to do with smoking. I have weeks at best, and I'm not proud to say that this diagnosis makes what happened last week less of a guilt in my mind. I just wanted you to know." He raised his hands and shrugged. "I just wanted to tell you in private."

Vicky held back a tear of sadness and guilt. "Oh, Alex. That is so sad. I...I...don't know..."

"Say nothing, Miss Vicky. You must go."

She looked up and reached for him with her right hand. "Kiss me, Alex."

He took her in his arms and gently kissed her lips. She responded with her arms around him and opened her lips for him to touch his tongue to hers. They embraced and held each other, until finally he gently stepped back. "You are a lovely young lady, Miss Vicky. I will deliver the clue to your cabin in a couple of hours. Now you should leave."

Vicky replaced the microphone on her bra and re-buttoned her blouse. "When you come to my cabin, Alex, I shall have a glass of white wine waiting for you. I might even join you."

He opened the door and she left; her head held high and not ashamed of the tears running down her cheeks.

CHAPTER ELEVEN

Vicky walked into the cabin, closed the door, and leaned back against it. Finally she could relax and her shoulders sank.

"What happened?" Ed asked as he jumped up from the chair. "Are you okay? It looks like you've been crying."

She looked over to him, shaking her head. "Of course I've been crying, dummy. Do you think I let my make-up look like this all the time?"

Ed waited a few seconds before he responded. "No, Slim, I don't. And no, Vicky, I don't."

Her head sank. "I'm sorry. That was totally rude of me and uncalled for. I sincerely apologize."

"No matter. Are you okay? Did something happen? Did he..."

"I'm fine. Honest. Let's just wait until Miss gets here, okay? I don't want to repeat my story. I only want to tell it once...ever!"

Ed nodded, and, not to Vicky's surprise, picked up the phone and ordered a pot of tea for three. "Always the answer," he said, turning to Vicky.

"I'm beginning to agree," she mused. "I must be getting old. I have to fix up my make-up, excuse me." She walked into the bathroom, closing the door.

There was a knock on the cabin door. Ed opened it and Carolyn walked in, looking around.

Ed nodded toward the bathroom, and pointed to his cheeks. "She's been crying," he said quietly.

Carolyn cringed. "How's she doing?" she replied, equally quietly.

"She's doing just fine," Vicky said as she left the bathroom. "Never better." She held the microphone out for Carolyn. "Thanks, Miss. I hope I never have to wear one again. Have to be on one's best behavior, yes?"

Carolyn put the microphone in her uniform pocket. "I don't doubt you are always on your best behavior, Slim. You did wonderfully. We are so fortunate to have had you join us."

"I've ordered tea," Ed added.

"Perfect," Carolyn said, "just what we need. After it arrives, I'll sum up and save Slim the trouble of having to tell us everything. In the meantime, the plan for tomorrow is as follows. We arrive in Izmir at 6am. We will be the first off the ship. We will be driven to a heliport just out of town and flown by helicopter to Athens. That's about a two hour flight. Then from Athens we will fly, courtesy of the RAF, to Brize Norton RAF airbase, just outside of Oxford. A direct drive to Stonebridge Manor, and we should arrive about 3pm local time…just in time for tea. Ah, speak of the devil." There was a knock on the door.

Ed opened the door and a large tray of tea was delivered.

"I'll be mother," Vicky said, getting up. "Gee, I'm really spending too much time with you English," she added. "I suppose I had better put milk in first, what?"

Carolyn took the cup of tea that Vicky had poured. "Actually, Vicky, I looked up the name Kilgour in a book of ancestry. It's really very English. Northern England mostly." She laughed. "Not bad news, I hope?"

"Not at all. Actually my father is rather proud of our British background."

"Could be worse," Ed commented. "Could be French."

"Let's get back to work," Carolyn said, not wanting to respond to Ed's comment.

They sat and Carolyn led the discussion.

"So to summarize considerably, here's what I heard. The Chernobyl accident, was an accident, but could have been prevented. It resulted from poor management of the plant, running an important test over three shifts, and the right people were not on duty. If Mr. Umarov had been on duty the right buttons would have been pressed and all would be well. But he wasn't. In fact he went out of his way not to be there. However the next incident, the one he warned us of, will not be an accident. He knows when, where, and probably how, but he did not organize it in any way. The only good news in all of this is that in less than two hours he will be here to enjoy a glass of wine, and give us; give Slim, a clue. As to what the clue will be we do not exactly know, but I have the impression it will provide us with enough data to prevent it from happening; if, and I think it will be a big 'if', we can break his code. He said it would not be easy. Slim, does that sound right to you?"

"Yes, Miss. Well summed up."

Ed clapped his hands quietly. "Outstanding result, Slim. You should be proud of yourself."

"Maybe," she replied, unenthusiastically.

Ed shrugged, expressing his confusion.

Carolyn assumed responsibility for control of the conversation. "Let me explain what I think she is saying. When the tape is reviewed in London it is clear that for a short while Slim took off the microphone and spoke privately with Mr. Umarov; at his specific request for privacy. He'd made it clear he knew the conversation was being recorded and Slim, wisely I might add, didn't disagree with him." She smiled. "And before she took the microphone off she made it clear she wasn't going to let him kiss her. You had full control, young lady. Well done. Now I must ask you, Slim; was there anything said during that short period of time that relates to our role here?"

"Let me top us up," Ed said, wanting Vicky to have the time to think. After he finished topping them up, he sat down and they sipped their warm tea.

Vicky sipped her tea and took a deep breath. "Okay, I…er, he…"

"Do you know, Vicky, why we talk about milk in first?" Ed interrupted. "No, of course you don't. Let me explain. Many years ago fine china was just that; fine. And those posh types that could afford the finest of china always put milk in first so that the hot tea would not crack the cup. Nowadays, of course, fine china is bone china and hot tea will not crack the cup. So those posh people today put the milk in last, and in doing so can better control the perfect cup of tea. However, we lowly types still put milk in first in order to act as posh as we can." He smiled. "Interesting, eh?"

Carolyn turned to Ed. "What are you…?"

Vicky laughed. "That's okay, Carolyn. Ed's just getting me to relax; and learn something at the same time. I'll be sure to mention this bit of, otherwise useless, information to my father who still does milk first. Thanks, Ed."

Ed nodded his understanding.

"What Alex told me," Vicky began calmly, "is that he is dying; weeks, not months. Cancer. He tried to make me feel better by saying it is not related to his cigar smoking, which I had convinced him to stop doing. Not sure I believe him on that small point, but I certainly believe he is dying. He understands that I will relate that to you, but he did want to tell me in private. I do hope that's not a problem?"

"Oh, my God," Carolyn exclaimed, "what terribly sad news. And, Vicky, you're not required to do anything for us. Everything you do is strictly up to you, but let me tell you again, you are doing a super job in a very difficult set of circumstances."

Vicky began to cry and dropped her head low.

"I'll go for a short walk," Ed got up and left.

Carolyn reached over and put her arm around Vicky and held her for a while. "And I'll bet you let him kiss you," she said warmly.

Vicky nodded. "Yes I did. I wanted him to know I like him; and if he's soon to die, I…"

Carolyn squeezed her gently. "I understand, Vicky. You're a wonderful human being. The world needs more like you." She stepped back. "Now why don't you freshen-up your make-up, and get ready for Alex to join you and Ed in a little while?" With a wave she left the cabin.

Vicky smiled and walked into the bathroom.

Several minutes later Ed entered the cabin with a wine bucket filled with ice and a bottle of white wine, and three glasses. He set them down and sat on his bed. He wanted to think through the possibility of how they could gain further information over a friendly glass of wine with Alex. He knew they shouldn't do anything that would discourage Alex from speaking freely and potentially provide them with more information. His thoughts were interrupted when Vicky stepped out of the bathroom. She had refreshed her make-up and looked happier and more relaxed than just a short while ago.

"So how do I look?" she asked happily.

"As beautiful as ever," Ed replied.

"Hmmm, I'm not sure I can trust you on that one, bloke. You're just trying to butter me up."

"Just telling the truth, Vicky. I never lie."

She shook her head. "Maybe. But more to the point, how do we put this whole thing to bed?" she asked.

"Is that a play on words?" Ed enquired with a straight face.

She waived the question off. "Let me re-phrase the question, Mister. How do we handle this friendly glass of wine with Alex?"

"Good question, Slim. I was thinking about that…"

His response was interrupted by a gentle knock on the door. Ed jumped up, opened the door and invited Alex in. He bowed gently to each of them and took the chair offered by Vicky.

"Let me get the wine," Ed said pleasantly, and started to un-cork the bottle.

"Let me give you this," Alex offered Vicky an envelope. "But please don't open it until after I have left. I do not want to discuss it, if you don't mind."

Vicky took the envelope and put it in a drawer by the side of her bed. "Thank you, Alex. Enough said."

Ed passed wine to Vicky and Alex. "Would you prefer water?" he asked Vicky as he handed it to her.

She took the glass of wine. "This is fine, but thanks for asking."

"To a great cruise," Ed toasted, and to his surprise Vicky took a small sip of wine.

"A short cruise for you perhaps?" Alex toasted.

Ed replied. "Yes, we must leave very early tomorrow morning. We have a wedding to attend on Saturday and to add to the timing issue, I am the best man."

They drank their wine and chatted about cruising and the increase in cruise ships being added to the world's fleets. It was friendly and just banter, until Alex changed the conversation as he turned to Ed.

"Have you listened to the tapes?" he asked.

"No, sir I have not. And to be frank I'm not sure I ever will. But the general conversation has been outlined to me. May I, however, raise a point?"

Vicky got nervous, but didn't speak.

Alex nodded. "Please."

Ed waited a second before he spoke. "If you don't mind my saying so, sir, I think you're telling us a bit of a porky."

Vicky put her glass down. "A what…?'

Alex smiled. "Pray tell."

"Pork pie, sir; London Cockney slang. It rhymes with lie. I think you're telling us a lie."

Vicky jumped up, knocking over her glass. "Ed, how dare you! That is totally offensive. Alex has been totally honest…." She threw up her hands and left the cabin slamming the door as hard as she could as she left.

Ed finished his wine. "More wine, sir?" he asked.

Alex shook his head. "What makes you think I am not telling the truth, Ed?"

Ed topped up his own wine. "Oh I think you're telling the truth, but not the whole truth and nothing but the truth. In fact I think you are reluctant to tell Vicky the truth because you do not have long to live and you want her to remember you as a gentle and kind man and not someone who would deliberately kill people, some of whom you would have known personally. Perhaps if there was more time you could explain your reasoning to her, but alas, that cannot be. She has obviously taken a liking to you and you are certainly enough of a gentleman to not want to hurt her feelings."

Alex nodded his thanks. "Ed, I..."

"Let me add, sir," Ed said interrupting, "that Vicky is a very nice, but also a very strong young lady. She is certainly capable of handling the truth. What I am trying to say, sir, is that she is no softy; far from it."

Alex sat up straight. "Are we being recorded?"

"I believe so, yes."

"Well there is another side to the story, but like anything related to a nuclear power operation it is not as simple as ABC. In fact it's more like A to Z only five times over. Therefore I will not try to explain my personal involvement, except to say that I was fully aware that the test would not be successful and damage would be done. The damage was worse than I had expected and that was due to the poor management of the plant. In fact time will tell that even the KGB was concerned about how nuclear plants are mismanaged in the USSR. Now that I have addressed your concern, I will now leave."

They shook hands and Alex left. Ed waited a few seconds and said aloud, but softly. "Well that was a good guess."

Five minutes later Vicky entered the cabin and sat down, obviously still shaken. Ed didn't speak, not wanting to create a scene.

"More wine thank you," Vicky said flatly.

Ed jumped up, filled her glass and then sat back down.

"Thank you." Vicky said, not looking at him.

They sat in silence.

Ten minutes later Carolyn entered the cabin closed the door with a bang, and turned to face them. She smiled but got no response. Stepping into the centre of the cabin, she removed a small recorder from her pocket, placing it on the table.

"Mister, Slim I don't want either of you to speak until after I have turned off the recorder, and I have said a few words. Thank you." She pressed the play button and they listened. Alex's voice began:

"What makes you think I am not telling the truth, Ed?............

Carolyn let it run and turned off the recorder after Ed's final comment:

..........*"Well that was a good guess."*

Carolyn looked at them with a cheeky grim. "Well done team. Good acting on both your parts."

"That was no acting and you know it," Vicky shook her head. "Ed, Mister, I apologize. I over-reacted and you were right. Sorry."

Carolyn jumped in, not waiting for Ed to respond. "No apology is required, Slim. You took a chance when you decided to tell him you two weren't married and Mister took a similar chance in questioning his facts. It's what we do and you both did it well. And before Mister speaks, I want to say that I think we've learned something about the so-called accident in the last half hour, although I confess I'm not sure what. Speak, Mister, or forever hold your peace.....and no smart response to that; it's peace with an 'a' not an 'i'."

Ed raised both hands in submission. "All's well that ends well."

"Oh God," Vicky groaned; "now he's quoting Shakespeare to us."

Ed stood and raised his right hand to his heart. "Let us then be wiser me sayeth."

Carolyn shook her head. "That's not Shakespeare."

"No, I know," Ed replied pointing to the drawer. "What I meant was should we see, perchance, what Alex left us, or more to the point left Vicky, as a clue to solve the problem of the future disaster?"

"Exactly what I was going to suggest," Carolyn agreed. "Slim why don't you have the pleasure of seeing what he left us?"

Vicky reached into the drawer and with some excitement pulled out the envelope. She carefully opened it and extracted the small sheet of paper and unfolded it. It contained only numbers:

40 7 30 30 9 30 4 30 5 9

She looked at it, shrugged her lack of understanding and passed it on to Ed and Carolyn who looked at it together.

"Well that's easy," Ed offered, "I have absolutely no idea."

"Agreed," Carolyn nodded. "But this is not for us to solve. Our role is to deliver it to London tomorrow and let them figure out what it means." She turned to Vicky. "If you're okay with it I suggest you invite Alex to dinner tonight with the three of us, strictly on a non professional basis. What do you think?"

Vicky nodded with a smile. "Absolutely, great idea." She turned to Ed. "Are you okay with that, Ed…oops! I mean, Mister?"

"Perfect," Ed replied, "and if you agree, Miss, perhaps we can now go back to our regular names, and relax somewhat?"

"Done." Carolyn replied quickly, "but I'll still be Nancy Watson tonight."

Vicky stood and walked toward the door. "Okay, I'm going to buy a bikini from the ship's expensive shop and sit out by the pool and try and get a tan for the wedding. I'll charge the bikini to the cabin which Ed said was okay, and that the British government would be happy to pay for it. I'll phone Alex and invite him when I return." She grabbed a bath robe and a towel and left.

Ed looked at Carolyn. "That's okay isn't it; paying for the bikini?"

"Well I should hope so, you're getting paid by the hour as a consultant, and I'm paid as a civil servant. The least we can do for Vicky is pay for a bikini."

"Is that a play on words; the least?" He grinned.

Carolyn shook her head. "Let's go for a cup of tea. It may keep your mind out of the gutter."

"Yes, boss."

They left for the atrium at a brisk walk.

Sitting in a quiet corner of the atrium they ordered a pot of tea for two – English Breakfast. It was delivered several minutes later, nice and hot. Ed waited the three minutes suggested by tea experts, and then poured; milk in first.

Carolyn raised her cup and held it towards Ed in salute. "Cheers," she said, "and congratulations on a job well done."

Ed returned the salute. "Cheers, but most of the work was done by Vicky. I give her one-hundred percent for intuition. She just seemed to know that it was best to change the story from married couple to brother and sister. Still a lie, but a better one in the circumstances. Good guess I'd say."

Carolyn laughed quietly. "That wasn't a guess, Ed. She could see that he liked her and she took advantage of his obvious feelings. Oh it was a wonderful decision, but certainly not a guess."

Ed understood. "Ah, the old 'city girls; open doors with just a smile,' eh?"

"Exactly, and in this case a very pretty city girl, very pretty indeed."

They sipped their tea and didn't speak for several minutes before Carolyn put down her cup and leaned forward. "So why did you order separate beds, before the brother/sister decision?"

Ed shrugged. "Vicky felt better about that. Wasn't going to argue with her. We had this story of my having nightmares from the Falklands, but brother/sister worked wonders. So we're up with the crack of dawn tomorrow?" Ed asked, wanting to change the subject.

"First off the ship. The wake up call is set for 5am."

"Looking forward to getting back to London and getting involved in the wedding."

"My too," Carolyn nodded. "Still not sure if we've added anything to the 'More to come' problem, but one can only do one's best."

"Right on," Ed added, "I'll order some more tea."

Vicky lay on a swimming pool lounge chair with the back up. She rubbed suntan lotion on the front of her body and then lay back and closed her eyes to relax. The bikini was not large, but certainly not skimpy. She felt more than comfortable in it; especially at the price she didn't have to pay. She had almost nodded off when she felt someone take the lounge beside her. She opened her eyes. It was Alex. He wore a pair of shorts and a golf shirt; totally unlike him.

"May I join you?" he asked.

"Of course you may, Alex, please do."

He sat and stretched himself out. "I never dress like this," he said, "but I saw you here and didn't feel comfortable joining you in a jacket and tie. Actually I feel rather strange; comfortable but strange."

"You look fine, Alex. Just fine." She sat up. "Maybe you could do me a favor? If I roll over, perhaps you could put some sunscreen on my back?"

He looked nervous at the thought. "If…if that's okay…I…"

"I'll tell you what," Vicky interrupted, "I'll do the back of my legs and you just do my back. Okay?"

He nodded. "That would be fine. I appreciate your trust."

Vicky quickly rubbed suntan lotion on the back of her legs, gave Alex the sunscreen and rolled over, resting her head on her arms. Carefully he poured the sunscreen on the middle of her back, looking around to see if he was being watched. Slowly and gently he started rubbing the cream in, trying not to press too hard. As he got close to the bottom of her bikini he stopped several inches shy.

She turned her head to him, still resting it on her arms. "You don't want the lower part of my back to burn do you, Alex?"

"No, no I wouldn't want that, Miss Vicky," he smiled, and rubbed the cream into all of her lower back. He added a touch more cream, spread it all over her back and then sat back into his lounge.

"Thank you, Alex. That was very nice. And while I'm talking with my back to you," she chuckled, "would you join us for dinner tonight? No business, so to speak, just a relaxing dinner before we have to leave tomorrow morning. There will be three of us. We have another associate with us."

"That would be lovely, and no doubt the other associate would be Nancy Watson?"

"Why, Alex," she smiled, lifting her head somewhat, "I do believe you have been spying on us."

He leaned forward. "When you live with the KGB, you always keep your eyes open for 'other associates'."

"Well said, Alex, well said. But please keep in mind, no more hidden mics, just a friendly dinner. Let's say seven-thirty in the main dining room. I'll order a table by the window, with a nice bottle of white wine."

"I shall look forward to it with great pleasure...and I'll make sure I turn off my microphone also." He stood up, bowed nicely and quickly left.

Vicky turned over and sat up, wanting to get his attention, but she was too slow. She shook her head. "Nahh," she mumbled, "he's too nice for that." She turned back on her stomach to get another few minutes of sun on her back, and wondered if he really had been recording their conversations. "No big deal," she muttered with a shrug, "most of what I said what true."

CHAPTER TWELVE

At exactly seven-thirty Alex joined Ed, Vicky, and Carolyn at the table Vicky had reserved for their dinner together. All three of them at the table knew that after this evening they would not see Alex again, and in the not too distant future he would be dead. He certainly did not in any way appear sickly or ill. His physical appearance was of a tall, healthy thirty-something with a smile and a pleasant personality. Given his personal circumstances he was friendlier and more relaxed than would be expected.

He reached over to Carolyn and shook her hand. "It is a pleasure to meet you, Nancy Watson. I am Alex Umarov, although you no doubt are aware of me through your friends and associates here at the table." He shook hands with Vicky and Ed, motioning Ed not to stand, and then took the empty seat between Vicky and Carolyn.

"I have heard both about you, and indeed from you," Carolyn replied with a cheeky smile. "It is a pleasure, sir, to finally meet you. I trust my friends haven't been too intrusive?"

"Not for a minute, and please call me Alex."

"And please call me Nancy," she replied.

The waiter opened the bottle of white wine from the ice bucket, Ed tasted it with a nod, and then the waiter poured all four a glass of wine each, bowed nicely and left.

"If I may," Alex said holding his glass high for a toast, "I would offer a toast to new friends and positive international relations."

All four shared the toast, raising but not clinking their glasses.

Vicky tapped her fingers on the table. "Let me call this meeting to order," she grinned, "and declare the motion to adjourn carried. Please review the menu, select you choice of meals and then enjoy the fun of cruising with new and not-so-new friends."

The meal was served, another bottle of wine was ordered and the four sat and enjoyed themselves chatting and talking about everything and nothing in particular. At nine-thirty Carolyn knew what she had to do to end the evening in a perfect fashion.

She stood and turned to Ed. "Well, Edwin, I do believe you should walk me back to my cabin. We must be up early tomorrow. Perhaps, Alex, I could ask you to walk Vicky back to her cabin? Ed and I have some business to talk about for a few minutes."

Alex stood and offered Vicky his hand. "I will be honored if you would allow me the pleasure."

She took his hand. "Of course, kind sir."

After the required 'good-byes' the two couples went their separate ways.

Walking through the atrium Ed and Carolyn walked close together, waiting to be out of all hearing before they spoke.

Carolyn said quietly "Of course, I can't really have you walk me to my cabin, Ed. It is in the out-of-bounds area. It would be nice to spend some time together, however."

"Well you certainly can't come to my cabin," Ed added.

They sat in a quiet area, close to the now closed Photoshop.

"You'll be ready by six in the morning?" Carolyn asked.

"Ready and more than willing to head back to England and put this all behind us. I'm really not sure we've done any good, but only time will tell."

"I agree. But all said and done we file our report, and then get ready for the wedding."

"I suppose so."

They sat in silence for a while.

"Ed?'

"Yes, Carolyn."

"How do you think Vicky feels about all of this? One minute she seems on top of the world, and the next…I don't know; sort of depressed."

Ed thought before he replied. "I think, and I stress 'think', she will suffer somewhat in the short term. She is a super strong person, but given what she went through, without prior warning, how could we not expect her to struggle."

"Agreed. I'll keep in touch on a regular basis after she gets home. I'll let you know." She stood. "Walk me to the no-go zone please, Ed. I'll start my report and get it out of the way so as not to take away from the wedding."

They walked slowly to the 'Crew only' area on a lower deck. They kissed holding on to each other for as long as they could, making sure no-one was watching.

"Good night, Ed."

"Good night, Carolyn. Sweet dreams."

They kissed quickly again, and Carolyn opened the door and entered. Ed waited a few seconds and then walked even more slowly toward his cabin.

Vicky and Alex strolled hand in hand from the Dining Room to her cabin.

She turned to face him. "Good night, Alex, and thank you for everything."

He bowed slightly with respect. "Thank you for everything. You are clearly a very special person. You have made the past couple of days the best for me in a very long time; perhaps ever. I wish you the very best in life."

"Thank you, Alex. It was a pleasure to meet you." She held out her hand to shake hands.

He took it gently, leaned forward and kissed her forehead. "You know that I..."

She shook her head, interrupting. "Please don't say it, Alex. Let me dream my own dreams...please."

He nodded, kissed her again on her forehead and then whispered in her ear. "The clue is a combination tactic. Goodbye, sweet Miss Vicky." He stepped back, turned and walked down the hallway, not turning back.

Vicky entered the cabin and quickly walked into the bathroom. She knew Ed would not wait too long before he returned. This was business after all. She washed off her make-up ensuring all of her eye shadow was gone. Then standing straight and looking at herself in the mirror, she used the 'Major General' lesson Ed had taught her just a few months, but a lifetime, ago. She spoke aloud:

"There are men in the ranks who will stay in the ranks, and I'll tell you why: because they don't have the ability to get things done!"

And then louder:

"There are men in the ranks who will stay in the ranks, and I'll tell you why: because they don't have the ability to get things done!"

And then louder, almost shouting while pointing to herself:

"There are men in the ranks who will stay in the ranks, and I'll tell you why: because they don't have the ability to get things done!"

She shook herself to waive off all the shackles and left the bathroom feeling one heck of lot better. "Okay, Miss Kilgour," she said, still speaking aloud, "let's get packing and get ready for the wedding."

Five minutes later Ed knocked on the door, counted ten seconds and entered. Vicky was busy packing her clothes into her new and expensive suit case. Ed's older case was on his bed.

"Let's go," Vicky said with authority, "we've got things to do and places to go."

"Yes, ma'am," Ed replied, more than pleasantly surprised, "let's go."

They packed their luggage leaving out only the clothes they would need in the morning. When they finished, Ed turned to Vicky and gave her a serious look.

"You seem rather chipper, Vicky, did something happen?"

Vicky winked mischievously. "There are men in the ranks, right?"

Ed laughed. "Yes, there are men in the ranks, and I can assure you, you are not 'in the ranks' by any stretch of the imagination. If fact you're a true leader. Well done!"

She waved him off. "Just a woman of the eighties…with an ex-boyfriend with unusual circumstances, eh?"

"Whatever you say, Vicky. Whatever you say."

"Well I say that I'm going into the bathroom and get ready for bed. You change and get into your bed while I'm changing. And put on some underwear please. I don't want to be sleeping in the same cabin with a naked man; even if it's you."

Ed stood and took of his shirt. "On my way, boss. I'll set the alarm for five-thirty. Looking forward to heading back to dear ol' Blighty for a fun wedding."

"And other events," Vicky quipped as she entered the bathroom; referring to the fact that Ed was planning on asking Carolyn to marry him, the day after the wedding.

"That too," Ed agreed. "That too indeed." He jumped into his bed, keeping his undershorts on.

Vicky exited the bathroom ten minutes later, wearing her long granny style nightgown. She turned off the lights and got into her bed.

"Good night, Vicky," Ed said with a phony yawn.

"G'night, bloke."

They both lay facing away from each other, both wishing they were tired: but they weren't. Vicky was the first to speak.

"Ed?"

"Yes, Vicky."

"Since I sometimes call you Mister, and sometimes I call you Ed; is it okay if I call you Mister Ed?"

"Neigh," he replied quickly.

"That's funny," she giggled. "Have you been asked that before?"

"Nay," he responded, almost before she had finished the question.

She laughed aloud. "That's clever, Edwin. Maybe I should call you Edwin?"

"You, my mother, and Lady Stonebridge would be the only ones, so you'd be in good company, Victoria."

"Okay. Ed it is. Good night."

"Good night."

Several minutes later Vicky rolled over in her bed to face him.

"Ed?"

"Yes, Vicky."

"Can I ask you a favor?"

"You may."

"Okay, smartass; 'may' I ask you a question?"

"Of course."

She waited a few seconds before asking. "May I come over to your bed, and would you just put your arm around me? No naughty stuff, just a comforting arm."

Ed rolled over to face her. "On one condition."

"Oh, wow! And what is that, Oh Mighty One?"

"That you're not going to pretend I'm Alex."

She sat up in bed. "Of course I'm not going to do that. I want 'you' to put your arm around me." She jumped out of her bed and into Ed's. Once she settled in with her back to him he put his arm over her and held her at her shoulder.

"Good night, Slim." Ed said, squeezing her shoulder gently.

"Good night...spoilsport."

In just a few minutes they were both asleep and very much at ease.

Carolyn was in her cabin, finalizing her report for the next day.

Alex sat out on his balcony enjoying a relaxing glass of wine. In his pocket was a letter addressed to Vicky at her office address.

The cruise ship moved slowly through the quiet waters on its way to Izmir.

CHAPTER THIRTEEN

Friday, May 2nd 1986

By six am Ed and Vicky were both showered and ready to go with their luggage fully packed. They had gone out of their way to not been seen in any way undressed by the other. A good night's sleep had helped immensely and both were relaxed and wanting to get off the ship and head to England and their good friends' wedding. The phone rang and Carolyn asked them to be on the deck at 6:30 and ready to go.

At exactly 6:30 the three of them walked down the gangplank to a waiting limousine. They threw their luggage into the trunk and jumped in. The driver tramped his foot heavily on the gas and they sped off quickly.

Ten minutes later the steward from Alex's suite walked down the gangplank with the stamped letter addressed to Vicky.

Fifteen minutes after that, Alex sat in his suite with an unlit cigar in the ashtray on the table next to him. He smiled, remembering his promise to Vicky. He picked up a glass of water, popped two cyanide pills into his mouth and swallowed them with the water.

Three minutes later Alex was dead.

The helicopter flight to Athens was very loud. Ed, Carolyn, and Vicky were seated together at the rear, not able to speak clearly to each other. Each had their own thoughts about the past few days. Ed was pleased with the results and more than impressed with Vicky's input and self-direction. As usual, he had a great deal of respect for Carolyn's ability to lead in a manner that allowed each member of the team to share their thoughts and to use their own personal abilities to keep the plan moving in the right direction. Carolyn, while pleased with the results and the final outcome, seriously wondered if the clue they had received would lead to a positive solution to the message: 'More to come.' She doubted that it would. Vicky couldn't get her head around what had happened, what she had seen and done in just a few days. She knew Alex had done a terrible thing, but somehow understood that his intentions were, at least in part, understandable, given his Chechen background. She cleared her mind of the recent events and looked forward to the wedding of her good friend Pat. She smiled with a nod to Ed and Carolyn and gave them a thumbs-up. They both returned the message, knowing they each had to calm down and get on with life.

The transfer at Athens Airport from the helicopter to the huge Lockheed TriStar was quick and easy. Their luggage was carried by RAF personnel, the plane had been warming up for ten minutes and was ready to go. As small and as noisy as the helicopter had been, their new plane was anything but. Although today there was a crew of only four, as a passenger carrier, it once carried 187 passengers and a crew of ten. It had since been converted into a fuel carrier for jets, and had been used in the Falklands. The three of them sat together and buckled-up along one wall at the centre of the plane. The door was closed and within two minutes they were in the air. Fifteen minutes later they were at 30,000 feet

"My first and last trip to Greece perhaps?" Vicky commented dryly. "I'll have to try it for a bit longer sometime!"

"You should," Carolyn said. "You'll love it, especially the islands."

Ed laughed. "England, Turkey, Greece; why Vicky you're a world traveler."

Vicky nodded. "First I want to see more of England, enjoy the wedding and perhaps get to see London. Big Ben, Trafalgar Square, Piccadilly Circus, and maybe visit a real English pub. Warm beer and cold toast, eh?"

Their discussion was interrupted by a member of the crew joining them from the cabin. "The captain would like to see Miss Andrews up front please."

Carolyn un-buckled and followed him, giving Ed and Vicky a 'don't know' shrug.

"What do you think, Mister?"

Ed shook his head. "No idea. Perhaps a message from London? Maybe they've solved the clue! That would be nice."

When Carolyn returned five minutes later, the look on her face said it was not good news. She stopped twenty feet from them, and motioned to Vicky. "Can I see you for a minute?" she asked.

Vicky looked down and rubbed the back of her neck. When she looked up, there were tears in her eyes. "No thank you, Miss. I'll stay here if you don't mind. He's dead, isn't he?"

Carolyn nodded and walked over to join them. She put her arm around Vicky. "He committed suicide this morning. I am so sorry." She gave her a squeeze. "He did leave you a bit of a message, Vicky. Beside him was an expensive Cuban cigar; unlit and in an ashtray. A 'Thank you' I believe."

Vicky sniffed back a tear. "Really? That is nice. He never did have a smoke after he told me he wouldn't. A true gentleman."

"Every ounce a gentleman," Ed agreed. "Should I see if we can get some tea?"

Carolyn nodded, and Ed left quickly to the front of the plane.

Vicky wiped her eyes. "What a world, eh?"

"I know this won't change anything, Vicky, but I believe he loved you. His last few days were so nice compared to his not having met you, talked to you, and kissed you." She nudged Vicky. "And not smoking to boot!"

"Maybe that was the best part for him?" Vicky laughed.

"I think not, young lady. I think not."

They ended their conversation as Ed walked down the centre of the plane with a tray of tea and biscuits.

"I hope that's milk in first, bloke," Vicky said with a grin.

"MIF in the tea and some McVities Digestives for the ladies," Ed replied. "What else could a lady want?"

"Don't ask, Ed," Carolyn replied. "Just don't ask."

Ed didn't ask; he just served the tea and biscuits with a smile.

They drank their tea and really relaxed for the first time in several days. After a few minutes while Vicky was not looking Carolyn motioned to Ed to leave. "Why don't you get us some more tea?" she asked. Ed took the hint, picked up the tray and headed to the front of the plane.

Carolyn turned to Vicky. "May I ask you a somewhat personal question?"

"Ask away."

"I know you're not a big drinker, and actually thought you didn't drink at all. Was there something that had you change your mind in the last couple of days? I'm not suggesting anything, but I cannot help but wonder."

Vicky gave a hearty laugh. "Nothing to worry about, but if I explain where I'm coming from you must promise to say nothing to anybody; even as Miss."

Carolyn held up her hand. "I promise."

Vicky took a deep breath. "I used to drink when I was younger, not a lot but I did drink. Like many kids that attend university, I drank more and more."

"Been there, done that."

"Well one night I got totally pie-eyed drunk, as did my then boyfriend. We ended up spending the night in his room making.... well, you know. Lot's of 'you know'. In the morning I thought I was going to die. I wasn't on the pill and he hadn't used anything. I was sick to my stomach for more than one reason. As it turned out, I did not get pregnant; I thought my parents would have disowned me. God I still feel sick when I think about it! Now the good news is that we then got engaged a little while after, and the bad news is that he was the man that dumped me and is now living with his boyfriend – excuse me, his partner - in San Francisco."

"Yikes," Carolyn cringed.

"Yikes indeed. However to answer your question, since that night I haven't had a drink until this trip. So no problem, I do not have a drinking issue. And to be honest I haven't had a good reason to have a glass of wine until we met with Alex, knowing that he would be telling us something that might save some lives. That seemed like a good reason to me. What do you think, Carolyn?"

Carolyn moved over to her, put her arms around her and gave a huge hug. "I think you are one of the nicest people I have ever met, and I've met some pretty nice people. Thanks for telling me, and it will go to my grave with me."

Ed returned from the front of the plane with a fresh pot of tea. "Not interrupting anything important am I?" he asked.

Carolyn shook her head. "Nothing important at all, Ed. We were just talking about you."

Ed eyed them suspiciously. "Boring I'm sure."

"Bang on, tea boy," Vicky said, "bang on."

He put the pot of tea on the tray. "Tea for two very charming young ladies."

Carolyn's shoulders sank. "If you're trying to make us both feel guilty; it worked. Okay?"

Ed poured the tea and raised his cup in a toast. "Just stating a fact, ladies. Just stating a fact."

The three toasted each other, and Ed was glad to change the conversation away from himself. So were the 'two very charming young ladies' glad to change the conversation.

They enjoyed their tea without further conversation for a few relaxing minutes. Eventually Carolyn looked at her watch and stood. "I have to make some arrangements for today and tomorrow. I'll be back in a while." She headed to the front of the plane.

"We weren't really talking about you, Ed. In fact we were talking about me. Carolyn wondered way I started drinking wine, knowing that I don't usually drink. I told her why I quit some years back. Would you like me to tell you, Ed?"

"Do you want to tell me?"

She shook her head. "Not really."

"Then I don't want to know. We all have our secrets, and often it is best when we keep them as such."

Vicky smiled. "Really? What secrets do you have, Ed? Just tell me one."

He thought for a moment. "Okay, but it relates to you."

"Oh, oh! Now I've done it. Fire away."

"Well I'm really, really happy that your ex-fiancé dumped you and then left town. I'm sorry, but it's the truth."

Vicky thought for a while, and Ed wished he hadn't said what he'd said. "So am I, Ed. So am I. It hurt at the time, but since then my world has changed in many ways, and all positive. You're part of that, of course. But it's mostly my head that's changed. I see the world with a totally new perspective." She laughed. "And this trip certainly opened my mind to new and different thought processes." She saw Carolyn leave the cockpit and head toward them. "I owe you a secret, Ed. Later."

Carolyn joined them. "Here's the deal, team. I just spoke to Lord Stonebridge. We'll be at the manor in about an hour. I need to spend a few minutes with him alone, and then we'll all get together. Both of you are spending the night at the manor, as his guests. In separate rooms, of course."

"Hooray," Vicky interrupted, "no more snoring."

"Ed; your mother will be driven by limo to the manor tomorrow, and she'll spend the night as Lord Stonebridge's guest. While I'm with Lord Stonebridge for the few minutes, Lady Stonebridge will show you to your rooms. She has arranged for dry cleaners to drive out tomorrow morning with a commitment to have everything back in plenty of time for the wedding. She has also arranged for her hairdresser to be available tomorrow all day for all guests to the wedding that need a touch up." She looked at Ed. "That includes you, of course."

"That's subtle," Ed replied.

"My mother is never subtle," Carolyn answered quickly. She turned to Vicky. "She would like you to accompany Ed to ensure that his hair is cut short enough."

Vicky nodded with a smile. "Done. Friend, life insurance agent, wife, sister, and now his caretaker: not much left is there, Ed?"

"'Friend' is the important one," Ed replied with candor.

"Well said," Carolyn agreed. "Now let's get ready to see a little bit of rainy England as we head to the manor."

They buckled up as the plane started its descent.

CHAPTER FOURTEEN

The drive from Calgrove airport was quiet as they sat in the limo driven through the narrow back roads of Oxfordshire in order to miss the Friday afternoon traffic. It was drizzling rain for a while and then suddenly the sun broke through the clouds and everything seemed so much happier.

Ed started humming 'Jerusalem', getting louder as the sun shone. When he arrived at the last line, both he and Carolyn broke out in joyful voice;

"...in England's green and pleasant land."

The driver gave a short honk on the horn to acknowledge their singing.

Vicky sat up straight to get attention. She started humming 'O Canada', getting louder as she moved through the verse. On the last line she, Ed and Carolyn sang out loud:

"...O Canada we stand on guard for thee."

The driver gave two honks on the horn, just as the limo turned in through the gates of Stonebridge Manor.

As was expected by both Carolyn and Ed, Lady Stonebridge was at the massive front door to the manor; and as usual dressed ready to meet them, or the Queen, should she unexpectedly show up. Carolyn led the way in with Vicky, while Ed was happy to help the driver take in all their luggage; a job which was not for the faint hearted.

Lady Stonebridge invited Vicky and Ed into the huge library while Carolyn went straight upstairs to meet with Lord Stonebridge to present her initial report.

Tea and crumpets were available at the table in the centre of the room, and Lady Stonebridge was more than happy to play mother.

"So tell me, Miss Kilgour," Lady Stonebridge enquired, "how was your short cruise? I trust you, Mr. Crowe, and my daughter enjoyed yourselves?"

Vicky took a sip of her hot tea, before she carefully replied. "I think everything went as well as expected. Isn't that right, Mr. Crowe?"

"Absolutely," Ed agreed. "Istanbul is a beautiful city, and we had the chance to visit all the usual sights. The Blue Mosque, the..."

"Yes, yes, yes," Lady Stonebridge interrupted, "but what about the purpose of the trip. How did that go?"

Ed began to enjoy her attempt to pry some information from them before they headed upstairs. "Well we're back safe and sound, Lady Stonebridge, and on this trip I didn't have to pretend we were on our honeymoon." Referring to his previous trip with Pat, of which Lady Stonebridge was aware due to the news reports at the time.

"Nothing like that," Vicky agreed. "Just a quickie cruise."

Ed cringed at her comment, but it didn't register with Lady Stonebridge who sipped on her tea knowing nothing would be forthcoming. "Well let me show you to your rooms, which are no doubt larger than your cabin on the ship."

"Cabins," Ed added with a smile.

"Yes of course, of course. Please follow me."

With a quick grin to each other, they followed Lady Stonebridge up the grand oak staircase to the rooms which would be theirs for the next couple of nights.

Half an hour later Ed and Vicky were summoned to Lord Stonebridge's office. He and Carolyn were there along with Mr. Cooper. Lord Stonebridge rose from behind his desk and shook hands with them both, offering them seats in front of his desk.

"Let me first give a brief update on the situation at Chernobyl. First the size of the explosion. It has been estimated, with some precision that is, that the amount of radioactive material released was four hundred times more than the atomic bombing at Hiroshima, and we all know the amount of terrible suffering that created. This is truly a disaster, with most of suffering yet to occur. Secondly, in addition to Ukraine, twelve other countries have found increased levels of contamination, and more are expected into the future. The town of Pripyat has been evacuated. The people were told to be away for approximately three days. It is most unlikely they will ever return. And lastly the death toll so far is now forty. So anything we can do to eliminate a second 'accident' is critical. But let us turn to your trip. An eventful trip I would say," he nodded. "Very eventful perhaps." He turned to Vicky. "What we don't have recorded, of course, is what you and Mr. Umarov spoke of in private. Was there anything you can add to the records – strictly confidentially of course – that might increase our knowledge?"

Vicky offered a friendly smile. "That was very nice of you to put it that way, Lord Stonebridge. While I covered up the microphone is what you mean, of course." She thought for a moment. "Did Carolyn say anything about what he said?" she asked.

Carolyn shook her head. "No I didn't. You told me in confidence, and I have lived up to that."

Vicky continued. "Thanks. Well let me see. He told me he was going to die; in weeks, not months; from cancer, but not from smoking. He told me I was a very nice person, and then I asked him to kiss me…which he did, and that is something I am not ashamed of, sir."

Lord Stonebridge stood from his chair, walked around the front of his desk and leaned back against it. He wanted his message to be clear. "Miss Kilgour you have nothing to be ashamed of, but a great deal to be proud of in your work on this assignment. And I want to make it clear that I say this not because this is your first involvement with this type of activity, I would say that if you were a regular member of this department."

"Hear, hear," the General added quickly. "Totally professional."

Vicky blushed. "Thank you for that. It was a lot of fun in its own way and certainly a learning experience for me; one I will never forget." She laughed. "Besides I got a new swimsuit out of it, courtesy of the British government."

"And may you recall this event with pleasure each time you wear it," Lord Stonebridge added. "Now let us move out of this of this office, turn into our true selves and get ready for the wedding."

They all stood and gladly left the office and headed downstairs where they knew a fresh pot of tea would be waiting.

As they entered the library, they were happy to see tomorrow's bride and groom sitting at the large table covered with tea and biscuits, and Lady Stonebridge at the head of the table inviting everyone in to relax, enjoy, and share some time with Pat and Roy before their big day on Saturday. Lady Stonebridge was unusually relaxed, enjoying the company of so many young people together in one room: her room.

CHAPTER FIFTEEN

Saturday May 3rd, 1986

THE WEDDING DAY

Ed was up and dressed by six-thirty, ready for the busy day ahead. When he went down to the breakfast table in the large dining room, the only other guest was Vicky. She was dressed casually and looked totally refreshed and happy.

"Morning, bloke," she said. "Good night's sleep?"

"Never better," he replied. She gave him a dirty look. "Well, you know: I could relax after a busy three days. What about you?"

"Perfect. No snoring or heavy breathing. Made for a nice change." She paused. "By the way, you didn't say anything about my letting Alex kiss me. Any comment?"

"Only that he was a very lucky guy, and I agree with everything Lord Stonebridge said about your activities during the trip."

She nodded. "Okay, just wanted to know. Now that part of our life is over – for me anyway – let's enjoy the wedding in jolly old."

Carolyn walked into the room. "Okay late-risers; please join me in a walk around the estate before my mother sends you both off for Ed's shampoo and haircut."

The three left through the beautiful garden doors that led into the many acres of trees and forest of the manor which had been in Lord Stonebridge's family for hundreds of years. Carolyn pointed out some of the largest oak trees that been planted several hundred years before, explained how the several man-made lakes were managed, but avoided her 'special place' where she and her first boyfriend had agreed to marry when they were just age eight, and where she and Ed had made love to make it 'their' special place. When they returned Lady Stonebridge was standing at the garden door with her hands on her hips. "When you are ready, Mr. Crowe. Our hairdresser awaits you and Miss Kilgour."

Ed and Vicky were driven to the nearby town of Halton and the car stopped outside The Fate hairdressers' shop. They entered with Vicky pushing Ed in through the door. It was a small but very cozy with just three chairs. Standing over one chair were a man and a young woman.

Vicky took over. "This is the gentleman that needs a good haircut," she nodded toward Ed.

"Indeed he does," the man said, "indeed he does." He was about five-eight with a natural tan. "My name is Dominic, and my assistant is Tori Lee. Tori will wash and shampoo your hair, sir. Unless, that is, you want it colored?"

"Colored?" Ed gasped. "Good lord, no! Who would want his hair colored?"

Tori stepped forward. She was tall and slim, very good looking with a short fashionable hair style. "You might be surprised what Lord Stonebridge asks of us for some of his friends, isn't that right Dominic?"

"Indeed, that is so," Dominic replied pointing Ed to a sink at the back, "but this gentleman is a guest of Lady Stonebridge, and her guests are considerably less interesting…from a hairstyling perspective that is."

Ed sat in the chair in front of the sink and Tori began to gently wash Ed's hair. "Are you the groom?" Tori asked.

"Just the best man," he replied. "No-one wants to marry me I'm afraid."

"For many good reasons," Vicky added quickly.

Dominic turned to Vicky. "Ah, a combination of good looks, nice hair style and a sense of humor."

Vicky closed her eyes, looked up and groaned. "Oh crap," she said loudly. "I forgot all about that!"

Ed assumed it had something to do with their trip. "Hold on, Vicky. We'll get back as soon as I'm done here. I know it must be important."

Dominic and Tori carried on as if nothing had happened. They were used to strange people being referred to them from the manor. It was just another day with the Lord and Lady's weird friends.

Tori finished washing his hair, led Ed to Dominic's chair and offered everyone coffee. Ed declined but Vicky accepted, annoyed at herself for neglecting to mention a part of Alex's clue.

Dominic refused to accept a tip from Ed, explaining that he and Tori were paid in full for the day, and only expected a few more guests. He didn't mention the word 'weird,' just guests.

Ed and Vicky jumped into the waiting car and asked the diver to make it back as quickly as he could. The driver nodded, and drove away faster than either Ed or Vicky had expected.

"I'll tell you when we get back to the manor," Vicky whispered, looking out the window as the English countryside passed very quickly. "If we get there," she added.

The car slid to a halt at the main door of the manor and the driver jumped out to open the door closest to the entrance. Ed realized he had over emphasized the need for speed, but he and Vicky quickly ran up the steps to be consistent with the driver's sense of urgency. Once in the manor, they stopped to catch their breath. Lord Stonebridge was in the library reading. Ed motioned Vicky to approach him, which she did calmly but deliberately.

"Lord Stonebridge, I forgot to mention something earlier. I..."

He raised his hand to stop the conversation. "Upstairs in my office please, Victoria." It was the first time he had used her Christian name. For some reason, which she couldn't explain to herself, it made her feel more comfortable. The three of them walked up the stairs and into his office.

"My apologies, Miss Kilgour," Lord Stonebridge offered, "I prefer to separate my personal and government responsibilities as much as possible, for reasons I'm sure you understand."

"Of course, sir," Vicky replied honestly. "I shall try to do that more often in my own career. But what I wanted to mention is something Alex…I mean Mr. Umarov said on the last day of the cruise. The three of us met with him for dinner, and it was on a strictly no-business basis. When the drinks were over Ed walked Carolyn to her cabin and Mr. Umarov walked me to my cabin. I did not invite him inside, he kissed me nicely on the forehead and he told me the clue was a combination…" She held her hand to her head to think. "There was another word he used with combination, but I don't recall what it was. I'll think more about it, but my point is that he said it was a combination."

Lord Stonebridge nodded his understanding. "We, of course, thought it might be a combination, but then we also thought it could be some kind of code where a number represented a letter. And I might add that given Mr. Umarov spoke several languages, which resulted in our back room techies working late into the night. They are not happy until they break a code." He laughed. "Not exactly the most socially-skilled people, but put a computer in front of them, then sit back and watch. So the fact that we are dealing with some form of combination limits our need to look further in many directions. I shall contact London immediately. Thank you, Miss Kilgour."

Ed and Vicky left the office, and Lord Stonebridge picked up the phone.

The two walked into the library and sat. Ed was going over his best man's speech and Vicky was thinking back to the 'combination' comment from Alex.

"Are you a hypnotist?" she asked Ed.

"Of course, one of my special skills. How can I help?"

"I'm trying to recall the other word Alex used. I think it's important."

Ed moved over closer to her on the large couch. "Okay, close your eyes, and listen to me carefully."

"Yeah, right," she huffed, but closed her eyes anyway.

Ed spoke close and quietly. "So you're outside the cabin door, and you're both chatting." He paused. "He kisses you nicely on the forehead. That felt very nice."

"Hmmm."

"Then he slowly reaches over and gently caresses your beautiful breasts..."

"He most certainly did not!" Vicky said loudly opening her eyes.

"I knew, I know, but he probably wanted to."

"Maybe! But he didn't."

"Close you eyes again." He waited as she relaxed and closed her eyes. He spoke in a whisper. "Think deeply, now. He likes you a great deal and he wants to assist you. You like him because he is such a gentleman. So quietly he says...."

Vicky's eyes opened wide. "Tactic! That's it! He said it was a 'combination tactic'. Damn, I remembered!"

Ed raised his hand to his chin. "You remembered? I think it would be more accurate to say 'I' delved deep into the depths of your mind to release your inner-most thoughts and hidden secrets."

"Bullshit! You'll never know what goes on in my mind. Never in a million years, bloke. But I have to run upstairs and tell Lord Stonebridge that I remembered." She got to the door and turned. "Thanks, bloke. I owe you."

Ten minutes later Vicky returned and joined him on the far end of the couch. "You were kind of right, though. He was going to tell me that he loved me, but I stopped him.'

Ed spread his hands. "See I can read your mind. I'm not just a pretty face."

"No you're not. A pretty face that is. But it was a good guess."

Ed shook his head. "Not a guess, Vicky. An assumption maybe, but not a guess. He obviously liked you a great deal. You're an easy person to get to like. Been there, done that, eh?"

"Don't get all wishy-washy with me, bloke. We're here for a wedding and the future, not to look back." She shrugged. "Even if it was a bit of fun. Now let's find out where everybody is and start getting ready for the wedding."

"As you say, Vicky, as you say."

Fifteen minutes later the manor was ablaze with activities, deliveries, and phone calls, as the wedding plans started to fall into place. Ed and Vicky stayed out of the way: but were happy to help by carrying in the myriad of flowers both for the wedding event and the 'best wishes' floral arrangements from friends and family. The local florists hadn't had a day like this for ages. The flowers added tremendously to the spirit and fragrance of the wedding.

Vicky was caught off guard when a lovely rose corsage arrived for her from her parents in Canada. Attached was a note:

'Dear Victoria. Enjoy the wedding.
Regards to Edwin.'
Your loving parents.

While she couldn't hide it entirely Vicky did her best to not show the emotion of the moment. Her parents were not inclined to show their love in such a way, so she was especially happy as a result. She showed it to Ed.

"Lovely," he said with a nod. "Perhaps you will allow me to pin it on you later?"

"That would be lovely, Edwin," she grinned.

"I suppose I'll have to cancel the one I ordered for you," he added with a straight face.

"Yeah, right!" She ran upstairs to leave the corsage in her room.

At 2pm, an hour before the service, guests began arriving at the manor. Tea and biscuits were available to one and all. Many long time friends who had not seen each other for some time, especially on Roy's side, met, chatted, enjoyed the tea and at 2:30 started to head to the chapel at the north end of the manor. It held over one-hundred and was soon filled to overflow. Lady Stonebridge greeted each guest individually, especially Pat's parents and family from Canada.

"It is lovely for you to host the wedding," Pat's mother expressed sincerely.

"Our pleasure," Lady Stonebridge replied, escorting her to the front of the chapel. In her heart she had expected that the next wedding at the manor would be her daughter Carolyn's, but that was not to be. 'Not yet anyway', she mused as she walked back to the entrance. With ten minutes to go, all guests were seated or standing and ready for the big event.

At five minutes to three, the groom Roy Johnston and his best man Ed Crowe entered the chapel and walked carefully to the front. They each wore black tuxedos with a grey vest and a dark grey tie. The minister stood on a step above the floor, wearing a full white cassock and gown for this important ceremony. He smiled at the guests, holding a bible in front of him. He enjoyed weddings and his smile and composure made that evident.

At exactly three o'clock the familiar music of 'Here Comes the Bride' began and Pat entered the chapel with her father at her side. She wore a white gown of French silk with a short train. The bodice was lace appliquéd with seed pearls. Carolyn, wearing a light blue gown, slowly walked three steps ahead of them, endeavoring to have Pat reach Roy just as the music ended. The timing was perfect. Roy and Pat quickly exchanged sideway glances at each other and then both looked ahead to the minister. The minister nodded, looked out to the gathering and commenced.

"Dearly beloved, we are gathered here today….."

Ed walked over to Vicky to ask her to join him for the third dance of the evening. There were four of his old school friends standing around her, obviously interested in wanting to dance with her and make a new lovely looking friend. He smiled as he approached them:

Mick Collins; tall, blond and always the 'leader',

Tony Holloway; even taller, dark haired, and a gentleman at all times,

Johnny Pearce; short, funny, always active and the life of the party.

Peter Rose; tall, slim, good looking, and dressed impeccably.

"Gentlemen," Ed said with a smile and a hand out to greet them each, "I see you have met my friend and life insurance agent. May I interrupt and take the opportunity to share this dance with Miss Vicky Kilgour?"

"Just for one dance," Mick responded with a nod of his head. "The rest of us would like to learn so much more about Canada than we ever did in geography classes."

Vicky stood, took Ed's hand and joined him on the dance floor.

"Nice bunch of blokes," Vicky offered with a smile. "I might need a dance card."

"Save one for me."

The DJ started the music with an announcement that this song was for good friends and lovers.

Vicky laughed as the song began. It was 'The Twelfth of Never,' by Johnny Mathis. The very same song Vicky had played for Ed over the phone a few months ago to let him know how much she liked or loved him; she wasn't sure then, and she wasn't sure now. But circumstances had changed considerably since then, and you cannot go back.

"Nice song,' she said without emotion.

"Very nice song," he replied with a gentle hug. "I trust you will save another dance for me?"

"Of course I will. Nice 'Best Man' speech by the way. I wasn't aware of your public speaking capabilities."

He replied quietly. "There are men in the ranks, eh? Always works for me."

After the dance finished, Ed escorted Vicky back to her waiting new friends. He spent several minutes catching up with them, and then left Vicky in good hands – many good hands.

After the cutting of the cake, Vicky pulled Ed to one side and nodded for him to join her in the garden. It was a lovely clear night with a million stars adding to the wonderment of the wedding.

"So here's the up-date, Ed," Vicky began. "Tomorrow at 6:30 am Peter Rose, who is staying at a local pub, is going to drive me to London to see some sights. On Monday he's going to drive me to Heathrow, via Windsor Castle, and I'm flying home on the same flight we booked, but a day early."

"Oh, okay."

"No naughty stuff, Ed. I'm still staying at your mum's place tomorrow night, and she's going to join us to visit Windsor." She smiled. "And it will give me an opportunity to find out a whole bunch about you, that I don't already know."

"Er, okay."

She spoke quietly. "If there is any 'stuff' about the 'business' that I need to know, which I very much doubt, please phone me on my cell phone. I know there'll be international fees, but guess what," she whispered, "if I can get a bikini out of 'them', I'm sure they'll be happy to pay my phone charges."

"Of course they will, Vicky. More than happy."

"Okay," she said quickly, "I'll see you back home sometime. And, Ed, I do hope you 'conversation' with Carolyn goes well. She's a super lady. I'll update her before we all call it a night." She gave him a quick kiss on his cheek. "See ya, Ed." With that she left him standing and returned to the activities inside. He walked slowly back to the dance floor and looked for his mum to have a dance and spend some time with her.

CHAPTER SIXTEEN

Sunday, May 4th 1986

"Wakey, wakey," Carolyn called from just inside Ed's bedroom. "Time to move your booty!"

Ed sat up in bed. "Hey, Carolyn, nice to see you. Can you stay…?"

"Afraid not, Ed. This isn't a friendly call. Lord Stonebridge needs to see us in his office in fifteen minutes. Something's come up."

Ed looked at his watch. It was 7:35. "I'll be there – with bells on," he added.

Carolyn gave him a wink and left him to get dressed.

He washed up quickly; still not quite sure why Vicky had decided to leave early. He was happy knowing that Peter Rose would look after her extremely well. He was a good friend and a person to be trusted. Ed had heard that Peter was thinking of emigrating to South Africa. He chuckled and wondered if spending some time with Vicky might have him thinking of Canada. He set that thought aside, finished dressing and walked quickly to Lord Stonebridge's office.

The mandatory tray of tea and biscuits was available and he, Lord Stonebridge, Carolyn, and the General were settled in with their hot tea before Lord Stonebridge led the discussion. He sat behind his desk, and looked serious; more serious than Ed had seen him look before. He scratched his chin, wanting to give the correct message.

"In the words of American history, ladies and gentlemen, 'Houston, we have a problem.'" He raised his eyebrows reflecting it was that kind of message. "Gorbachev phoned President Reagan in the early hours, Washington time. The timing itself is noteworthy since it is a known fact that President Reagan does not like being woken during his regular hours of sleep, and I'm told Mrs. Reagan took some convincing to agree to wake him. Apparently she runs the White House."

"Nothing like that around here, right sir?" Ed commented without thinking.

Lord Stonebridge shrugged with a grin. "Well not in this office. Not yet, anyway. But back to Gorbachev. His message was very clear and very serious. As we know the KGB is aware of the 'More to come' note from Mr. Umarov. But the message from the KGB, in no uncertain terms, is that if the second incident is not stopped he, Gorbachev, is gone. Not just out of power, out of life. As totally ridiculous as it sounds, it makes sense to the KGB leadership. Gorbachev was at fault: Gorbachev is gone. No arguments, no discussion: gone. Now there is no clear replacement for Gorbachev, and we doubt anyone would even try to assume Gorbachev's role. He too might be gone. Thus the end result could be the KBG assuming full power."

The General shook his head. "Sir, that would be disastrous. I couldn't even imagine..."

"Indeed, General, neither can I," Lord Stonebridge agreed. "The second event would be bad enough, but given the fact that Mr. Umarov – a Chechen – was responsible for the first event, then to the KGB, and likely all Russians, it would only make sense that Chechens as a nation would have been responsible for the second event. For those of you that have heard the tape of Mr. Umarov speaking to Miss Kilgour, it would not be unreasonable to assume that Russia, now headed-up by the KGB, and indeed the Russian people themselves, would want to get revenge. That would be a disastrous repeat of history. And to make matters worse, we must recall that the majority of Chechens are Muslim." He shook his head sadly. "And if Iran, or

Syria, or even Turkey were to consider defending their Sunni Muslim brothers, the world order could be in grave danger."

They sat in silence for a few moments, before Ed asked the obvious question.

"Excuse me, Lord Stonebridge, and at the risk of sounding stupid, what can we do to prevent the possibility of preventing those circumstances, other than doing our best to prevent the second event?"

"Therein lays the problem, Mr. Crowe. Nothing! All we can do, the only thing we can do, is prevent the second event. It has simply become more important that we do so."

Carolyn spoke for the first time. "Perhaps to help matters I have a complete copy of the tapes from the cruise for Mr. Crowe to take with him. There maybe something he hears that we haven't picked up on. It's worth a try." She stood and handed Ed a tape. Ed smiled his thanks, now desperate to listen to it all for the first time.

"One further issue, sir," Ed added hopefully. "As I recall there was a representative from the Canadian nuclear power authorities that visited Chernobyl very shortly after the explosion. Could I perhaps get his name and telephone number, just in case?"

Lord Stonebridge nodded. "Good thinking, Mr. Crowe. Perhaps, Miss Andrews, you could obtain that information and pass it on?"

"I will get at it as soon as we're done here, sir."

Lord Stonebridge stood. "Then I think we're done. Our cryptographers are working tirelessly, but their last communication suggested that they have been unable to make any progress. They need more information. So I wish you all good searching, and indeed good luck, in these very confusing and dangerous circumstances."

Without further ado, they headed downstairs where Lady Stonebridge was waiting for them to join her for breakfast. Both Pat's parents and Roy's parents were at the table, and there was cheerful and bubbly chatter about the wonderful wedding and the couple who were 'born for each other', if not in height. They were honeymooning in Paris. Pat had selected the location with no hesitation in spite of her business 'honeymoon' with Ed. However she had carefully selected a different hotel, in a different arrondissement, on the other side of Paris.

Carolyn left the breakfast table to gather the information on the Canadian nuclear representative for Ed. She also wanted to spend some time together with Ed in private. Ten minutes later she waved to Ed, motioning for him to join her in the garden. He excused himself and entered the garden through the French doors. Carolyn was walking slowly toward the trees at the top the hill, and toward 'their' spot. Ed quickly caught up with her, and she slide her arm though his.

"Things are getting worse by the minute," she said glumly.

"No doubt about that," he agreed.

She handed him an envelope, which he slipped into his pocket without opening it.

"All the information on our Canadian friend is in there. He visited Chernobyl as was planned, and is currently working on his report. He's suspicious, but can't identify anything, at least not at this stage of the game; perhaps never. Keep in mind he does not know what is included on the tapes, which is highly confidential. He lives in Chalk River and works at the Chalk River Nuclear Laboratories. It's about a five hour drive from Toronto, so not a great distance. He's been told you may be contacting him. For security purpose, he'll ask you where you were born and the answer is Whitemouth. Only the head of Atomic Energy Canada Limited, you, me and the contact know the password Q. and A. By the way his name is Robert Helbrecht."

Slowly they walked, enjoying the crisp cool air with the knowledge that it would be a warm spring day. Still it was difficult for them to enjoy the 'green and pleasant land', knowing what they now knew. There wasn't a cloud in the sky, yet they felt as if there were thin clouds all around them, with darker clouds yet to show themselves. They felt better as they entered 'their' spot; a small area of wild grass surrounded by a variety of trees and shrubs that allowed a certain level of privacy, except, of course, from the many birds nesting and mating in their world.

"Let's sit and enjoy the peace and quiet here," Carolyn suggested.

They sat with their backs snuggled against each others.

"I see one of the most common birds in England," Ed said quietly. "It's sparrow size, with two white bands on its wing. What is it?"

Carolyn grinned to herself. “That would be a male Chaffinch, and it has a blue-grey cap. It is correctly named a Common Chaffinch, but who wants to refer to such a lovely bird a common?”

Ed turned around and gave Carolyn a hug from the back. “Hey, well done. Since when have you…?”

“Since you started getting me interested in birds when we first met in Turkey. And there couldn’t be a better place than the manor to spy birds, at least in England.”

“So you’re a Birder now?”

Carolyn tipped up her nose slightly. “More of an Ornithologist, actually.”

Ed chuckled. “Oh, lah de dah, I’m sure.”

Carolyn turned to him and kissed him gently on his lips. “Let’s make love, Ed. I don’t want to get naked, but I want you to make love to me. Right here, right now.”

Ed returned her kiss, and was happy to do as he was asked.

Twenty minutes of total happiness later, they once again sat back to back.

“Do you have a question for me?” Carolyn asked.

“Yes I do,” Ed replied, reaching for her hand.

CHAPTER SEVENTEEN

Wednesday, May 7th 1986

The Queen's Head.

It was quieter than on a Friday night, but some of the regulars were enjoying an early evening beer before heading home for supper. Ed walked to up the bar, nodding to Seana, who was managing the bar.

"Hey, what are you doing here," she laughed, as she began pulling him his regular Double Diamond. "It's not Friday, is it?"

"First day back at work, and still struggling with jet lag," Ed replied. In fact he was exhausted. The jet lag, and no further news or up-dates on the nuclear issue, kept him tired and unusually irritated. He took a long, deep mouthful of his pint. As he placed the glass on the bar, he was astonished to see a reflection in the mirror behind the bar of Vicky walking toward him. She did not look happy.

He turned with a smile. "Hi, Vicky. Heard you had a fun day in London. My mum likes you."

She didn't return the smile, but stood close. "I need to see you."

"Sure, let's take a table and catch up." He nodded to a quiet area.

She shook her head. "I need to see you, Mister."

He got the message. "Your place or mine?"

"Yours. Five minutes." She turned and left.

He knew Seana would be watching. He waited a minute, and without turning back to the bar to finish his beer, he left. He'd apologize and explain as best he could later. He didn't like to appear rude.

Vicky was waiting at his apartment door when he arrived. They didn't speak until they were inside and the door was closed.

Vicky raised her hand in order to speak first. "I phoned you at work and your boss Diane told me you went for a mid-week beer. If you don't mind my saying so, you look like you've been drinking beer full time."

Ed shook his head. "No such luck. Just been busy with everything. And if you don't mind my saying so, you look like you need a beer...or a glass of white wine. But more to the point, what brings you to me, Slim?"

"Yeah, right Slim," she muttered. "Wish I'd never heard of the name."

Ed led her to the kitchen table, and she sat. "Listen why don't I…"

"Make a cup of bloody tea," she snapped.

"Well to be more precise I was going to say a bloody cup of tea. That way there's no blood in the …"

"Give over, Ed."

"Of course. Sorry. Just trying to calm things down."

Vicky raised her hand. "No, Ed, I'm sorry. And yes, please make us a nice cup of tea. And further, let's not speak until we're drinking it."

Ed nodded, and put the kettle on.

Vicky waited impatiently while Ed heated the tea pot, put in two tea bags, filled the pot and waited three minutes before he poured.

She took a sip before she spoke. "I didn't know making a pot of tea was so time consuming."

"Only if you do it right, Vicky. Just like everything else in life." He smiled and didn't release his smile until she smiled back. "So what brings you to chasing me down on a Wednesday? Miss me too much already?"

She shook her head and reached into her purse. "Don't kid yourself, Ed. This did, Mister." She handed him an envelope. "This arrived at my office today. As you can see it was posted in Izmir, and no prize for guessing who it is from."

Ed opened the envelope and removed a sheet of photo-copy. He unfolded it and read the note:

Dear Miss Vicky
40 7 30 30 9 30 4 30 5 9

Numbers are clever. They can be added to make more and less.

Clearly there was more to the original note. Ed looked at Vicky chewing on his lip. "Where's the rest?"

"It's private. Miss said I didn't have to share everything, and in this instance I don't want to."

"Fair enough. But obviously the rest is personal, and bothers you considerably." He waved the paper. "This is a further clue, so that is good news; very good news. Are you sure...?"

"Positive."

He nodded and looked again at the note. "Added to make more and less," he mused aloud. "What do you think, Slim?"

She looked floor before she looked back at Ed. "I don't think anything. I don't want to think anything. I just want to get on with my life. My life without you, and without MI bloody 6."

"Would you like another cup?" Ed asked.

She shook her head.

"How was London?" he asked.

That brightened her up. "Terrific. Peter took me to London and in one day we saw just about everything. Trafalgar Square, Buckingham Palace, Tower of London, Big Ben, the lot. We even had lunch at The Sherlock Holmes pub. Ever been there?"

"One of my favorites."

"Then he drove me to your mum's and we sat up until 2am talking. Your mum and I, that is."

"Oops."

She laughed. "Nothing to worry about. She thinks a great deal of you. I'm not so sure she likes the idea of you living in Canada."

Ed nodded his understanding.

"Then the next morning Peter picked us up and we went on a full tour of Windsor Castle. What a wonderful palace. It's my favorite place of all. Peter drove me to the airport, and then took your mum home. Nice guy; or nice bloke I suppose." She paused. "Okay, maybe I will have another cuppa tea please."

As Ed topped up their tea Vicky sat up straight, feeling much better than just a little while ago. They sat and drank it, not speaking for several minutes.

Vicky finally broke the silence. "Part of what bothers me, Mister; in addition to the rest of Alex's note, is that numbers are a part of my life, part of me. And I don't understand his comment about more and less. I think he assumed that I would catch on, that we would solve the problem. I think he wanted us to understand; to stop the second explosion. Damn it all, and damn Alex. Anyway, I've got to go. I obviously haven't eaten yet. Not that I'm hungry anyway."

Ed raised a hand. "You know, Slim, we should phone Miss and tell her what we have."

Vicky stood to leave. "You go ahead. You two don't need me." She gave him a little grin.

"Slim, things have changed. To be honest, things are a lot worse than we thought just a couple of days ago. There was a meeting in Lord Stonebridge's office Sunday morning…"

"What! Should I have been there? What happened for crying out loud?"

Ed shook his head. "No, you didn't have to be there. But if you have a minute?"

"Tell me some good news, Ed. What about you and Carolyn. Are you…you know?"

"No."

"No?"

"No."

"She said no?"

"No."

"Stop this right now, Ed. I don't want to hear the word no again. You understand?"

"Yes."

She took a deep breath, and asked slowly. "Did you ask Carolyn to marry you?"

"The opposite of yes."

"You didn't ask?"

"Correct."

"Why not for crying out loud? You love each other, what else matters?"

"Have a seat, Vicky. And I won't ask you if you want another cup of tea."

Vicky sat back at the kitchen table. "It feels more like I need a glass of wine, but don't ask; I might say yes."

Too bad, Ed thought to himself. "It's not as easy as you think, Vicky. You see the way they live, and you see the way my mum lives. She loves going to Stonebridge Manor, but really it's a different world. Oh I know Lord and Lady Stonebridge would be happy to have me as a son-in-law, but I'm also sure they would be happier if I lived in their world, knew their friends, and had their formal education. And keep in mind that Lady Stonebridge was not to-the-manor-born, as she puts it. But I can assure you Lady Stonebridge has had to change her lifestyle considerably since they married. And to be even more frank, it is easier in England to 'marry up' if you're a female than is it for a male. It might not be fair, but…"

"Yeah, yeah, I know; life's not fair. But that still sounds ridiculous. Okay, I'll stop asking you anything further in that respect. If we have to phone Carolyn, let's get it done. If this clue can help someone solve the issue, so much the better."

Ed picked up the phone to dial, but Vicky held his arm to stop him. "Look I'm sorry I lipped off, Ed, and I'm sorry things haven't worked out for both of you as they should have. Let's make the call and then I'll buy us supper. Over supper you can up-date me on the Sunday bad-news meeting. Okay?"

Ed nodded and dialed the number.

The phone was set on audio in order that they could both hear and speak. It rang several times before a sleepy Carolyn spoke. "Hello. Who's this?"

Ed spoke. "Carolyn it's me…"

"For God's sake, Ed, it's gone two a.m. I thought we'd…"

Vicky quickly interrupted, speaking quickly. "Miss, it's me. Mister and I have an up-date. I received a letter in the mail today from Alex. It was mailed from Izmir the day we arrived. It has another clue." She waited.

"Good morning, Slim and Mister. My apologies. Haven't slept well lately with everything going on. What's the message, please?"

Ed read the message.

"That's it?" Carolyn asked.

Vicky responded. "There is a private message to me below that. I'd prefer…"

"Of course. I understand. Could I ask that you fax the main part to me as quickly as you can? You have the number do you, Mister?"

"Yes. I'll fax it from my office in fifteen minutes. It makes no sense to Slim and me, but knowing Mr. Umarov as we do, I believe it is important."

"I suspect you're absolutely correct. I'll get the copy to everyone involved first thing in the morning. Thank you both. And Ed, I'm sorry for…"

Ed interrupted. "Understood, Carolyn. Try to get some sleep for the rest on the night." He hung up.

"That went well," Vicky said enthusiastically.

"Oh, spectacularly, I'm sure."

She jabbed him in the arm. "You know what they say about sarcasm, don't you?"

Ed nodded to the door. "Let's go eat…and have a drink if that's okay?"

"Sure, you deserve one…maybe two, but no more."

He saluted her. "As you say, boss."

"Yeah, right. I'll drive you to your office, I'll decide where we're going to eat, I'll listen, I'll pay, and then I have one personal question for you. Let's boogie."

Ed bowed and waved his arms for her to lead the way. "Looking forward to it all," he said graciously. "Or most of it anyway."

An energized Vicky led the way.

CHAPTER EIGHTEEN

Vicky managed to get a table by a window, looking over Lakeshore Rd. in a downtown Oakville restaurant. They sat at right angle instead of across from each other, wanting as much privacy as they could get

"You must have clout," Ed said, looking around at the almost full restaurant.

"It's Wednesday, and they had a cancellation. Besides I wanted us to have some level of privacy. People can't hear through glass."

Ed nodded. "Good point. By the way you owe me a dance."

Vicky looked up from the menu. "Excuse me? Oh, you mean from the wedding. Some time, I'm sure."

"You also owe me a secret."

"What?"

"From the plane ride."

"Do you ever forget anything?"

He grinned. "Only when I want to. No rush. Some time, I'm sure."

She looked back at the menu. "Just figure out what you want to eat, Ed. It's getting late."

Ed replied without looking at the menu. "Calamari appetizer and their sea-food special, please. And a glass, or two, Pinot Grigio; preferably from Italy."

Vicky put down her menu. "Sometimes, Edwin..."

"I can be a pain in the butt?"

"Au contraire, mon frère. Let's share the appetizer, and I'll have the same main course. I'll order us a bottle of Pinot Grigio, and hopefully they'll have a choice from the Lombardy area of northern Italy. Of course it was originally grown in France where it is known as Pinot Gris. Over the years..."

"I give up," Ed conceded, raising his hands in defeat. "Just a young travel agent trying to move up a station in life."

"You are not a 'just' anything, young man. Now since you're the male at the table, put in our order please."

He nodded, and raised his hand to get the attention of the waiter. "Monsieur. S'il vous plait."

Vicky sat up in her seat, enjoying every minute with this 'young travel agent': her 'young travel agent'.

Waiting for the appetizer to be delivered and their glasses of wine poured, Ed led the discussion. "First let me say that I didn't realize how potentially destructive the Sunday meeting up-date was until I heard the full tapes of you and Alex."

Vicky cringed. "Yikes!"

"No, no, not what you think. What I learned from the tapes was the historical bad feelings, to put it mildly, between Russians and the Chechen peoples. Keep Alex's comments in mind when I tell you what is happening. But first," he said happily holding up his glass, "cheers, and it is nice to see you again. As Vicky, I mean."

They touched their glasses. Vicky motioned for him to continue.

For the next half hour Ed explained the circumstances of what was going on in Russia between Gorbachev and the KGB, and the possible international-relationships risks involved. She didn't speak, couldn't speak, as she took it all in. Her only reaction was to finish her glass of wine ahead of Ed; which he topped up, but only slightly. He stopped speaking as their main course arrived. He ate his quickly so that he could finish the story.

"Now what amazes me," he went on, "is the potential, and let's keep that important word in the forefront of our minds, that things could get worse and more dangerous because of religion for God's sake."

"A play on words?" she managed to ask.

"Intentional," he lied with a broad grin.

The waiter cleared their table and offered to add more wine to their glasses. Vicky covered her glass with her hand with a smile to the waiter. Ed encouraged the waiter to pour to a full glass. Vicky asked him to bring the check in about fifteen minutes, wanting to finish the business.

"So what you're telling me," she said quietly, "is that all hell could break loose – and that's my play on words, smarty-pants – with more than the two main countries getting involved simply as a result of religion?"

"Yes."

"Couldn't you soften that a tad?"

"No."

"However..."

"However," Ed interrupted, "we now have a further clue to help us solve the problem. A further clue due mainly, if not only, because of your excellent work on the cruise and in particular your friendship with Alex. Whatever the rest of his message to you says, you should take great pride it what you did."

"What we did. What the three of us did."

"Fair enough, but the challenge now is to interpret his message in order to find the gold at the end of the rainbow – so to speak."

"And there goes a good night's sleep."

"Afraid so."

They both leaned back in their chairs and looked out onto Lakeshore as people casually walked the downtown area and enjoyed the coming of spring. They turned to each other both of them wishing they knew what to say next that would help the situation. Neither came up with anything worth mentioning, so they waited for the check.

Vicky drove slowly to Ed's apartment and pulled up in the front driveway. She wasn't going to stay.

"So my personal question," she said, turning to Ed, "is did you two kiss when you got together?"

Ed shrugged. "Of course we kissed."

She gave him the eye. "Ed, I don't mean kiss, I mean did you two, you know… 'kiss-kiss'? You know what I mean."

"Yes."

Vicky smiled. "Good. Glad to hear that. Now one final question…"

"Another? Really?"

"Do you recall the first time you kissed a girl?"

"I do."

"Pray tell."

Ed chuckled at what he was about to say. "I walked her to the garden gate. Her mother was at the front door and said it was time she came in. She apologized for her mother, and then I moved forward a couple of inches and we kissed. Just for a few seconds, but what was nice was that she was kissing me. It may sound silly, but it was wonderful. Then her mother called her again and she went in"

"Good. Now, Ed, I want you to kiss me like that please."

He leaned toward her and they oh-so-gently kissed, their lips barely touching. They separated, both smiling.

"It's time for you to go in now, Edwin," Vicky said in a motherly tone. "Good night."

He did as he was told, got out of the car, waved good-night as her car pulled away, and headed up to his apartment. As soon as he arrived he phoned Vicky's number and left a message. "That was wonderful, Vicky. Good night."

CHAPTER NINETEEN

Thursday, May 8th 1986

He looked at the clock by his bed. 4:27. He couldn't sleep. He had tossed and turned all night. Nothing could get his head clear of the message – added to make more and less. It made no sense. He tried thinking about that special kiss with Vicky, but the message kept forcing its way to the front of his brain. He got out of bed and walked around the room naked. He wanted to think, he needed to think. The phone rang. He picked it up immediately.

"Can't sleep, eh?" It was Vicky.

"Barely a wink."

"Thanks for the message, but that's not why I phoned. It's improper English!"

"Sorry?"

She spoke slowly, wanting to make her point clear. "Remember we were in the grocery store one time and the fast lane was for people with not many items. The sign said, 'Less Than Twelve Items,' and you said…"

"Fewer!" Ed shouted. "It should be fewer! Yes, you're right. His message should read 'They can be added to make more and fewer'. I think you're onto something, Vicky."

"What?" she asked quietly.

He thought for a few seconds. "I don't know. I have to think about it, but I'm sure you're right."

"Good. I'm going back to bed."

"No, no, not yet." Ed pleaded. "I'll give you Carolyn's phone number, and *you* phone and tell them what we think. They have to know. It's important. Please?"

"I have her number. I'll phone right away…and then I'm going back to bed.

Thanks again for the message. Get some sleep, Ed. I'm beginning to worry about you." She hung up.

He picked up the photo-copy of the message and walked into the kitchen area. He laid it on the table and looked at the numbers: 40 7 30 30 9 30 4 30 5 9. He started talking to himself out loud.

"Okay, how does an engineer think? With precision, clear and simple, no loose ends." He shook his head. "No, no, more than that. He loved Vicky. He wouldn't make it totally impossible for someone to figure it out." He looked down at the numbers. "Forty, seven, thirty, thirty, nine... Mostly it has to make sense, especially to an engineer. Not simple, but…Shit I've got it!" He banged the table with his fist. "The numbers are more, but fewer!"

He grabbed a pen and wrote below the original numbers:

47 30 39 34 35 9

"More, but bloody less. It makes sense. It does, it does."

He looked at the new numbers. They added up 194 just like the old set of numbers. Nothing new there. No, there was another message. What's he trying to tell us? Think, think, think… Finally the penny dropped. His shoulders relaxed and he grinned as big a grin he'd ever grinned. "You smart old bugger, you. You've just told us where it is."

He did a little jig in the middle of the kitchen, picked up the phone and dialed Vicky's number.

"Now what?" Vicky groaned, staying under the bed covers.

"I've got it. I've got it. The numbers are more, but fewer." He read out the new numbers. "He's told us where it is."

Vicky sat up in bed, throwing off the blankets. "Where is it, Ed? For God's sake where is it?"

"I don't know."

Vicky was angry now. "What! What the hell are you…?"

"Listen, listen, please. The new numbers are co-ordinates; Longitude and latitude. But I don't have a bloody atlas. A travel agent with no bloody atlas. How stupid is that? I'll phone Carolyn and find out…"

"Ed, stop talking. If you're right, let's do it correctly. My father has a large National Geographic World Atlas. Get your ass over here right now. I'll be waiting at the front door. Ten minutes. Are you dressed?"

"No."

"Fifteen minutes. And guess what? I'll put the kettle on for a cuppa tea, and I won't open the book until you get here. Move it!"

"You're a genius, Miss Kilgour. How did I ever manage without you?" He hung up.

Vicky stood with the phone in her hand. "I'm a genius? Nah; I'm just an MBA. He's the bloody genius." She reached for her housecoat and headed to the kitchen, mumbling to herself... 'Boiling water, heat the pot, two tea bags, exactly three minutes to brew, milk in first… What! Am I turning into an English maid?' She shrugged. "Oh well, could be worse; could be an English old maid."

Ten minutes later Ed pulled his car in front of Vicky's parents' house and jumped out. Vicky met him at the door and they entered the huge living room area. To the left was the library with a significant number of books in the many shelves against the wall. Sitting on a table, unopened, was the World Atlas…and two cups of tea. They each took a sip of their tea and set the cups to one side. Ed put the piece of paper with the new numbers on the table, crossed his fingers and opened the atlas to the first page which showed the pages that contained each map.

"It has to be Europe," Ed said. "Let's try Europe."

Vicky carefully opened the page on Europe. "You do Longitude, and I'll do Latitude," she said, peering into the map. They started on the sides and top of the page and carefully each ran their hand along the respective lines as best they could.

"We need a bigger map," Ed grumbled.

"Deal with what we've got," Vicky replied. "Just take your time."

Agonizingly slowly they moved their pointing fingers toward their goal.

"Got it," Ed said. "It's in Ukraine, just north of Crimea, but where exactly...who knows?"

"Let's check the larger maps," Vicky said enthusiastically.

Flipping back to the inside cover, they identified the best page for Ukraine. "Page 73," Vicky announced proudly.

Opening the map on page 73 made it easier to find. Again they ran their hands across and down the page. Their fingers met on a lake. Ed moved in as close to the map as he could. "I'd say it's on that lake near the town of Nikopol."

Vicky peered in. "I agree. The good news, as it were, is that it makes sense that it's in Ukraine, again, and it really makes sense that there's a lake. All nuclear power stations need water! I think we've got it."

They stood, now not exactly sure what to do. A phone call to Stonebridge Manor was a certainty, and the sooner the better. But what if they were wrong?

"I'm kind of scared," Ed said, suddenly drained of energy. "What now?"

"Now?" Vicky asked. "Now we give each other a big hug, and then we do what we have to do. Have another cup of tea."

Ed laughed aloud, turned to Vicky and pulled her to him with a hug that almost took her breath away. "Right on, Slim. Right on." He stepped back.

"I'm not Slim here and now, Ed. I'm Vicky."

Ed nodded his apology and moved back toward her. He gave her an even bigger hug and kissed her gently as they separated. "Thank you, Vicky. Thank you for everything."

"Not good enough, Ed," she moved back into his arms and kissed him fully and sensually.

"Everything okay, Victoria?" Mr. Kilgour asked as he entered the room wearing his bath robe and an enquiring look. "Hello, Ed. How are you doing?"

Separating quickly both turned to Vicky's father.

Ed managed to speak first. "I am doing fine, Mr. Kilgour, we were…"

Vicky interrupted. "We were planning a trip to Europe, Father, and we needed a map…"

"Nice places to visit," her father said, looking down at the map. "You'll particularly enjoy Kazakhstan, especially at this time of year." He nodded and left the room, heading upstairs and back to his bedroom.

Vicky picked up the atlas. "Let's go up to my room. We don't want to get my parents involved in any way. He's already suspicious enough of my trip to the wedding. He only has my best interest at heart, but he is my father after all."

Ed picked up the two cups of tea. "No sense wasting these, eh?"

They took the elevator up to her room. As they entered her room Vicky turned to Ed. "Okay, no more kissing and stuff, right?"

"Hey, I was just going along. Happily going along for sure. But no more kissing and stuff." Ed grinned. "What is 'stuff' anyway?"

Vicky waved him off.

They sat at the window that looked over Lake Ontario. The timing was good with the sun just raising its head over the calm and wave-less lake.

"You make the call this time," Vicky said bluntly.

It was way past noon in England, so timing wasn't an issue. Ed put the phone on speaker and dialed the number. Carolyn answered.

He wasted no time. "We know the location, or a least we think we do."

"Hang on," Carolyn said immediately, "I'll make this a conference call in his office. Thirty seconds."

Less than thirty seconds later Lord Stonebridge came on the phone. "Good morning to both of you. I understand you have some interesting news for us. We can use some. Please proceed."

Ed spoke clearly. He wanted to say it just once. "We turned the ten numbers into six, sir." He read the new numbers carefully. "We think they are geographical co-ordinates. Our map is not very large, so the best we can come up with is a lake in Ukraine close to a town called Nikopol. We can't be certain..."

"Hold on, Mr. Crowe. What you're saying makes a great deal of sense. Let me make a phone call regarding those co-ordinates and see what my people can tell me. I'll be a couple of minutes."

Vicky picked up their cups of tea and handed Ed his cup. "It may not be hot, but it may be the most interesting cups of tea we both ever enjoy...or not."

It seemed like forever, but seven minutes later Lord Stonebridge returned. "As in the world of real estate, ladies and gentlemen; location, location, location." The tone of his voice made it obvious he was smiling, and there was the sound of clapping in the background. "My sincere congratulations to both of you. We have just made a major step in the right direction. I will be happy to phone Prime Minister Thatcher as soon as this conversation is complete. She will determine who and how to tell this good news, particularly Mr. Gorbachev. As we know he has the KGB to deal with. In the mean time, this is strictly confidential. Well done."

Ed spoke on their behalf. "Thank you, sir, from both of us. May I ask what else we know of this reactor?"

"Certainly. The difficult part is the name. It is the Zaporizhia reactor, or I should say reactors, since there are currently five of them at that location. They are all recently built with one more currently under construction. When complete they will produce twenty percent of Ukraine's total energy needs."

"Is that good news or bad news?" Ed asked.

Carolyn replied. "That was also our first question. Good news because they are new and up to date technologically, bad news since there are hundreds of workers in and around the reactor sites and that creates security concerns that are not normally an issue. And if I might just add an interesting fact. The co-ordinates were precise, almost to a yard. Our Alex knew his stuff." She paused. "Listen, I realize you two have been up all night. If you want to check in with me in a day or two, I'll keep you informed."

"Thanks," Ed responded, "we appreciate that. In the meantime, I'm still going to contact Mr. Helbrecht and see what he has to say. You never know."

"Good thinking. Let me know. Lord Stonebridge is already on the phone to the prime minister, so I'll say keep in touch. Thank you, Ed and thank you, Vicky."

Ed and Vicky said good bye and hung up the phone.

"Oh my God," Vicky said, spinning on one foot. "What a day. What a world."

Ed laughed. "Okay, I've gotta go. I still have to work today. Give me another hug before I go, Vicky." Ed hugged her gently. "You're not wearing a bra, are you?"

She gently pushed him away. "That is none of your business, bloke. And no, I'm not! Now go home please."

"I'll keep in touch," Ed said as he headed for the door with a broad smile. "And don't forget you owe me a dance and a secret."

She waved him off, and he left for home.

When he arrived home there was a message on his phone. It was Vicky.

"By the way, I hope that last hug wasn't just an excuse to hold my lovely, small, soft and sexy breasts – as you refer to them –against your body. That would make you a naughty, naughty bloke. And yes, keep in touch. But that will be figuratively, excuse the play on words, not literally. Bye now."

The thought of her breasts had him remember and smile. He needed a shower. He decided to take a cold one.

CHAPTER TWENTY

In spite of the little sleep he had managed to capture, Ed felt relaxed as he headed into work. They still didn't know what was planned at the reactors, but at least they knew the location of 'More to come'. He grabbed a cup of tea and sat at his desk. It all seemed so obvious now, but without Vicky's pointing out the improper English they wouldn't be limiting their search to one location. One location, but five individual reactors. Was it the location or one reactor that was the target, he pondered. His phone rang, and he was happy to turn his mind to work as he picked up the phone.

For several hours he was busy arranging his many and varied clients' business trips and vacations. Vacations were much more interesting to work with. The clients were excited about where to go, what to do when they got there, what kind of deals and packages were available, and of course cost was always an over-riding issue. The business people wanted to get there and back as quickly as their business meetings would allow. The earlier they could get home to family and friends the better. The recent increase in the need for security at airports made business travel even less desirable. Everyone knew it had to be in place, but it certainly slowed the boarding of a plane to a process of going from one line up to another. To a vacationer it was an annoyance, to a business traveler it was reason to travel less and use the significant technical changes resulting from cellular phones, conference calls, and the significant reduction in costs of international phone calls.

His stomach began to rumble, telling him that he hadn't eaten for hours. "Is that your stomach?" Vicky stood by the door of his small office.

He stood and welcomed her in. "Good morning, Miss Kilgour. Where in the world may I send you?"

She shook her head. "You're not sending me anywhere, Mr. Crowe. I'm taking you for lunch." She waved an envelope she held in her hand. "We're going to celebrate this. Or more to the point, I'm going to celebrate it, and I would like you to join me."

They walked to a local pub and sat in the corner where they could chat in private. Not to Vicky's surprise Ed ordered fish and chips and tea while she ordered a salad and a coffee for herself.

Ed leaned across the table. "So what is in the envelope that has you celebrating?" He assumed it wasn't their business, and he didn't want it to be either.

"This envelope has in it an application for life insurance, for one of my wealthier clients, for one million dollars." She smiled and kissed the envelope. "Quite a few cruises for me in here, but then I'll need a friend to go with won't I?"

"A million dollars. Yikes, I am impressed. I'm too well mannered to ask how much for you, but…?"

She sat up straight and proud. "More than I made last year in total. So my treat for lunch."

He laughed and bowed his head in thanks. "Glad to celebrate it with you."

The food arrived and they both enjoyed the first meal they had had for many hours. Vicky paid for the meal and walking close to each other they headed back to his office. When they arrived, Ed closed the door to his office. Intuitively he knew she had a reason more than a life insurance sale, even one that large, to pay him a visit. He waited for her to speak.

"There is an application for insurance in here," she said waving the envelope.

Ed nodded. "I don't doubt it for a second."

"Okay, okay, that's not the main reason I came to see you. I have two confessions to make. The first is that I looked at your passport on the flight over to know where you went on your 'business' trips."

"Well done."

"The second is, and I know this will sound weird, but I really enjoyed our assignment; the trip, the challenge, getting to know the people we did. It was wonderful. Especially the phone calls last night. That was just plain exciting." She paused "I just wanted you to know, that's all." She stood to leave.

"Not thinking of giving up your sales job, then?"

She waved the envelope. "Not a chance in the world. This is for a million, and it took me several weeks to finalize. Actually I recommended an amount less than a million, but he liked the idea of being worth a million bucks."

"Dead."

She shrugged. "There's a cash value and it could end up being tax advantageous. He's got a wife and kids. It's the right thing to do."

"Having a wife and kids?"

She winked. "Works for some. I gotta go."

Ed walked her to her car. "Might I see you at The Head tomorrow night?" He asked casually.

She shook her head. "No, I'm, er...seeing a friend."

"I shouldn't give you a hug, eh?" Ed said grinning.

"I'm fully clothed this time, bloke. Gimme a hug, and that's an order."

After a longer then normal hug, they separated and she left with a wave and a smile.

When he got back to his desk he phoned the local florist and ordered a delivery of six roses to Vicky's home. The card read:

'Thanks a Million for lunch...Bloke'.

He couldn't help but chuckle. But he had to get back to reality; he looked up Robert Helbrecht's telephone number.

Ed dialed the number and it was answered immediately. "Helbrecht."

"Hi, Mr. Helbrecht I'm Ed Crowe…"

"Where were you born?"

"Whitemouth."

"Oh, okay, Ed, what can I do for you? And it's Bob."

Ed felt more comfortable. "Well, Bob I'm not sure how much you've been told..."

"Next to nothing, actually. I've been told you would give me a call and we might have to get together about which I know nothing. Except, of course, it relates to Chernobyl, and it's top secret. My big boss has made it clear that I should help you as much as possible, and when he speaks, I listen."

"Thanks. To get to the nub of the issue, we do have to get together. I can drive up to where you…"

"No. I much prefer to come down to Toronto. It's rather quiet up here and I'm ready for a change of pace. When is good for you?"

Ed shrugged, thinking. "Tomorrow?"

"Done."

"Great. Let's do this. Let's meet in the lobby of the Royal York Hotel at one tomorrow afternoon. I'll get a room so we have some level of privacy. I suspect it will take two or three hours. If you like you can stay overnight in the room."

"I'll take you up on that. I'll wear my Winnipeg Blue Bomber jacket. Not too many of those in Toronto. Should I bring anything else?"

Ed thought for a moment. "Just your brain."

"Well that's not very heavy. I'll see you tomorrow."

They hung up. Ed's phone rang and thirty minutes later he had booked a Caribbean cruise for one of his regular clients; balcony, centre of the ship and one happy customer.

He was nodding off, trying to stay awake until ten o'clock. It had been a long and successful day, but they were still a long way from knowing when and exactly where the next 'accident' was going to be. His phone rang.

It was Vicky. "Hey, bloke, thanks for the roses. They're lovely. You shouldn't have." She laughed. "Actually you should have. Getting me up at some un-godly hour; having my father catch us in the early hours with me in my housecoat; and then the roses. My parents are totally confused as to where we, that's you and me, are going. So am I by the way. Gotta go. Bye." She hung up before he could respond. 'So am I,' he realized. He decided not to think further about that subject, and turned his thoughts to tomorrow's meeting with Bob Helbrecht from Whitemouth.

CHAPTER TWENTY-ONE

Friday, May 9th, 1986

He had selected The Royal York hotel in downtown Toronto for a reason. It was a beautiful old hotel and where he had stayed when he had arrived in Canada for his introduction on 'being a Canadian' for his first assignment with MI6, just two years earlier. Having booked, and checked out, the room he waited in the lobby, sitting in one of the many chairs and reading a newspaper.

At exactly one o'clock Bob Helbrecht walked into the lobby. He was tall and slim and as mentioned on the phone he wore a Winnipeg Blue Bomber jacket that celebrated their 1984 Grey Cup win; their first win in twenty-two years. He looked around briefly and then walked to the centre of the lobby. He stopped, held his hands behind his back and waited.

Ed walked up to him with his hand out. "Hi I'm Ed Crowe from Whitemouth." They shook hands and Ed motioned for then to step to one side. "Have you eaten?" Ed asked.

"Eaten and ready to get at it," Bob said quietly. "Whatever 'it' is."

They headed up to the room on the eighth floor. The room was large and high enough to look over Union Station across the street, and see Lake Ontario in the distance. They exchanged business cards.

"Travel agent. That's interesting." Bob remarked.

Ed nodded, and not wanting to delay the process opened a desk drawer, pulled out a tape recorder and placed it on the table.

"Now that is really interesting," Bob said cautiously.

"Nothing to fear," Ed replied, "I'm going to play a tape, not record. Let's sit and I'll explain the situation as best I can, then I'll play the tape."

They sat. Ed sat leaning forward. Bob sat back in his chair.

Ed began. "So this whole thing might sound a bit weird, but it is what it is. The recording is a number of tapings of me, a friend of mine who, as she mentions on the tape, is a life insurance agent, and a gentleman by the name of Alexi Umarov. He is..."

"I know who he is," Bob interrupted. "Keep in mind I was flown in to see the Chernobyl accident several days after the explosion. My report uses the word accident very loosely. There is more to what happened there than what is being reported by the Soviet Government. Everyone involved in reviewing what is known at this time suspects that. I more than suspect it. Mr. Umarov's absence from the reactor at the time of the accident was noted by many, mostly as an unfortunate circumstance."

"Good. That helps. The recordings were made on a cruise ship that left Istanbul last Wednesday, four days after the Chernobyl accident. Keep in mind that Vicky is neither my wife, nor my sister. But she is my life insurance agent."

"And you're her travel agent."

"Correct."

"I'm all ears."

"That would be very good, because as you will hear Mr. Umarov, or Alex, tells us a great deal about the accident, the USSR nuclear power operation, and some interesting history between Russia and Chechnya. He is Chechen. He is very bright and speaks several languages. As you will hear, he speaks to us about the nuclear issues in plain English. But you will also understand he is very clever, and for lack of a better word – sneaky."

"Sneaky?"

"Yep. You'll understand as we go through the tapings. Now, why are we here today?"

"Indeed, that's my question."

"What I would like you to do, what *we* would like you to do, is listen to the tapes and see if you can pick out anything that he says that we did not pick up on. Feel free to take notes. Keep in mind that we started taping the conversations after we had introduced ourselves to Alex, and not from the start. To be honest, we didn't expect to meet with him as much as we did. And the main reason for that is because Vicky and Alex got along well; very well. Ask any questions as we go through. It will take several hours, and it will be better if we address your questions as we go."

"Question one. Who are 'we'?"

"Now that's a good one," Ed said rubbing his chin. "Let's, for now, say we are the good guys and I'll let your boss decide how much he can tell you in more detail. Okay?"

"Good answer. Ready when you are."

Ed pressed the play button.

Bob listened intently to the first tape where Vicky had breakfast with Alex, and where he made it clear that he knew Vicky knew more about him than she was letting on, and resulting in Vicky re-introducing herself as Vicky Kilgour. It was easy to be impressed by Alex's demeanor and historical knowledge. Ed paused the recording as the breakfast taping ended.

"I see what you mean by sneaky," Bob said smiling.

"Just wait. There's a lot more to come."

Ed pressed the play button, and they listened to the recording of Vicky and Alex having lunch in his cabin. It was fascinating to hear it, even for Ed who had heard it before. Bob took notes as they listened. When this portion was finished, Ed turned it off.

Bob looked sideways at Ed. "May I ask what he said in private?"

He knew there was no reason not to reveal what was said. "He told Vicky that he was going to die from cancer: weeks not months. And he further explained that it had nothing to do with his cigar smoking which, while not captured on tape, Vicky had convinced him to quit.

To finalize the story he committed suicide the next day, the day we disembarked at Izmir."

Bob shook his head. "And all this involving a travel agent and a life insurance agent! It boggles the mind."

"I'll take that as a compliment and will pass it on to Vicky. She's quite a lady. But before we move on the final taping, let me ask you a question. You went to Chernobyl, and here you are full of life and energy. If the damage was four hundred times the level of Hiroshima and they've cleared the local town of Pripyat; how can that be?"

Bob raised a hand and nodded. "Excellent question and one that will be asked for years to come. Hiroshima was an atomic bomb, a bomb that was designed to explode and thrust outward with the goal to blast everything in its way. That is what killed so many. Of course many died from radiation, some in the short term and many weeks, months, and years later. But the largest number died immediately or shortly thereafter from the actual explosion. The radiation from Chernobyl will no doubt kill more people, but not like a bomb blast. A slow and terrifying death, no doubt. In the case of Pripyat and the surrounding area, the risk is contamination. Any food grown such as vegetables, grain, and of course livestock have been contaminated. That contamination will last for years. The reactor that was damaged was reactor 4. Although located on the same site units 1, 2, and 3 would have remained operable as long as radiation fields and fallout from the accident did not impact the working environment. That is, the explosion did not damage the other three units physically. Following the explosion and initial release of radioactivity, the dangerous radiation fields would have been confined primarily to the affected reactor. The internal environment of the other three operating units was likely controlled by their separate ventilation control systems and the fact that deposition of radionuclides would impact the outside rather than inside of structures, although that would be dependent on stopping ventilation systems from drawing in outside air until releases were under control. In short the accident in an adjacent unit likely had limited impact on operation of the three other units, other than requiring additional controls on staff entering and working in these units. I suspect that the level of radiation doses that personnel could now be exposed to in the aftermath and containment of unit 4, including my own short visit, have been somewhat relaxed relative to current international standards. The same thing may be true to keep the remaining reactors operating into the future. Consideration of the significant impact that closure of the remaining units would have on Ukraine's demand for electricity is no doubt a factor into the decision to keep them operating. The biggest question, at this time, is the matter of keeping the three other reactor units, potentially with the same flawed design as unit 4, in operation at all. If that is the case that leaves open the door to another possible accident and that would be an absolute disaster."

Ed listened, hoping he fully comprehended what he was hearing. The only thing he knew for sure was that if there is another 'accident' the USSR, and likely the world in general, would be in chaos. He shuddered at the thought. "Well, when you listen to the last tape I think you'll believe, as we do, that if there is another so called accident, it won't be at Chernobyl. We did get a clue from Alex, and I'll explain what that led us to, but first the recording." He pressed the play button.

Bob listened intently at the recording of Alex bringing the clue to Vicky, and the two of them and Ed enjoying a glass of wine. His body reacted with surprise as Ed called Alex a liar, using the expression 'pork pie'. The confession that then followed of Alex admitting his involvement in the Chernobyl incident totally surprised him and it showed in his shaking his head in disbelief that anyone would do what he did, knowing what would happen to some of his own friends. Ed turned off the recording.

"So you simply guessed?" Bob asked.

"I'd like to think of it as intuition, but really it was a guess. A good one, but just a guess. Now before I ask you if you heard anything that we didn't pick up on, let me finish the story so far. The clue Alex gave us was a set of numbers that meant nothing to us…or anyone else. But finally we put our heads together…"

"The travel agent and a life insurance agent, that is?"

Ed smiled. "Yes, actually. The bottom line is that the next incident, unless we prevent it, is at the Zaporizhia reactor, or one of the five reactors at that location. It's located..."

"Yes, I know where it is. New, more modern reactors. Good new, bad news."

"Exactly what other people have said." He paused. "So, Robert Helbrecht from Whitemouth, did you pick up on anything that we didn't capture having heard what was said during the recordings?"

He looked down at is notes, turning them over to see all of his comments. "Nothing jumps to mind," he said, somewhat sadly. "But let me think about it all. There were a lot of opportunities for Mr. Umarov to sneak something in. And as you said, he sure is a sneaky, if highly professional, gentleman."

Ed stood, picked up the tape recorder and they shook hands. "You have my number. Don't be concerned of thinking something might not matter. We only figured out one clue because of his improper use of English in a note to Vicky." He chuckled. "And it wasn't bad English of that I'm certain. He intentionally used an incorrect adjective, and that led to a different interpretation of his clue. Sneaky for sure."

"I wouldn't hesitate to phone," Bob promised.

"I trust you won't," Ed replied and left for home.

CHAPTER TWENTY-TWO

The Queen's Head
7:30 pm

Ed was on his third Double Diamond, relaxed but somewhat lonely after the busy week before. Peter was running the bar, and as usual on a Friday night it was busy. They had chatted briefly about the F. A. Cup to be played at Wembley Stadium the next day, between Everton and Liverpool. Peter's team, Manchester United, had beaten Everton for the Cup the previous year, so he automatically wanted Liverpool to win. Ed couldn't get into the discussion with any enthusiasm; it was a bit of a world away from his recent thoughts, and he still was concerned that he – they – hadn't finalized the entire matter of 'More to come'.

Against his better judgment, he walked out of the pub, and into the far end of parking lot. He didn't want to be heard. Looking around to ensure he was alone, he took out his cell phone. He knew he shouldn't, he was positive it was the wrong thing to do, but he dialed Vicky's number anyway.

"Is this business?" Vicky asked quietly, recognizing his number.

"No."

She spoke softly but bluntly. "I told you I am with a friend."

"Yes you did."

"So why are you phoning?"

He gulped. "I have a song to sing you; it's one of my mum's favorites."

She couldn't believe what she was hearing. She wanted to hang up, but she could not convince herself to do that. "Ed, I have a friend here with me."

He started singing:

"Put your sweet lips a little close to the phone.
Let's pretend that we're together all alone.
I'll ask the man to turn the juke box way down low.
And you can tell your friend there with you, he'll have to go."

"Oh my God," Vicky groaned. "I can't believe this. Hang on."

She held the phone against her side, turned to her friend and shrugged. "Can we catch up tomorrow? This is business."

"Of course," her friend replied with a smile. "Anyone one I know?"

Vicky nodded.

"Ed?" Seana asked.

Vicky nodded.

Seana grabbed her two bags of new clothes from their shopping expedition, gave Vicky a wink, and left with a broad smile on her face.

Vicky counted to ten in order to act as calmly as she could, and raised her phone to her lips. "My friend has left," she said.

Ed grimaced at the tone of her voice. "Is he mad at you?"

"My friend has left," she repeated.

"Are you mad at me?"

She paused. "Not yet, but you better have a good reason for me to send my friend home. And by the way, you're no Jim Reeves."

"Thanks."

"The reason you phoned?"

"Ah, yes. I have two." He tried hard to think of a second one.

"And they are?"

"Well it seems to me that I might need more life insurance, and who else better to discuss that with than a fully qualified life insurance agent, especially one that has recently sold a million dollar policy to a customer, and of course…"

"Baloney. And you second reason?"

He hung his head. "I'm lonely."

She almost dropped her phone at the tenderness of his voice, but she held it all together. "I wasn't."

"I'm sorry. This isn't like me."

No it wasn't she thought. "I'll be at your place in half an hour. Right now I'm half naked and surrounded by my underwear." She looked at her recent Victoria Secret purchases spread across her bed, and couldn't help but grin.

"Are you sure? You could phone your friend…."

"Half an hour?"

"Half an hour," he replied eagerly. "I'll have a bottle of wine and some snacks ready for when you arrive. And thanks."

"Bye, bloke." She hung up the phone, selected the sexiest underwear from her afternoon shopping trip, decided on her blue, tight, and somewhat short dress, and then moved quickly to get ready for a glass of medium-priced wine and some just-unfrozen appetizers. She was really looking forward to the rest of the evening, and was so happy he had phoned.

Ed ran into the pub, finished his third pint of beer and headed home via the Liquor Commission. He was just a little ashamed of his actions, but was looking forward to seeing Vicky, especially in a 'non-business' environment.

With his expensive bottle of Pinot Grigio tucked under his arm and his mind on a fine evening ahead, it took him several seconds to recognize Bob Helbrecht standing inside the lobby of his apartment building. They shook hands, and didn't speak until they were on the elevator.

"I've been phoning you," Bob said quickly

Ed banged his head with his hand. "Shit. I didn't give you my cell phone number. Sorry about that. How did you get here?"

"A very expensive cab ride."

They waited until they entered Ed's apartment to speak.

"I hope this is good news," Ed said.

"Maybe a reason for a bottle of wine?" Bob replied motioning to the Pinot Grigio as Ed put it in the fridge.

No sooner had he spoken, there was a knock on the apartment door. Ed motioned for Bob to stay seated. He walked to the door hoping to speak first, but he lost.

"Hi there, big guy," Vicky said in a deep sexy voice. "Watcha doing tonight?"

Ed opened the door fully. "Good evening, Miss Kilgour. I'd like you to meet Mr. Robert Helbrecht."

Her legs wobbled, and she almost fell. Giving Ed a dirty look, she turned to go. Ed chased her down the hallway, and gently took her arm. "Vicky, please stop. I didn't know he was going to be here. We just got here ourselves. It's business. Please!"

She turned and looked at him face to face. "You owe me big time, Mr. Crowe, and don't you ever forget it. Capisce?"

"Big time, Vicky. Big time."

They walked back into Ed's apartment and Vicky carried on as if nothing had happened. She extended her hand. "Good evening, Mr. Helbrecht. I'm Vicky Kilgour. I'm Mr. Crowe's life insurance agent. I always drop in to see him on a Friday night, just to make sure he is still alive." She smiled sweetly. "Tonight he only just made it…alive that is."

Bob nodded his understanding. "First, Miss Kilgour, please call me Bob. Secondly let me say I feel like I have already met you, having listened to the tapes from – and I quote - the travel agent and life insurance's agent's cruise." He paused with a smile. "Having said that, I do want to say that while I don't know everything about the cruise, you and Ed did a wonderful job of gathering information that will, I have no doubt, be helpful into the future." With those comments, he turned to Ed. "Would you please re-play the last recording when you suggested Mr. Umarov was lying; or telling a porky as you referred to it."

Ed moved to collect the tape recorder ready to play.

"You see," Bob continued, "it was the porky bit that distracted my attention from his response, and I think, in fact I'm rather sure, that he provided another clue to the issue at hand."

They sat and watched Ed speed through the taping. It seemed to take forever.

"And please call me Vicky, Bob," Vicky said, waiting for the final taping to be found.

Ed finally found it and pressed the button.

"If you don't mind my saying so, sir, I think you're telling us a bit of a porky."

"A what...?'

"Pray tell."

"Pork pie, sir; London Cockney slang. It rhymes with lie. I think you're telling us a lie."

The sound of Vicky knocking over her glass "Ed, how dare you! That is totally offensive. Alex has been totally honest...."

The sounds of Vicky leaving the cabin.

"More wine, sir?"

"What makes you think I am not telling the truth, Ed?"

"Oh I think you're telling the truth, but not the whole truth and nothing but the truth. In fact I think you are reluctant to tell Vicky the truth because you do not have long to live and you want her to remember you as a gentle and kind man and not someone who would deliberately kill people, some of whom you would have known personally. Perhaps if there was more time you could explain your reasoning to her, but alas that cannot be. She has obviously taken a liking to you and you are certainly enough of a gentleman to not want to hurt her feelings."

"Ed, I..."

"Let me add, sir, that Vicky is a very nice, but also a very strong young lady. She is certainly capable of handling the truth. What I am trying to say, sir, is that she is no softy; far from it."

"Are we being recorded?"

"I believe so, yes."

"Well there is another side to the story, but like anything related to a nuclear power operation it is not as simple as ABC. In fact it's more like A to Z only five times over. Therefore I will not try to explain my personal involvement, except to say that I was fully aware that the test would not be successful and damage would be done. The damage was worse than I had expected and that was due to the poor management of the plant. In fact time will tell that even the KGB was concerned about how nuclear plants are mismanaged in the USSR. Now that I have addressed your concern, I will now leave."

Long pause

"Well that was a good guess."

Ed and Vicky turned to Bob. His head nodded and his eyes were open wide.

"As I suspected, there is a message, but only one that a nuclear person would understand. Umarov mentioned the issue was not simple, not like ABC; more like A to Z five times. What he was referring to is the SCRAM emergency system that, if initiated, would insert all control rods into the water to shut down the reactor. This is done by pressing the EP-5 button, also known as the AZ-5 button; A to Z five times! I won't try to get into too much detail, but the bottom line is basic. Nuclear reactors use uranium rods as fuel. Through the process of nuclear fission, heat is generated. Water pumped through the reactor core is heated to create steam. This steam drives turbines, which in turn drive generators. And then, as in all power facilities, the generators create electricity. If the control rods are not inserted correctly into water to cool the system down, the reactor overheats in a fashion that, eventually, is uncontrollable. In such an event the reactor would increase its fuel temperature resulting in a massive steam buildup and rapid increase in steam pressure. Eventually, but quickly, this would cause destruction of the reactor containment…and in the case of Chernobyl, if I am correct, this resulted in the explosion that tore of the roof of the reactor. Like I said, the purpose of the AZ-5 button is to inject shutdown rods into the reactor to rapidly reduce power to zero. If it wasn't pressed or if it was pressed at the wrong time…" He didn't have to finish the sentence.

"I have no idea what to ask." Ed said honestly.

"Was the AZ-5 button pressed?" Vicky asked.

Bob motioned uncertainty with his hands. "I have absolutely no idea, and that won't be known for some time. But the point, or the clue, that Mr. Umarov is offering is that the explosion had something to do with the AZ-5 button. That is a significant clue. It narrows the question of where to look, but it certainly doesn't tell us exactly what to look for." He turned to Ed. "And I most certainly don't know what to do with this added information."

Ed took over. "Not a problem. We know where to start; England." He picked up the phone and dialed.

Bob turned to Vicky. "A travel agency?"

"No," she smiled.

"A life insurance company, perhaps?"

She shook her head, maintaining her smile.

The phone rang several times at the other end, before a tired sounding Carolyn answered.

"I wonder who this might be at two twelve in the morning."

"Us again," Ed said, knowing that was obvious. "But we do have something very serious to pass on to you. Robert Helbrecht has heard the tapes from the cruise, and is sure he has some very good news for our assignment."

Carolyn slipped out of bed. "Give me five minutes and we'll be in the office."

Ed replied quickly. "I think you should record the conversation. It's likely to be very technical in nature and while it won't all make sense to those in the room, it will make sense to a nuclear physicist… or whomever."

"Done," she replied. "Five minutes."

Ed turned to Bob. "We will be speaking to a department in the British Foreign Office. Because of the political circumstances in the USSR, their government – or more to the point Gorbachev – has asked for outside help in dealing with concerns of a potential second nuclear 'accident' in Ukraine."

Bob nodded his understanding.

The line came alive, it was Lord Stonebridge.

"Good morning, Mr. Crowe. Always nice to hear from you… especially at this time of the day."

Ed grimaced. "Thank you, sir. I am here with Miss Kilgour and Mr. Robert Helbrecht, of whom you are aware. Just to summarize, sir. Mr. Helbrecht heard the tapes this morning and upon reflection this evening, he wanted to hear them once more. This just took place, and he is sure he has some news which was, once again, hidden in a clue by Mr. Umarov." He handed the phone to Bob. "You are speaking to Lord Stonebridge the head of the British Secret Service; better known as MI6."

Bob looked surprised and took the phone. "Good morning, sir. It is a pleasure to speak to you."

"It is our pleasure, Mr. Helbrecht. Please proceed. As you know this conversation is being recorded, so don't be concerned about my understanding of your message. Please be as technical as you need to be."

Bob swallowed to clear his throat and began. "Well, sir, here's what I believe…"

Bob spoke close to fifteen minutes using words and terminologies that meant nothing to Ed or Vicky. They just listened. During the conversation, Ed gently pointed to Vicky's dress and gave her a thumbs up. She sniffed her lack of interest in his opinion.

Toward the end of the conversation, Bob answered a couple of questions, thanked Lord Stonebridge and pass the phone back to Ed.

"What do you think, sir?"

"I think, Mr. Crowe, that we have just come a great deal closer to resolving the 'More to come' issue. I will report this to the prime minister, and through her we will contact whomever Mr. Gorbachev tells us to get this important information to. A job well done to both you and Miss Kilgour. And I now have to rush." They hung up.

"Now what?" Bob asked.

Ed shrugged. "Well it's Friday night, and I doubt you can get hold of your boss, but I would up-date him as soon as you can as to what you think and what is happening in England. Would you like to join us for a bite to eat?"

Bob shook his head. "I'll pass thanks. If you could get me a cab, I'll head back to downtown Toronto and get an early night."

Ed phoned for a cab, they all shook hands and Bob left, still wondering about the whole somewhat loose process.

Ed could see Vicky was not amused. She stood with her back to the window with her arms crossed. Instead of starting the conversation he opened the fridge and took out the bottle of wine, now just the right temperature. He held it up.

"Shall we?" he asked smiling.

"I thought we were going to eat."

"Yes, yes we are," Ed replied opening the wine. "I'm going to make us a pizza."

She laughed. "You're going to make us a pizza. That's funny. You mean you're going to take a frozen pizza out of the freezer, and pop it into the oven, right?"

He shook his head, handing her a glass of wine, motioning for her to sit with him on the sofa. She sat on the loveseat. "No, I'm going to make it myself. I recently bought a dough maker, and I have the instructions for pizza dough." He gave her a wide grin. "You see, you make lots of dough by selling life insurance, and I make small amounts of dough for a pizza for my good friend Vicky."

She shook her head not replying to his comment. "And just how long does it take to make a pizza for your good friend?"

"About two hours."

"What! Two hours. What the heck are we going to do for two hours?"

He thought, rubbing his chin dramatically. "Well I could come over and join you..."

"No."

"You could..."

"No."

"We could..."

"Are you going to get the dough going, or we'll be eating at midnight?"

He jumped up, moved quickly to the kitchen area and started working on the dough. Vicky topped up their wine, enjoying watching him pull together all of the ingredients in his new machine.

"You ever done this before?" she asked.

"Nope. First time." He pressed the button to start the process for dough. "In an hour and twenty minutes, we'll be ready to roll the dough and move on to cooking."

They sat down again, looking across the room from each other.

"Nice wine," she said.

He took a sip and nodded his agreement. "Only the best for my friend Vicky. I spoke to the wine person and she recommended it."

"Sommelier." Vicky added.

"No, it's a Pinot Grigio."

She banged her head in frustration. "Not that. I meant..."

"I know what you meant," he grinned. "It's just fun getting you upset sometimes."

She tried not to smile, but she couldn't hold it back. "I'll make you a deal. If I can convince you to take me to your bedroom and make mad passionate love to me, I'll show you something very interesting."

He stood up and reached for her hand. "If we make mad passionate love, I'll have seen everything interesting I'd want to see for a long time to come."

She took his hand. "Hmmm. Speaking of coming."

He took her in his arms. "God you're beautiful, Vicky. Both physically and emotionally."

She reached up and kissed his cheek. "Let's do the physical thing first, and then worry about the emotions, eh?"

Ed did as he was told.

Thirty minutes later they were laying naked in each others arms with just a bed sheet covering them. Their love making had started slowly but ended with them both happily exhausted.

"Not bad, eh?" Vicky said.

"Better than good," Ed replied, kissing her forehead.

Suddenly a loud bumping noise had Ed sit up and throw off the bed sheet. "What the hell is that?"

"That, my friend," Vicky said, covering herself up, "is the difference between a teaspoon and a tablespoon of yeast."

"Shit," Ed said, running naked to the kitchen area. The dough maker was pouring semi-liquid dough out of the machine and onto the counter. He ran to the machine un-plugged it, grabbed some paper towels and started cleaning up.

Vicky stood at the bedroom door, covering herself with Ed's housecoat. "I could have told you," she said coyly, "but it's just fun watching you get upset sometimes."

Ed knew when he was beaten. He turned and bowed to the winner.

Vicky continued with a smile. "Clean up, get dressed and I'll treat you to a late dinner at a nice restaurant…with my dough."

CHAPTER TWENTY-THREE

There were few other customers at the restaurant Vicky had selected, so they could enjoy a casual, relaxed meal with few interruptions. To Ed's surprise Vicky ordered a bottle of red wine, and at a price that was not in his normal price range.

"Cheers," he said raising his glass.

"Cheers indeed," Vicky replied, taking a sip. "I know this is expensive, but I did want to thank you for the song and the 'other' part of the evening."

"My pleasure," Ed added. "And I do mean my pleasure." He leaned forward and whispered. "I do love sucking on you breasts…"

"Stop that, Ed," Vicky interrupted, "you'll get me all excited again."

Ed shrugged. "Whatever turns you on."

Vicky raised her hand. "Okay stop this now. I told you before I'd show you something interesting if you made mad, passionate blah, blah, blah, to me. Since you met that commitment, here's my end of the deal." She opened her small purse and pulled out an envelope. Seemingly reluctantly she offered it o Ed. "This is the full note from Alex. I think it's only fair that you see it; you're being the leader of the assignment and all."

Ed took the envelope reluctantly. "Are you sure?"

"Read it quickly or I'll take it back!"

Ed opened the envelope and unfolded the note. He read it to himself:

Dear Miss Vicky

40 7 30 30 9 30 4 30 5 9

Numbers are clever. They can be added to make more and less. You are a wonderful person to have befriended me, given what you knew. I enjoyed your company, our conversations, our glasses of wine and more. I wish we could have been alone together longer to enjoy these even more, and perhaps finally-some unmet natural desires…and you.

Thank you and farewell.

Alex

Ed re-read the note several times, his mind spinning. He closed his eyes to think. He didn't want to open them to see Vicky.

"Ed, what's the matter?" Vicky asked, not caring who heard.

He raised his finger to his mouth. "There's something..."

"Of course there's something for crying out loud. He wanted to make love to me. I knew that, you knew that. Just because he wrote it doesn't..."

He quickly reached over and took her hand as tears rolled down her cheek. "Vicky…"

She snapped back. "And no, I wasn't thinking of him earlier this evening. Oh my God."

Ed counted to ten, not letting go of her hand as she tried to pull away.

"Vicky, please listen. It's not what you're thinking. Of course he wanted to make love to you. He makes that clear. And, Vicky, he did it in such a lovely way as only Alex could." He squeezed her hand. "But he also gave you a final clue while expressing his love."

She sat up, wiping her eyes. "Where?"

He pointed to the last part of the note, and read it out loud. "And finally – some unmet natural desires – and you." He waited, but she shook her head in silence. "It's a crossword process; it's 'final', now look at the beginning of each word after that." It took only a second. "Sunday! Oh for God's sake, it's this Sunday." She bowed her head briefly then looked up. "Okay I missed that. Now what do we do?"

"Let's make the phone call. There's nothing else we can do." He took out his cell phone. "I've never used this to phone overseas, let's see if it works." He dialed the number for Stonebridge Manor.

Carolyn answered "This must be serious."

"It is," Ed replied. "Vicky just found a clue in the personal part of the note from Alex. It's this Sunday. We're sure it's a clue. Rather complex process, but that's Alex."

"Well done, both of you. I won't get Lord Stonebridge on the line. I'll take it from here. If it's not too late, grab yourselves a glass of wine. You deserve it. I've got to run. Bye now." They hung up.

Vicky shook her head. "You can be such a liar."

He smiled. "Coming from you, that's a compliment. Let's take Carolyn's advice and enjoy the…"

His cell phone rang. "I forgot to tell you," Carolyn said quickly, "it's reactor three. When I said the co-ordinates were precise and down to the yard, we didn't realize how accurate that comment was. Bye again." She hung up.

Ed shook his head in amazement. "The AZ-5 button, this Sunday, and it's reactor three. That's…that's…"

"Effing amazing," Vicky added finishing off his thoughts. "Pour the wine, bloke. I think we might need another bottle."

They decided to pass on another bottle of wine at the restaurant, and Vicky drove carefully back to Ed's apartment. She agreed to come up for a cup of tea, but when they sat down, they decided on another glass of wine. They sipped it slowly, both reminiscing about what had occurred in the past couple of weeks.

"It's Saturday in Ukraine, you know?" Vicky observed, stating the obvious.

Ed nodded. "Yes, it is. Surely there's something we can do."

"Pray?"

"No thanks, I'm not into that."

"Me neither."

She raised her glass in a toast. "Thanks for lying, by the way. It was foolish of me not to share the full note from Alex earlier."

He nodded his understanding. "I chose my words carefully. I said you found the clue, which you kinda did."

She gave him a questioning look, but decided not to drag the conversation any deeper.

They sat across the room from each other, neither knowing what to say or do. Finally Ed stood up and reached for her hand. "Okay let's do something."

She looked at his hand, but didn't take it. "Like what?"

"Well, we could go into my bedroom…"

"No."

"Or I could come over there…"

"No."

"You didn't let me finish."

"Finish."

"I could come over there, take you by the hand and do what every young Canadian couple wants to do given the current circumstances."

She grinned. "You're going to take me to Tim Hortons for a double-double."

"Exactly what I had in mind," he lied.

As they headed for the door, Ed had a thought. "Now if we went into the bedroom, we could both have a double-double. You know, twice in one day."

Vicky shook her head and opened the door to the hallway. "E. for effort, bloke. A Tims is hotter and lasts longer."

"Ouch!"

Their departure was interrupted by his land-line phone ringing. He looked at his watch. "I had better take it," he said turning.

"Maybe a girlfriend?" Vicky asked cheekily.

Shaking his head, he answered. "Crowe's nest."

It was Pat. "Houston, we have a problem."

"Just a minute, Boss," he replied, waving for Vicky to come back into the room and close the door. She did so, knowing it wasn't a girlfriend; it was business.

Ed walked over to Vicky so that they could both hear the message. "Go ahead, Boss. Slim is here and listening."

Vicky interrupted. "Pat, you're on your honeymoon!"

"Not an issue, Vicky. This won't take long, and what I'm going to tell you is happening in Canada, so I had to get involved. It can't be handled from the manor. First I want you to know that I am up-to-date on your recent conversation with Miss. All very good news, and well done. The problem we have at hand is the KGB; or at least some of their rogue members. To cut to the chase we found out that the stateroom steward for Mr. Umarov was contacted by these KGB members and, with the help of a few bucks, they were able to determine the, shall I say, friendship between him and Vicky. And before you ask, we found out by the same method. He won't need to work cruise ships after he finishes his tour. But the point is we now know that there are three KGB agents in Canada..."

"Looking for me," Vicky added.

"Exactly," Pat continued, "but hear me out. They want you to tell them what you know; that being that Mr. Umarov - the Chechen Mr. Umarov that is - was responsible for what happened in Chernobyl."

"Oh shit," Ed said. "They want to expand their hate against the Chechen people."

"Correct," Pat said quickly. "But there is a time limit to their goal. On Sunday Gorbachev, as General Secretary of the Communist Party will be speaking to over a thousand delegates. He will be stating clearly that Chernobyl was an accident, precipitated by bad planning and mismanagement. He will also outline significant changes to their nuclear program. Any information that would upset that planned speech would be..."

"A disaster." Ed finished.

"Correct again," Pat said, "an absolute disaster."

"Where are the agents now?" Ed asked.

"They flew into Toronto this afternoon, they've rented a van and the last time the van was seen it was headed west; toward Oakville. And you'll never believe the colour of the van."

"Red!" Vicky laughed. "A red van."

Pat smiled. "That's correct, and they tried every car rental agency to get a van that was not red, but alas. So here's the plan. First, Mister; you have to protect Slim for the next thirty-six hours. You will receive some assistance shortly in the form of a pizza delivery. Slim; I know you're your own strong person, but this is business. Mister has more authority than you do to, let's say, break the law. Okay?"

Vicky nodded vigorously. "I'm with you, Boss. In fact I should perhaps say; I'm with you, Mister. Boss, we were just about to go out for a Tims double-double. Is that not safe now?"

"Hmm. I'd wait until you get the pizza delivery before you go out. Having said that, the two of you do want to move around. Staying in one place is not a good idea, even Crowe's nest. Mister, you have my cell number. Phone if you need to. Whenever it rings, Roy goes for a walk. The two of you together for another thirty-six hours should be fun, eh?" They could feel the grin on her face. They all said their good-byes and hung up.

They took their seats across the room from each other, neither sure what to say. Finally Vicky broke the silence.

"No double-double in your bedroom tonight, bloke."

"No indeed. So aren't you just a little scared? I know I am."

She thought about his question seriously before she replied. "Let's see what the pizza brings us. I suspect it's not pepperoni and mushroom."

As she spoke there was a knock on the door. Ed motioned for Vicky to stay away from the door and walked over and opened it. The man was tall and husky. He wore a loose fitting suit. Not your average pizza delivery man. He handed Ed a large pizza box. He spoke seriously. "I'd suggest you tell your friends in the lobby not to open the door to pizza delivery people." He turned and left.

Ed walked the pizza box over to the kitchen table and Vicky joined him. He shook it gently. "It's full of pepperoni."

Vicky gave him a look. "How do you know that?"

"Because there's not much room inside." He couldn't stop himself from laughing, almost dropping the box.

Vicky's mouth dropped open; she couldn't believe what she was hearing. "Not much room..." she groaned. "Here we are concerned about the KGB, and you're cracking jokes." But she couldn't stop herself from smiling. "Open the thing, for crying out loud...or I will; cry out loud that is."

Putting the box on the table, Ed lifted the lid. Sitting in the middle of the box, surrounded by its holder, was a hand gun.

Vicky stepped back. "What the hell...?"

"It's a Smith and Wesson, Model 36, probably the most popular handgun in the world."

She briefly closed her eyes trying to understand what was happening. "Have you ever used one of these things?" she asked gently.

Ed nodded.

"Have you ever...?"

"Killed someone? No."

"Have you ever...forget it, I don't want to know." She took a deep breath. "Are you licensed to carry one of these things in Canada?"

He shrugged. "Knowing Pat as well as I do, I'd be surprised if I'm not licensed as of today."

She looked at him, then at the gun, and then back to him. "Now what?"

"We go for coffee."

"All three of us?"

"All three of us."

"Well at least I can honestly tell my parents that just the two of us didn't spend the weekend together."

Ed picked up the pizza box and walked into his bedroom to arm himself. When he returned, he was wearing a thin spring jacket. When they reached to hallway door, she turned to him and gave him a hug, feeling for the gun around his waist. She felt nothing.

"You wearing it?" she asked.

"Yeah, it's on the inside upper-part of my leg."

"Yuck! I'm not reaching down there."

He grinned. "Neither should you. It's a dangerous weapon."

She grinned back. "So is the gun."

They laughed and left for Tim Hortons.

The Tim Hortons was quiet and relaxing. Most people were home watching television, or partying on their Friday night escape. The customers were mostly older and probably regular to this store. It was comforting.

Vicky leaned forward to speak quietly so only Ed could hear. "You know I feel rather overdressed. Why don't we go to my place and let me get a change of clothes, or two."

Ed nodded. "While I think you look quite lovely, that's probably a good idea. If we're going to keep on the move for a while you might as well get comfortable. Maybe I could help you select your undies?"

She shook her head, finished her coffee and stood to leave. "Let's go, Mister."

"Yes, yes, you're right of course. It's business, Slim. Let's go and not be found; at least by those KGB types."

They left for Vicky's, keeping their eyes out for a red van.

While Vicky was up in her bedroom changing and packing some additional clothes, Ed spoke with her father. Mr. Kilgour asked questions about the wedding and the cruise Ed and Vicky had been on. Ed lied about the details of the cruise, knowing that Mr. Kilgour didn't expect the truth. His knowledge of Ed's 'Honeymoon' with Pat to Paris that had erupted in street fights was not done as a travel agent. He nodded and simply accepted the facts as Ed explained them. More importantly his daughter had changed considerably since she had met and travelled with Ed, and that was most certainly good news. She was not now limiting her time and thoughts to life insurance sales, but was socializing more which was reflected in her day to day approach to life; more positive, greater interest in friends and family. He was a very happy father. Mr. Kilgour offered Ed a glass of scotch which Ed declined with thanks, just a Vicky joined them. She was now wearing slacks; a woolen sweater buttoned to the top, and had a small travelling bag.

"Okay, Mr. Crowe, let's go see Niagara Falls at midnight." She turned to her father. "We'll likely be up all night, so tell Mother not to worry."

Mr. Kilgour gave her an uncharacteristic hug and wished them a fine weekend. They left and jumped into Vicky's car. She turned to Ed. "What did you say to my father that had him give me a hug? That's not like him."

"I just told him we were eloping."

She turned sharply to face him. "I hope that's a bloody joke, Ed!"

He kissed her quickly on her forehead. "Of course I didn't. And if I had, he wouldn't have believed me. He knows you'd never marry me."

She turned away and faced forward. After thirty seconds, which seemed like a lifetime, she spoke calmly and clearly. "Ed, that conversation is over. Period. Don't apologize, which you should, just nod that you understand what I just said."

He nodded, wanting desperately to apologize.

"Okay," she smiled, "where are we going, and what are we going to do to keep ourselves motivated and awake?"

"You've got a change of clothes, so let's drop by my place and I'll grab a change also."

She started the car. "Maybe I could help you select your undies?"

His head dropped. "Vicky, I am so…"

"The nod was enough," she interrupted, and drove away at a good speed to Ed's apartment.

Vicky waited downstairs while Ed ran up to pack a bag. She turned up the music to keep her mind away from the earlier conversation. When Ed returned he threw his back into the back of the car and jumped in.

"You said Niagara Falls," he beamed, "so let's go to Niagara Falls."

Vicky nodded and headed off to pick up the QEW. As she turned onto Lakeshore, two blocks behind them a red van started and carefully started to trail them.

CHAPTER TWENTY-FOUR

The drive to the Falls was easy driving once they were past the busy city of Hamilton. They listened to the latest hits, and Ed made sure he didn't make any comment when they played The Moody Blues, 'Your Wildest Dreams'. Vicky didn't let it pass.

"Thinking of Carolyn are you, bloke?"

"Carolyn who?"

"Very funny."

"Oh, you mean the Carolyn that I said I would ask to marry me on October 29th 1989?"

"What! You've asked her to marry you! You said…"

Ed raised his hand to calm things down. "What I mean is that I told her I would ask her on that date, and before you ask, I said that on that same date, five years earlier – in 1984."

Vicky slowed down to get a better control over both her driving and her temper. "So what changed your mind when you decided to ask her, or not ask her, after Pat's wedding?"

"Well I mentioned before the family issues are real, and I'm not sure either of us are ready to be engaged. Certainly not with her job at MI6 and my consulting with MI6. It just didn't make sense."

Vicky pulled the car over to the right side of the QEW and put on her emergency flashes. "So tell me in detail, please, exactly what you did say when the two of you met after the wedding. And I do mean in detail."

"Well she asked me if I had a question for her, and..."

"This was after you ...you know."

Ed nodded. "Yes, after. She asked me if I had a question for her, I said yes, and then I asked her if we could put off any 'engaging' questions until October in 1989."

"Engaging questions; very clever. And?"

Ed replied looking straight ahead, not wanting to face Vicky. "She agreed. Now I'm not sure she was totally happy, because if I had asked her to marry me, I'm almost positive she would have said no."

"Oh shit!" Vicky exclaimed loudly.

He turned to face her. "What? It wasn't that bad..."

"Listen, Mister," Vicky said, pointing through the front window, "your wishy-washy decision making process just resulted in a red van passing us, no doubt 'the' red van. Hang onto your seat." She put the car in gear and pulled back onto the highway picking up speed as fast as she could. "Now we've got you, our KGB chums, on the run. Now we've got you." She giggled in delight.

Ed appreciated the luck. "That's great, Slim, but what are we going to do with them?"

Vicky took her foot off the gas somewhat. "Good question. I don't know. I'm just the driver. You tell me."

Ed thought about the situation for a few moments, and came up with an idea. "Let's make sure, as best we can, that the red van ahead of us is the KGB van. He's slowed down and in the right lane. He obviously wants to get behind us. So speed up enough to pass him in the second lane, but not too fast. In the meantime adjust the side mirror on the passenger side so that as we pass it, we can see inside the front widow of the van."

"Eww, very clever," Vicky said adjusting the mirror, "aren't you a sly one. Almost a spy perhaps?"

Vicky passed the red van, not looking at the side mirror until they had passed the van be fifteen feet. "Looks like a couple of big guys to me," she said. "I think that's them."

Ed looked and nodded. "I agree. Let's speed up a bit more and just keep them in your rear view mirror. I don't want them to see me turning around to look."

"Got it." She speeded up. "That was clever thinking, by the way." She paused. "Now what?"

Ed scratched his chin. "Let me think out loud. They got into the country, so they're not known as bad guys. The chance of them having guns is most unlikely. The message we got was they wanted to have you identify Alex as the person that helped blow up Chernobyl; by that I mean they don't want to hurt you, except perhaps to scare you into telling them what they want to hear. From what Pat said, police and others are also looking out for them, although there is nothing they can do to them. So perhaps we keep our distance, enjoy a couple of bad nights' sleep, and enjoy each others company – professionally that is." He turned to Vicky. "Whaddaya think?"

She thought about his comments, hoping he was correct, but she didn't think he was. "Why did Pat get a gun to you? They may not have guns, but they could easily have purchased a couple of Crocodile Dundee knives. You know, 'That's not a knife, THIS is a knife.' And while I may enjoy your company for an extended time, I do need to a change of clothes once in a while. I suggest we meet with them face-to-face in a location and environment where we feel comfortable. Let them ask me what they want to ask me. I tell them I won't, and they go home saying they did their best; outdone by a life insurance agent and a travel agent." She turned to him with a sly smile.

"Well, let me see," Ed said slowly, "perhaps we should meet them in a Tim Hortons, buy them a coffee and tell them we, you, know nothing about a man named Alex. Then maybe, just maybe, you could sell them some Whole Life Insurance with a Guaranteed Purchase Option; just like you sold me."

Vicky replied quickly. "Maybe I should sell them life insurance. At least they will admit to being in the spying business, which is more than *you* told me; even if it's part-time. So there!"

"Yeah, but…"

Vicky interrupted. "And if you do get bumped off on your part-time role and the insurance company finds out about you, they will not pay the claim. And even worse I will have to refund my commissions. So double there!"

Ed chuckled, reached over and squeezed her arm. "You win." He thought some more. "Although I do like the idea of meeting them face-to-face – on our terms. And before you say it, I don't mean Term Insurance."

"You and your play on words. It's something I will always remember you by."

"Good bye?"

She shook her head, not bothering to respond.

They drove carefully along the highway, both wondering what their actual next steps should be. Doing nothing was not an option, of that they were both certain.

Vicky spoke first. "Seriously, where is the gun? I know it can't be strapped to your leg."

"It's strapped to my side, just below my left armpit. I'm no expert, but should the occasion arise it would only take a second or two to have it ready to use. I've used a gun before, but I'm no James Bond."

"No indeed." She managed to keep a straight face.

Driving on they passed a sign indicating Niagara Falls was twenty kilometers further. An idea flowed into Ed's head. It made sense, and he hoped it would work.

He turned to Vicky and started singing;

'*Somewhere over the rainbow, way up high*
There's a land that I've heard of once in a lullaby..'

Vicky managed to keep her eyes on the road, but took her foot of the gas to slow down a little.

"What the hell are you singing for? This is serious..."

Ed interrupted. "Where are we going, Slim?"

"Niagara Falls. So?"

He started singing again:

'Somewhere over the rainbow...'

Vicky laughed aloud. "Of course, of course! We're heading over the Rainbow Bridge to the US. You're a very sneaky man, Mister."

"I try my best. You obviously have your driver's license. I have mine, and I also have my Canadian Citizenship card. We're good to go!"

Vicky picked up speed, now looking forward to getting rid of their Russian friends, and spending a good night's sleep in the real Land of Oz. They both started humming their now favorite song.

Vicky kept her eyes on the rearview mirror, seeing the red van keeping a good distance but clearly still following them. When they arrived at the 420 exit, they turned left onto it, heading for The Falls. Vicky reduced her speed. She didn't want to get a speeding ticket now, and speeding was one of her bad habits. They drove slowly through the not-so-busy tourist area on the outskirts of the town. When they arrived at the Rainbow Bridge entrance Vicky took a sharp left onto the bridge and followed it across the Niagara River to the US Customs booths. To their surprise the red van followed them across the bridge.

"Here we go," Vicky said as she looked for the least amount of traffic at the booths and pulled up behind the one car ahead of them on a very slow night of traffic.

The Customs officer, dressed in full uniform and no doubt with access to a gun, asked the usual information; where are they going, how long for, and proof of citizenship. He took their driver's licenses and Ed's citizenship card. He spent some time on Ed's card, obviously entering the data from the card into a computer. He waited for a response, returned the documentation and looking directly at Ed nodded and wished them a nice day.

"What was all that about?" Vicky asked, putting the car in drive.

Ed shrugged.

They drove about a hundred yards into the parking-lot size area of entry when Vicky slammed on the brakes. Ahead of them, blocking their way was the red van. The front doors were wide open and two men stood next to the van. The one standing directly in front of the van had his hands raised and a forced smile on his face. He was tall and slim. The other man was shorter and much larger. He didn't smile at all and kept his hands behind his back.

Vicky spoke slowly. "I think the expression 'Oh shit' fits the situation we are in. Now what?"

Ed unnecessarily squeezed his left arm to his body, confirming his gun was still in place. "Let's get out and meet our Russian associates. Stay on your side of the car and take a step away from the car. We want to be as far apart as we can."

Vicky nodded, put the car in park and turned off the engine. They both got out of the car and took an additional step sideways. The thin man noticed their actions with a knowing nod.

He spoke with very little accent. "My name is Vladimir. I must speak with the lady. It is important for my country. I am reaching into my pocket for a microphone, do not be disturbed." He reached into his inside jacket pocket and slowly and carefully pulled out a microphone. He took a step closer. "Please tell me that Alexi Umarov told you that he was responsible for the nuclear explosion at Chernobyl. We know that he did it, and we know he told you that was the situation."

Ed moved closer to speak, but Vladimir raised his hand, making it clear he did not want to hear from him. Ed took the step back, slightly further away from the car than before.

Vicky stood just a little taller and spoke clearly. "I met Alex on a cruise ship and we fell in love. He did not mention anything about that most unfortunate accident."

"You lie!" Vladimir screamed.

Vicky kept her calm. "I am a lady, and I do not tell lies. Alex and I were in love and intimate."

Vladimir shook his head. "Intimate, what...?'

"We fucked," Vicky replied in her most ladylike manner. "Do you know what that means, Vladimir?"

"Nyet, nyet," he replied, getting visibly angry. "You must tell me the truth."

Vicky reached for the top button of her sweater and undid it. "He particularly liked my breasts. Would you like to see them?"

Both men turned to look. Vicky undid three more buttons opening the sweater so that her bra and the top of her breasts were clearly visible. She counted to ten in her head and then motioned her head toward Ed. The men turned to see Ed holding his gun in his outstretched arm, pointing it straight to Vladimir's crotch. Vladimir raised his hands, making it clear he wasn't going to respond physically.

"Tell him to bring his hands up front," Ed demanded.

Vladimir thought for a moment and then spoke to his associate in Russian. The man waited, visibly annoyed at the situation. He began to bring his hands forward, and then in a flash ran headlong toward Ed, with a small baseball bat raised to kill.

In a second Ed turned his gun on him, aimed at his left leg and pulled the trigger. A second later it was aimed back at Vladimir's crotch. While the man on the ground rolled around in agony, everyone else kept their spots. Behind them there was a scream of sirens as police and custom officers ran and drove toward them. Thirty seconds later they were surrounded by fifteen officers all with their guns drawn. Ed carefully bent down and laid his gun on the ground.

No one moved or spoke, while the man on the ground screamed in Russian for help. After several minutes the customs officer who had passed Ed and Vicky through security walked up with another officer whose uniform made it clear he was the senior officer. He looked around at the situation, motioned for the man on the ground to be looked after medically and walked over to Ed. He motioned for Ed to join him further from the crowd.

"What goes on here, Crowe?" he demanded.

"There may be a third man in the van" Ed explained. "He may be dangerous."

The customs officer shouted instructions to the police and they moved carefully to the van, and searched it. They shook their heads indicating that is was empty.

Ed continued his explanation. "These men are Russian, members of the KGB. It's a long story, but they want my friend here to give them some information as it relates to the Chernobyl nuclear explosion."

The office looked over his glasses. "They are Canadian. They have Canadian passports."

"Really," Ed said, obviously surprised at the comment. "I can assure you, sir, they are not Canadian, and their Canadian passports are false. They have entered your country under false pretenses."

"As have you?"

Ed shrugged. "Only to the extent that we didn't tell your officer that we were being followed by KGB agents. And to be frank, we didn't even think they would get across the border, and neither did we expect your officer to believe us if we told him that we were being followed by the KGB. Sorry."

"Sorry doesn't really do it, does it? Can you prove any of this?"

Ed reached for his cell phone. "If you would let me make a call, sir, I can have someone in authority contact their counterpart in Washington and they can contact you."

"Go ahead," the officer replied nonchalantly. "It'll make my day."

Reluctantly Ed phoned Pat's number, once more disturbing her honeymoon.

The phone rang and Pat picked it up the first ring. "We were just about to go for an early breakfast," she said. "So tell me where you're at and what I can do for you."

Ed explained the details as quickly as he could, not mentioning the fact that he had shot one of the KGB agents.

"That is interesting," Pat replied after listening to the details. "Why don't you put the senior officer on the phone? I'll need the passport numbers of our guests. I know they arrived on their Soviet passports, so we could be in for some interesting international back-room discussions."

Ed passed his cell phone to the officer. "Her name is Pat," Ed offered.

"Hi, Pat," the officer began. "And your Mister Crowe forgot to tell you that he shot one of the men in the leg." He paused. "Yes, on the outside of the leg. Does that matter?" The man listened, and after a short chuckle, he headed off to get the passport numbers. On his way, he gave instructions for Vladimir to be put in a cell and the second man to join him as soon as he had returned from medical attention. As he left Vicky walked over to Ed.

"You know we weren't, don't you? Intimate I mean."

"Of course. This job can make it easy to tell lies sometimes. Often actually."

"Thanks. So where are we?"

'Somewhere over the rainbow...'

"Shut up, Ed. Where are we, Mister?"

Ed explained his call to Pat, indicating that he thought the matter at hand would be over in an hour or two, and they could then get on their way home. Just as Ed finished explaining the senior officer returned. He picked up Ed's gun and gave it to him.

He nodded to Ed, returning his cell phone. "You can both go now. And by the way we aren't trained down here to shoot a person in the leg, preferably on the outside where there are fewer veins and arteries. I'll suggest that at our next management committee and see what they say." He laughed and walked away.

Vicky shrugged her lack of understanding.

"I'll tell you later."

They jumped in the car, turned it around and headed back to Canada.

CHAPTER TWENTY-FIVE

After they crossed the border back into Canada, they headed to the closest Tim Hortons. As they drove, both were reluctant to speak about what had just happened; they needed to let reality set in. Ed was pleased with the results, while Vicky was adjusting to seeing someone shot in such unusual circumstances. Ed collected the coffee and they sat in the corner of the near empty Tims. He raised his coffee in celebration.

"Not a bad outcome, eh?" he offered.

Vicky looked him straight in the eyes. "Not bad? How the hell do you get there?"

He leaned forward and spoke quietly. "Look, I'm not proud of the fact that I shot a man, but he'll be fine. Heck he's going to get much better medical treatment than he would in Russia." He chuckled.

"That's not funny."

"Okay, it's not funny, but it is likely accurate. But, Vicky, the big picture. The bad guys are in the US, and for the CIA, FBI, or whomever, that is a grand opportunity to help Gorbachev. They'll be used as pawns so the US, and perhaps Canada, will gain some brownie points. They'll be okay back home, since they crossed into the US to do their job and got shot in the process. Sure Gorbachev didn't authorize this, but that's the point. He can now use this event to work in his favor."

"Maybe."

Ed shrugged. "Time will tell. But what matters more at this time is whether or not the experts have figured out the issues surrounding Reactor 3 in Ukraine. All I can say is that we did our part, and a large part of our success was your doing."

"By exposing my breasts!"

"Really? I didn't look."

"Well that's a change."

Ed laughed. "Oh, I wanted to. It's been a while."

"Shut up, Ed." She leaned forward. "Okay since I am now somewhat a part of your part-time business affairs, I'd like to ask you a question, and I expect an honest answer."

"If I can."

She squinted at him to make her point. "Oh, you can. On your left side, just above your waist there is a rather large scar. Is that from a gun shot wound?"

He rolled his head thinking, deciding whether it was safe to tell the truth. "Yes it is."

"And how did it happen?"

"Ahh, now that's another question."

"Listen, Mister, I want and expect a second answer, and more if need be."

He decided she was deserving of the truth. "It happened in Libya. Colonel Gaddafi shot me to show to his soldiers that he'd killed me because they thought I had killed one of them, which I hadn't – although I had shot him. Before shooting me he had drugged me, so I appeared dead when they sent me back in a body bag. I was in hospital for several days, and then fully recovered."

Vicky listened with her hands covering her face. She knew he wouldn't make up a story like this one, especially since she had seen his passport which had stamps to prove he had made a trip to Libya.

"Oh my God," she gasped. "Have you shot anyone else, other than today?"

"Yes. End of answers."

She took a gulp of her coffee. "End of questions! Take me home please."

"You're driving."

"Right, right. Let's go. I'll drive you home."

They moved quickly to the car and she drove carefully, but as quickly as the traffic allowed. They didn't speak for twenty minutes, and then Vicky broke the silence.

"By the way, you broke the law today."

He turned to her. "I did?"

"You brought a bloody hand gun into Canada without declaring it! You can't do that."

He cringed. "You 'shouldn't' do that."

She shook her head. "There's no place like home, there's no place like home."

He grinned. "Same movie."

She couldn't help but laugh. "Well if I'm Dorothy, who are you?"

"Toto. The cute one with a wiggly tail."

She laughed louder. "Okay, bloke, your new secret name is Toto!"

They drove home feeling safe and relaxed after their short but successful trip to the U.S. Ed was glad to see Vicky visibly more comfortable with what had happened and what he had told her about his scar. She was now one of the few that knew what had happened, and he was pleased with himself that he could tell her the truth about the shooting without having to tell her any more details of the assignment. They were now closer professionally, and that was comforting to him.

She pulled up in front of his apartment building, not parking her car.

"Good night, Ed," she said.

"Aren't you coming up…?"

"No thanks."

"Glass of celebratory wine?"

She shook her head. "Thanks, but no."

"How about a cuppa tea with your new friend Toto?"

"Okay then, but just a cup of tea. No personal stuff. Toto keeps his wiggly tail to himself." She drove to the parking area and they headed up to his apartment.

As they entered his apartment the phone in the kitchen area rang. He rushed over to answer it.

"Crowe's nest,"

It was Carolyn. "Good evening, Ed. I have some good news."

"So do I," he added.

He could hear her chuckle. "You tell me yours and then I'll tell you mine."

As he spoke he motioned for Vicky to put on the kettle, and turned on the speaker on the phone. "Slim and I have just returned from a very short but very successful trip to the United States of America. Have you spoken to Pat recently?"

"Yes, she updated me about the visiting agents, and the special pizza delivery."

Ed spoke carefully. "Good. We met the agents across the US border and shared the pizza with them. One got a bit sick, but he'll be all right. Two of them are now chatting to some of our US associates. Apparently there were some issues with their Canadian passports. We are not aware of where the third man is."

"Really? Very interesting."

"We are just about to enjoy a cup of tea, hopefully to toast your good news."

"Well I can report that a great number of international discussions have been held regarding potential events in Ukraine and the USSR in general. Your Mister Helbrecht has been on the phone several times with staff from Reactor 3, and after hearing him out, they had contact with the Politburo in Moscow and they got the go ahead to proceed with the agreed upon process. I won't go into all of the technical discussions, but as was suspected it was the AZ-5 button that would have created, let me say, a 'More to come' situation. Let me read you part of the report that somehow may make sense:

'The design at Reactor 3 of the EPS-5 button – also known as the AZ-5 button - was flawed and this had to be done intentionally. Applying the button was designed, in situations where the entire reactor system was overheating, to engage the drive mechanism of insertion of all graphite control rods into the reactor core to reduce the heat build up. In the case of Reactor 3, the control rods would not have fully entered the fuel pile. The result of this only-partial entry would result in a significant steam build up of uncontrollable heat and eventual explosion. The EPS-5 button at Reactor 3 has been disabled and will be replaced as quickly as possible with assistance and guidance from the International Atomic Energy Agency.'

Me thinks, team, we did the job!" Carolyn concluded.

Ed was dumbfounded and stood with his mouth open. Vicky took the phone from him.

"Hi, Miss, it's me Slim. I think you've just done the impossible; our Mister Crowe is stuck for words."

Carolyn chuckled. "Then the business is done, Vicky. We can go back to being our normal selves. Pinch Ed and bring him back to reality."

Instead of pinching him, she gave him a quick kiss on his cheek and handed him the phone. "Say something clever, Ed."

Ed took a deep breath. "When will it end, eh? All the distrust and hate around the world. I think we took but a minor step today."

Carolyn in England and Vicky standing next to him didn't know what to say. They couldn't think of an appropriate response. It took Lord Stonebridge in England who gently took the phone from Carolyn.

"Well said, Mr. Crowe. Well said." He paused briefly and then spoke more fervently. "On behalf of President Gorbachev I want to thank the three of you for your work on this very important and very difficult assignment. I can assure you that he is aware of exactly what happened, having been updated by both the British and Canadian governments. His thanks are most sincere. As planned, in several hours he will be speaking to a special meeting of the Communist Party's Central Committee regarding Chernobyl, and more interestingly he will address all Soviet citizens, and in fact the world, via television on Wednesday. He will make it clear that Chernobyl was an accident, and further that steps will be taken to ensure that such an accident will never happen again. On Wednesday he will make the very important statement that his telling the world of the circumstances surrounding Chernobyl is a major step in his policy of Glasnost – openness. I must leave you now, the prime minister is on the other line, and Mrs. Thatcher is not one to be kept waiting."

Carolyn came back on the phone a few seconds later. "I do believe Lord Stonebridge is rather chuffed," she said with a smile.

"Thanks, Carolyn," Ed said. "It would be nice if you were here to join us in a celebratory cup of tea."

"That would be lovely," she replied. "Next time, maybe."

They said their good-byes and hung up.

Ed walked to the door to the hallway, took off his jacket and the gun in its holster and hung them in the closet.

"Isn't that thing dangerous?" Vicky asked, pointing to the gun.

"Well it does have a safety catch," Ed replied, nodding his head, "and it is turned on. However I will have to get rid of it toot sweet," he said, walking back to the kitchen area. "Let's have that cuppa, eh?"

Vicky raised her hand. "You realize that toot sweet is a corruption of the French 'tout de suite' which means 'at once', don't you?"

"Of course I do," he lied, pouring the tea. "You know how much we English love the French." He grinned and presented her a cup of tea.

"Conneries!" she replied with a French accent.

"Bottoms up," he said, not wanting to ask.

"Most appropriate," she laughed, and sipped her tea.

They drank their tea, chatting about anything but their now complete assignment. Ed poured them a second cup, and they toasted themselves in silence. Ten minutes later, Vicky put down her cup and stood up straight and proud.

"Okay, bloke, I have to go. I need a good night's sleep. It's gone 2am." She walked around the table, kissed Ed quickly on his cheek and headed for the door.

"But, Vicky," Ed began..."

"Good night, Ed. Keep in touch."

He gave a little wave, accepting the inevitable. "Good night. Drive carefully."

Vicky walked across the room, happy with everything.

Half way to the door, their world changed. The door came crashing open followed by a huge man with both an ugly face and ugly demeanor. It was the third man. He held a small baseball bat high, smashing it on the now broken door. It was unquestionably metal and deadly. Ed stood and shouted for Vicky to move out of the way. "Go to the balcony! Stay out of his way! Phone from there!"

The man wasn't bothered by Vicky's moves; he was clearly and decisively after the male in the room. Ed moved to his right, away from the balcony side of the room and into the small kitchen area. Keeping his eyes on the man, he pulled out a butcher's knife from the knife rack. He held it high waving it to keep the man's attention. Now grinning at the man, he motioned with his finger for him to join him. "Come on Ruskie, let's see how tough you are."

As the man moved slowly toward Ed, Vicky took the opportunity to cautiously move to the broken door. She turned to Ed for direction.

Ed waved the knife at the man, threateningly. "Come on mister' come on." He paused, and keeping his eyes on the man, spoke forcefully to Vicky. "Go for God's sake. Get out of here! Phone for police and an ambulance. Go!"

Reluctantly she headed for the door, and then their world changed again. She silently opened the closet and pulled out the gun. As nervous as she was, she pointed it to the man, and looked at Ed for advice. He shook his head, and motioned for her to leave. That second that it took for Ed to motion to Vicky, the man made his move. He threw the baseball bat at Ed's head as hard as he could. Ed jumped to one side but not quickly enough, the bat hit him on the back of his neck. The man started to turn toward Vicky. Aiming the gun at the man's leg she pulled the trigger. It didn't move. She pressed a small catch on the side of the gun and pulled the trigger again. The gun exploded in her hand and the recoil forced her arm up and the bullet hit the man on the right side of his chest. He stood motionless for a second and then collapsed. She kept the gun on him, ready to fire again if she had to. Carefully she moved closer to him, now hating him and everything he stood for. She wanted him to move so she could shoot him again. He didn't move.

Dropping her arm by her side, she couldn't help but cry at what was in front of her. Ed lay on the floor unconscious, while blood poured from the fat man's chest and dripped onto the floor. "Fuck!" she screamed, "fuck, fuck, fuck!"

His head aching like it had never before Ed slowly sat up not believing what he was seeing. He had to move fast. Unsteady as he was he stood and stumbled more than walked over to Vicky. He took the gun from her, putting his arm around her. "Go home, Vicky. Go home now."

She shook her head. "I shot the bastard. I killed him. Oh my God!"

"He's not dead. Go home."

Vicky shook her head, unable to take her eyes off the man on the floor.

Ed shook her gently. "Slim, go home. Phone for the police and ambulance from the phone in the lobby. Don't leave finger prints. That's an order!"

"Fuck you too," she sobbed, turning to Ed. She wiped her eyes on her sleeves and quickly left the apartment.

Wiping the gun clean of Vicky's prints, he made sure it was now covered with only his prints. Not sure if it would do anything he wiped the end of the barrel with his finger and then spread any remains on his right hand. He needed it to be certain that any testing clearly indicated that he had shot the gun. He turned on the safety, put the gun on the coffee table and walked to the man on the floor. Knowing better than to try to help him in any way, Ed kicked the man's foot. The leg jerked and the large body moved in a shudder.

Ed looked skyward with a thankful nod. He didn't have to wait long before he heard sirens getting close. He sat on the sofa and waited.

In the silence of the room he clearly heard the elevator down the hallway as the doors opened and several people walked toward his apartment. They didn't try to keep quiet; they wanted whoever was in the room to know they had arrived. Then the steps stopped and there was a deadly silence for several seconds.

"Is that you in there, Mister Crowe?" a female voice asked.

He stood and raised his hands above his head. "Yes it is ma'am, and I'm standing with my arms raised."

"Where is the gun?" she asked calmly.

"On the coffee table and safety is on. It's a Smith and Wesson, Model 36."

"Nice gun. Please walk away from the coffee table turn your back to the door and keep your arms raised."

Ed did as he was told. "Ready ma'am."

In they came. Someone grabbed Ed's hands and in a second his hands were handcuffed behind his back. Two male paramedics ran past him to the man on the floor and started working on him, checking his breathing and pulse. They nodded positively to each other. One turned to the police, "He's alive, but bleeding badly." They didn't wait for directions, but started to patch him up and gently move him onto a stretcher. When they carried him out, it was obvious he was very heavy.

The female police officer directed Ed to sit. "What happened?" she asked. A male officer stood next to her taking notes.

Ed took a chance. "Do you know anything of a red van?" he asked politely.

"What kind of a question is that, Mister Crowe?"

Ed shook his head. "Sorry, I was just wondering if..."

She raised her hand, and turned to her associate. "Stop taking notes, Constable...but listen carefully."

He nodded and lowered his note book.

She crossed he arms. Ed noticed her sergeant stripes. "Proceed, Mister Crowe, but be sure to tell us all."

Ed related the story of his and Vicky's activities of the day without going into any background of the assignment, making no direct reference to the KGB. He outlined the events truthfully until their return to his apartment where he stated that 'Miss Kilgour had left his apartment approximately fifteen minutes before the man had barged through the door'. He then told his own outline of his fight with the man and his ultimate shooting of the man in self defense.

The sergeant listened, giving no indication of what she did or didn't believe. "I think, Mister Crowe you should escort me to the local police station." She turned to the constable. "Please remove the handcuffs from Mister Crowe. Then please contact the property manager and get this door fixed as soon as the photographers and SOC investigators have finished." She turned to Ed. "This way please."

The sergeant let Ed follow behind her to let it be known to the crowd in the lobby that he was not in any way under arrest. He waved to those that he knew, but didn't speak. He sat in the back of the police car which had a glass wall between him and the front seats; not an experience he had previously enjoyed, and not one he wanted to duplicate. He felt guilty knowing he had lied to the police, but somehow comforted himself in knowing that Vicky was not involved and that both CSIS and MI6 would ensure his limited involvement with the police; or hoped they would.

CHAPTER TWENTY-SIX

The cell was neither comfortable nor welcoming. It had the basics of a bed, a chair, a toilet, and a sink. Ed was told he would be in the cell for a short time, while a few details of the 'red van' were sorted out at a higher level. After an hour he began to wonder if things would be sorted out as quickly as he had hoped. He didn't want to lie on the bed; that would be accepting the place too much like home. Instead he sat on the bed, leaned his back against the wall and tried sleeping. Finally he nodded off.

He woke and jumped up as soon as he heard the large steel cell door open. He stood straight, expecting the sergeant to give him some good news.

The sergeant stood to one side and Vicky entered the cell, still wearing the same clothes from earlier. She looked around with her nose in the air. "Nice place you've got here. Rent okay?"

"Vicky, what are you doing here for God's sake? I haven't sorted out all the issues yet."

Vicky nodded knowingly. "I know you haven't, but I have." She pointed to the chair. "May I?"

Ed waved for her to sit. "Please. Make yourself at home. Perhaps a nice pot of English Breakfast tea? Some biscuits on the side perchance?"

She sat. "Carolyn asked me to tell you not to be a smarty-pants when I up-dated you. I assume that is the same as a smart-ass for us colonials?"

Ed took a deep breath, understanding he was getting nowhere fast. "What has happened please, Vicky?" He was tempted to call her Slim, but that wouldn't be playing cricket. She had the upper hand.

Vicky put her hands in her lap and turned serious. "I went straight home after I left your place. I didn't need to make a phone call; the place was already in high gear. The crash of your door and the shot had people heading for the lobby. It was full of your neighbors. I left through the back door, jumped into my car and headed for home. The police and ambulance were already within hearing distance, so I knew you'd be okay." She nodded with a smile.

"And then?" he asked leaning forward.

"Oh yes, and then? When I got home I decided I had to do something. I knew your plan. You would take all the blame and do all the work, and I'd be relaxing like nothing happened. Well that was not to be. I didn't want to phone Pat one more time since this would involve more than a quick call and really mess up their honeymoon. So I phoned Carolyn and Lord Stonebridge at the manor and asked for their advice." She gave a sweet smile.

"And then?" Ed begged.

"Well we had a good old natter about our Mister Crowe, and after a while they agreed with my suggestion." Vicky paused for effect. Ed groaned. "As approved by the head of MI6," she continued, "I went to the local nick – as they referred it – and told the truth. I explained how I shot the KGB agent, and you – being a gentleman as you are – wanted to take the blame; or get the credit, as the case may be."

"And?"

"And they phoned their senior officers, who phoned their senior officers, and eventually someone phoned Lord Stonebridge, and here we are."

"And where are we pray tell?"

She slowly looked around. "We're in a cell..."

"Vicky, please!"

"Sorry," she said quickly, "that was rude. As I understand it, we will be leaving this place very soon, and tomorrow you will meet with Sandy Dennison and give your statement, which will be documented this time for the records."

"Sandy?"

"Sandy Dennison the nice police sergeant that you met earlier and to whom gave a somewhat limited and adjusted story of this morning's events."

Ed couldn't help but chuckle. "You're enjoying this, aren't you?"

"Not really, Ed, but I am trying to keep everything level. The thing that allows me to do that is that I know the man I shot is in hospital doing quite well. Especially knowing that I shot him in the chest. But luckily for him and me of course, my hand was moving up as a result of the recoil. The bullet went through a muscle, cracked his Clavicle, missed his Scapula by a quarter of an inch, and he'll be fine in a week or two."

As she finished speaking Sergeant Dennison entered the cell. Ed and Vicky stood. "You may both leave now. And, Mister Crowe, please return tomorrow morning at ten, and we'll finalize the documentation of the events of today."

They both nodded and left as quickly as they could. Neither spoke until they were in Vicky's car and well away from the police station.

Ed turned to Vicky. "I owe you one."

"The only thing you owe me is a good night's sleep. Your door won't be finished until tomorrow and in the meantime there is police tape around it. My parents have invited you to stay at our place - in their guest room, that is. I accepted on your behalf. They will have breakfast ready for nine, so we'll get a few hours sleep. I have an appointment at noon, and you of course," she said grinning, "have one at ten. My father will drive you to the police station and then drive you home."

Ed was totally impressed and just a little in awe. “Do your parents know...?”

“Absolutely. It was my father who suggested that I confess. She didn’t say anything, but I suspect my mother is a lot prouder of her life-insurance-sales-agent daughter than she has ever been. And that does feel nice.”

Ed shook his head. “I don’t know what to say.”

“Change is as good as a rest, eh?”

“Yes indeed. Change is good. A change for you. A change for me. A new world for both of us.”

She nudged him with her elbow. “But first a good night’s sleep, Toto. The new world will seem a great deal brighter.”

Vicky parked the car in her spot at her parent’s house. She leaned over and gave Ed a quick kiss on his cheek.

“Before we go in,” Ed said reaching for her arm, “I would like to say something. If I may?”

Vicky nodded.

“Miss Kilgour, I think you’ve become a bit of a Wonder Women. When I think back to that somewhat confused, but lovely, young lady that I met just five months ago, it really is an amazing transition. Well done.”

Vicky closed her eyes and swallowed, determined not to cry. “Thank you, Ed. Thank you, Mister. And thank you, Toto. Now let’s go. I’ll see you at breakfast.”

They entered the large house, Vicky escorted him to the guest room, and they went their separate ways.

Ed fell asleep as soon as his head touched the pillow.

Vicky lay awake, thinking of what Ed had said. It made her smile and very, very happy.

CHAPTER TWENTY-SEVEN

Wednesday May 14th 1986
9p.m.

Vicky sat with her parents in their family room. She didn't want to be alone in her own large portion of the house. She needed company. The three of them watched television, none really interested in what was on. Both of her parents read books while watching the program, something Vicky could never understand. Her parents hadn't mentioned anything about the shooting since the three of them had talked early Sunday morning. Her parents didn't want ask, and she certainly didn't want to raise the subject. She hadn't seen or heard from Ed since Sunday breakfast. Three days seemed like a lifetime.

The calm of the evening was changed when the doorbell rang. Mr. Kilgour walked across the room and through the hallway. He returned a minute later with a large bouquet of flowers.

"Why, darling," Mrs. Kilgour said standing, "how lovely of you."

"Not this time, my dear. These are for 'Dorothy'." He shrugged. "The man said this is the correct address."

"They're for me," Vicky said enthusiastically. "They're from Toto." She took the bouquet and headed for the kitchen.

Mr. Kilgour shook his head. "Dorothy? Toto? Then I must be surely the Wizard."

Mrs. Kilgour gave him a look.

"Why you are Glinda the Good Witch, my dear. Who else could you be?"

"Who else, indeed," she replied "Pour us a glass of wine then, Wizard, and let us see what Dorothy has to say."

In the kitchen Vicky put the flowers in a glass vase, and only then opened the envelope. There was a message, clearly in Ed's handwriting. She smiled as she read it:

'To: Wonder Woman. Watch the ten o'clock NBC news. Peace on earth.'

'A big fan'

"That's a nice bouquet," Vicky's mother said, as Vicky carried the vase into the family room. "Does Toto have a surname?"

"Oh, Mother, you know it's from Ed. Who else would send me flowers?" She sat. "If it's okay with you, I'd like to watch the NBC news at ten."

"Some good news we hope," Mr. Kilgour commented.

"I'm not sure, Father. But I think it has something to do with the USSR."

"If you think that, then I'd bet on it," he replied.

Vicky simply smiled and kept her eyes on the lovely bouquet. It had been a long time since she had received flowers. She knew she would have to respond in kind, and turned her thoughts to what might be appropriate.

When the news started Vicky turned up the sound. After several minutes of national news, the newscast turned to Gorbachev's speech to the people of the Soviet Union which had been shown throughout the USSR on their national television news. Through translation he started by outlining that the worst of the accident was behind us, due in large part to the excellent work done by the firefighters and professionals who handled the immediate dangerous situation. He indicated that nine people were dead and many hundred injured. Vicky knew the number that had died was greater than nine. The latest number she had heard was thirty-one. She said nothing. Gorbachev then went on to complain that the West's news organizations details of the event as exaggerations and lies. Finally he reminded the world of the potential disaster in a nuclear war, and offered to meet with world leaders in any European capitol, or even Hiroshima to discuss reducing the threat of nuclear weapons.

"So what do you think?" her father asked.

"I think I'm going to bed," she replied, taking the bouquet with her. "A politician is a politician around the world. We need more women in politics. We're more honest."

"I'm sure Mrs. Thatcher would agree with you," her mother responded. "And so do I."

Vicky and her mother turned to Mr. Kilgour. He kept his head down reading the newspaper.

Vicky went to bed. She needed to think of a nice response to the flowers.

Ed turned the television off and walked out on his balcony sipping a red wine. He was impressed with Gorbachev, understanding that he had to lie about the number of dead. One has to manage expectations, he realized. He turned to face the area where Vicky lived. He toasted her with the last of the wine. "Well done, Miss Vicky. You're one of a kind."

CHAPTER TWENTY-EIGHT

Friday, May 16th 1986
The Queen's Head.

Six-thirty on a Friday night was just the right time for a beer. It was the long weekend – even better. Ed walked to the bar. His Double Diamond was waiting for him, and he waved thanks to Seana. It was a busy night and he enjoyed the atmosphere and sounds of people relaxing after a week's work. In his case it was a busy two weeks, remembering that fourteen days ago the team was on their way from Turkey to Jolly Old for Pat and Roy's wedding. He saddened when remembering that Alex has taken his own life that day. He shook his head to clear his mind of what had occurred during the past two weeks. He had to move on. The world had to move on. He took a long deep swig of his beer. Life was good.

He felt someone standing close behind him. The mirror behind the bar showed a smiling Victoria.

"Hi, bloke," she said as he turned to face her, "five days - long time."

He gave a broad grin. "Well if it isn't the lady that the weekend is named after; Victoria."

"That's an old one," she said.

"Can't be too old. How old are you any way?"

"You don't ask a lady her age, you should know that."

He bowed. "Of course, Victoria. Ah, such a nice name. I know that you are aware that Queen Victoria was the first child in England to be christened with that name. But did you know that her mother, of course, was born in Germany. Did you also know that Victoria was short and a tad plump? Obviously you are not related to the Queen. Also she…"

"Okay, bloke, you've been looking up information just to show my ignorance. I'll look up the name Edwin and see what I can find, should I?"

"Ah, now Edwin. Edwin, of course, was the king of Northumbria, which was basically the east and north side of what we now call the U.K. And, interestingly, after his death he was made a saint."

"Hmm! Then obviously you aren't related – in any way – to him. You're just a bloke."

"Indeed, indeed. But just think; Queen Victoria, King Edwin. It does have a certain ring to it, yes?"

"No."

He nodded. "You're right of course. Can I buy you a drink?"

She grinned. "I don't know, 'can' you?"

He bowed his head. "I stand corrected. 'May' I buy you a drink?"

"Sorry, I have to go. But thanks."

"Oh, I see," he replied, caught off guard. "I thought…"

"Not tonight, Ed. I'm busy. But I do have something for you." She handed him an envelope. "It's a poem. I wrote it for you after something you said."

"Wow, I am impressed. Is it a…?"

"A romantic poem? No. But please don't open it until you get home tonight. Deal?"

"Deal."

She leaned forward. "And thank you for the flowers. They are lovely. My parents were duly impressed. Whenever I'm around they refer to each other as Glinda and Wiz. How come I'm so normal?"

"It must be the friends you keep…like me."

"Yeah, right. Look I have to go. What are you doing tomorrow?"

He shrugged. “Nothing.”

“I’ll pick you up at eleven tomorrow morning. I’d like to buy you a drink in a place you’ve never been. We can catch up regarding ‘business’, and then I want to ask you a question I have for you.”

“I’ll be ready downstairs, and I’ll read your poem tonight.”

“Excellent.” She leaned forward, kissed him lightly on the cheek, turned and left.

He finished his one beer and headed home.

Sitting on his sofa he carefully opened the envelope and read the poem.

WHEN

When is the day, the World will sing
The trees will rest at last
When is the day the horns will cease
And all forget the past.

And when will they stop to gaze around
To see what they have made
And do their best to compensate
The errors of this day

Ever since the World began
It has always been the same
The hate, the scorn, the everything
That wars will never end

When will they see that the answer
Is not to hate and kill
And denounce the other as a man
With equal rights to fill

When is the day, that they will pray
For the good of all mankind
To live in peace and happiness
Until the end of time?

When is the day, I ask you
That the apocalypse will occur?
And when each of you have answered
Our Prayers have all been heard.

He was stunned. He couldn't get over the deepness of its meaning, especially given where the world was at; the Vietnam War, major changes in the USSR, Ronald Reagan's approval of bombing Tripoli in response to a discothèque bombing in West Berlin, the bombing of a TWA flight. It didn't seem to end. And here were Vicky's deepest feelings of despair, and a so simple and reasonable solution. He couldn't help himself; he picked up his phone and dialed her cell number. As he had expected, it went to message.

"Hey, Vicky, I just read your poem. It is terrific, I mean really terrific. So thoughtful and, and…er, so meaningful. I know you're intelligent and all that, but this is…I'm sorry I'm mumbling. Well done. I'm proud to know you…see you tomorrow."

He shook his head. *Nice mumble, Ed. She probably thinks I'm nuts.*

He grabbed himself a glass of wine and headed to his balcony. He read and re-read the poem. *Amazing. Bloody amazing.*

CHAPTER TWENTY-NINE

Saturday, May 17th 1986

As was his custom he was five minutes early for Vicky to pick him up. As was her custom, she was five minutes late – which to her was on time.

Ed slipped into the car and buckled up. "Look, I'm sorry about my mumbled message…"

Vicky raised her hand. "Let's talk about that and other things when we get where we're going. Okay?"

"Absolutely," Ed agreed, noticing her briefness.

They spoke little as she drove to down town Toronto on the QEW. After twenty minutes of silence, Ed turned to Vicky. "Are you mad at me?" he asked.

"No. Should I be?"

"No."

"Then why ask?"

He shrugged and gave up.

Five minutes later she spoke. "Look, I just want to get to where we're heading and then we'll have a good ol' natter, as you English types say." She smiled. "Okay, matey?"

"You're the boss. Looking forward to our discussion…I think."

"Time will tell."

Vicky parked the car, just a block from the Art Gallery of Ontario.

Ed nodded to the gallery. "Hey, you're going to try and get me some classical learning are you?"

Vicky shook her head and pointed to the building across the street from the gallery.

Ed looked and couldn't help but laugh. "Village Idiot Pub. Is there a message here somewhere?"

Vicky put her arm through Ed's and led the way. "No message. This is the pub I went to when I was at university, just down the street. Good place for memories."

Old or new, Ed wondered.

Ed opened the door and bowed for Vicky to enter. It was not a large pub, but decorated like a true English pub. There was a long bar on the far side, and tables and chairs throughout. It looked and felt friendly. It wasn't full, but there were guests at the bar and more guests enjoying their lunch with a pint of beer. All were dressed casually, and most were likely regulars.

A gentleman from behind the bar raised his hands when he recognized Vicky. "Miss Kilgour. It is good to see you again. Please come in." He was bald, medium build with a Mediterranean look.

"It's lovely to see you again, Atef," Vicky smiled as he escorted them to a small table in a quiet corner.

"I will have Eli look after you, Miss Kilgour," Atef said as he held the chair for her to sit.

Ed nodded. "Well aren't you famous in the pub. No-one holds my chair for me at The Queen's Head."

Before Vicky could respond Eli the waiter brought them a menu each. "Can I get you a drink?" he asked.

"You may," Vicky responded quickly. "My friend will have a Double Diamond, and I'll have a Virgin Mary."

After he left to get their drinks, Vicky leaned over to Ed. "Good looking guy, eh? Tall, slim, nice length of hair. Not like my friend the bloke."

"One out of three ain't bad. Hey, he doesn't get his haircut paid for by the head of MI6, and I won't lose weight if you keep feeding me beer, right?"

"Yeah, right. Pick your lunch, it's on me."

They enjoyed their lunch. Ed had fish and chips and Vicky her normal salad. Both passed on dessert, or pudding as Ed referred to it given they were in an English pub. They ordered a pot of tea, with Ed playing mother.

Ed sipped on his hot cup of tea. "Sooo, you had a question, young lady?"

"Yes, yes I did." She sipped her tea, not looking up at Ed.

"Should I guess the question?" Ed asked.

Vicky shook her head. "No. Here's the question I had. As you know I was engaged once. Obviously to the wrong guy, but I was engaged. Now the next step from being engaged is obviously to get married. I wanted to get married. Most people want to get married, and I wanted to get married young. We both had good jobs. It was the natural step. I still want to get married. No rush, but I do want to get married." She gulped. "So the question I had is…what would you think if we ended our relationship here and now? No bad feelings. Just no more dates, no more 'stuff'."

Ed cringed at the question, and then closed his eyes to think. He wanted to answer carefully, very carefully. He finally answered.

"I have a negative response and a positive response. I'll start with the negative. I would be heart-broken if we had to end that way. I understand our somewhat strange relationship would get in the way of your finding other friends, I really do. But it would hurt, that's all."

Vicky nodded her thanks. "That was nice, thank you." She waited briefly, and then followed up. "And your positive response?"

"Okay, I'll give you my positive response if you promise not to get annoyed at me."

She shrugged. "I promise."

He took a deep breath. "Well, not to be too picky, but you keep referring to the question that you 'had'. Now 'had' is the past tense, and of course 'have' is the current tense. So on a positive note, I'm hoping – perhaps beyond hope – that it remains a 'had' question."

"Really," she beamed. "Now that is interesting. Imaging *you* getting picky about the English language. Notwithstanding that I thought you might correct the waiter for asking 'can' instead of 'may' he get us a drink. My oh my, what a bloke."

"I'm sorry, I…"

Vicky raised her hand to stop him from continuing. "I'm going to tell you a short story, Ed. Please listen. Last night I had a date with a young man. A lawyer, in fact a very successful lawyer. We were having a really great time getting to know each other at a very nice restaurant, and then I received a call on my cell phone. I let it go to message. A few minutes later I went to powder my nose, and the message was from you about the poem I wrote."

"I'm so sorry…"

She waved him off. "I listened to your message, Ed, and guess what? I cried. I stood crying in the washroom of this fancy restaurant, while just outside was a charming young man with whom I was getting along very well." She gulped, holding back more tears. "So what did I do? Well I cleaned up my make-up and told this charming young man that the message was from my mother and that I had to get home. Which is to say I lied to him. He drove me home, and then I went to my bedroom and cried some more. And do you know why I cried? Well I'll tell you. I cried because I simply missed the thought of not seeing you, not being with you, again. What do you think of that, Mr. Crowe? Eh, what do you think of that?"

Ed was devastated, unable to think clearly. "Vicky, I don't know what to say. I…I…"

Vicky tapped the table gently. "Listen to me, Ed. That was the question that I had until I heard your message, and I had every intention of asking it until I heard your message. I therefore have, yes have, another question for you. I still want to get married some day, and I know, and you know, that you and I…well you know what I mean. So instead of asking you the question outright, I'm going to sing the first two lines of a song, and I want you to sing the next two lines." She smiled quickly, took a breath and very quietly sang;

"We'll sing in the sunshine,
We'll laugh every day."

Ed, just as quietly sang the next two lines;

"We'll sing I the sunshine,
Then I'll be on my way."

Vicky looked at him nervously, chewing on her lower lip. "I know you get the message. What do you think?"

Ed reached over and took her hands in his. "I think that sounds great. Now I know there are details to your proposal, so I suggest we sip up, pay up, and then drive to my place. It's a lovely day. We'll sit on the balcony and finalize the details to what sounds to me like a wonderful idea."

She squeezed his hands, picked up her cup and finished her tea. "Let's go, bloke."

They didn't speak during the drive back to Ed's apartment. They touched hands once in a while and smiled a great deal.

As soon as they entered Ed's apartment, Vicky turned to Ed. "Give me a hug, bloke. It's been a while."

Ed was happy to oblige and gave her a big hug. "So your lawyer friend didn't get to give you a hug last night?"

She gently pushed him away. "No he didn't. He was too much of a gentleman. He could see I was upset…Upset by you by the way."

He hugged her again, harder this time. "Sorry." He kissed the top of her head. "What would you like to drink on a lovely long weekend Saturday, as we sit on the balcony and enjoy the Lake Ontario view, pretty blue eyes?"

She snuggled closer. "I would like a nice pot of English breakfast tea. Be sure to heat the pot and let it brew for three minutes. Then I'll play mother, making sure I put milk in first."

He walked her to the balcony and opened the door with a slight bow. "Have a seat, and I'll join you in a few moments. When you're ready we can discuss the details of your – our – new and exciting relationship."

Ten minutes later Vicky poured the tea and they both sat back and relaxed. Ed waited for Vicky to start the conversation. She waited for some time before she began.

"First, Ed, I want to talk about what occurred over the past few weeks. The 'business', Stonebridge Manor, Chernobyl, Istanbul, the cruise, Alex, the red van, your shooting a man, my shooting a man; the works." She took a sip of tea. "I can honestly say that I will never experience anything like that again. At times I was scared, and other times I was having the time of my life. It is incredible when I think back about it all." She shrugged. "And here I can't tell anyone about it…ever. So I want to end that discussion to say that we worked well together, you, me, and Carolyn. I gained a great deal of respect for you and your funny ways of doing things; 'telling a porkie', yikes! So please let's set that experience behind us and not talk about it unless, for some weird reason, we have to. Deal?"

"Deal. And thanks. But you did do great, and we did probably save lives. Let's never forget that."

Vicky took Ed's hand. "So, as they say, to the future. Here's my proposal. There may be some flexibility, but not much. We stay together for a year. It ends next May long weekend, on Sunday. We then each go back to our separate lives. If it doesn't last, so be it. No other 'friends'. That ends it. That simply means that we can go out with, in your case, another girl, but our deal ends. But we stay good friends forever no matter what. What we do for the next year is entirely up to the two of us. I would like to travel, see the world. I love cruising…*real* cruising. We both have jobs and they are priorities." She squeezed his hand. "Comments."

Ed nodded slowly, thinking through the proposal. He raised a finger. "One question…"

"I know the question," Vicky added, interrupting. "If you have to go on 'business' and that in any way involves Carolyn, I'd accept that.

I won't want to know what, if anything happened. I'd just accept life as it is."

"That's very good of you. I doubt I'll be called upon any time soon. In fact I hope I'm not." He grinned. "Not for a year anyway. To your proposal, I'm one-hundred percent in."

"Okay," she laughed aloud. "One other issue; finances. I know you're gentleman enough to want to pay when we go out. That's fine, but once in a while it'll be my treat. Any travel is fifty-fifty. That's not negotiable."

Ed nodded. "Done."

She shivered as they squeezed each other's hands.

"One more final point," Vicky chuckle, "and I know this sounds weird, but! I don't want people to see us as boyfriend/girlfriend, and I sure don't want them to refer to us using the new tag – partners. Here's my suggestion." She paused. Ed waited.

Ed cringed. "I'm getting nervous."

"Okay, here it is. It's based on your English background. You're my Crowe, and I'm your bird." She giggled. "Get it? Crowe - bird."

"That's clever. If it's okay with you it's okay with me." He thought for a second. "Actually the word 'bird', many years ago, meant something young and pretty. So it fits perfectly. You're my bird…so young and pretty."

"You sure know some interesting information when it comes to the English language, so here's one for you." Vicky stood. "Since you've agreed to the proposal, I will now offer you a lagniappe." She stood looking down, waiting for a response. There wasn't one. "Well you sit here and I'll explain what lagniappe means." With a broad smile on her face she entered the apartment, closed the door and headed to Ed's bedroom. Ed stayed sitting on the balcony trying to figure out what 'lagniappe' could possibly mean. He wasn't often stuck for words. Two minutes later he found out.

The door to the apartment opened, he looked and stood up. Vicky was standing just inside the room wearing his housecoat. She opened his housecoat, holding her arms out. She wore a very sexy bra and panties. There was not much too them, but they looked wonderful on her slim body.

"Lagniappe," she said with a sexy voice, "means bonus. So this is your bonus, bloke. Come and get it.

"Oh my goodness," Ed managed. "You look so lovely." He took a step closer. "Is the clip on that beautiful bra at the front or the back?"

"That," she said taking a step back, "is for me to know and for you to find out."

It didn't take long for Ed to find out.

AUTHOR'S NOTES

This story is fiction, based on facts. There was, of course, a nuclear disaster at the Chernobyl Nuclear Power Plant in Ukraine on April 26th 1986. While some of the facts about the details of the event and the reaction to it from the Soviet authorities are documented in this story, the characters and story line are fictitious.

In April 2006, Mikhail Gorbachev said the following;

'The nuclear meltdown at Chernobyl 20 years ago this month, even more than my launch of perestroika, was perhaps the real cause of the collapse of the Soviet Union five years later.'